I0634174

KNIGHTS OF THE ANGEL REALM

Guarding Carthage

Gretchen Odette Rhue

KNIGHTS OF THE ANGEL REALM
Guarding Carthage
by
Gretchen Odette Rhue

Copyright 2011. Revised 2024.
The Just Kiddin' Company, LLC
Huntington Beach, Ca.

All rights reserved. No portion of this book may be reproduced, or stored in a retrieval system, or transmitted in any form or by any means, electronic, mechanical, photocopying, recording, or otherwise, without written permission from the publisher and author, except as permitted by U.S. copyright law.

ISBN: 978-0-9885386-0-3

This is a work of fiction. Names, characters, businesses, places, events, and incidents are either the products of the author's imagination or used in a fictious manner. Any resemblance to actual persons or actual events is purely coincidental.

COVER DESIGN: Lily Strozewski

For my parents.

"If you like to go behind the veil, into the spiritual realm, this book is for you. This book will take you there."

-foreenterprise (an Amazon reviewer)

Chapter One
Chosen

Carthage, Texas, 1954.

Four linebackers seized Sam Wright by his legs and arms. They paraded him, dangling like a hunting trophy toward the pond, while belting out the school fight song.

The onlookers clapped and chanted, "Sam! Sam! Sam!..."

Over the water's edge his teammates taunted Sam by swinging him back and forth like a jump rope.

"No! No! No! Stop!" Sam protested.

"Onnnne, twoooo, threeeee!" they yelled in unison, launching Sam into the air.

Still wearing his last-day-of-school clothes, including his letterman jacket, Sam plunged into the chilly water. He swam upward with all his strength, but instead of making headway to the surface, he sank like a boulder, an unseen force pulling him down. His sneakers collided into the marshy, dead-end bottom of the pond. He tried to push-off on the rebound, but his feet submerged into the slimy mud that congealed like cement. Panicked, he exhaled the last of his precious air.

He grabbed his knee, and then yanked it. It didn't budge. In the dim, murky water, he watched branches from a gnarled nest of underwater shrubs supernaturally coil around his ankles like tethers, trapping him. He clawed at the serpentine branches.

Everything started to spin from the lack of oxygen. Anxious for help, he looked toward the muffled crowd on the banks above.

The tradition of throwing the new quarterback into the old wash hole had gone terribly wrong. His friends had no idea Sam was about to drown. He tried to shout out to them, but instead, water rushed into his mouth and throat.

***

From his perch on the tallest pine tree, Armada stood boldly, as if he were standing on solid ground. He observed the rowdy crowd of teens who were waiting for Sam to surface.

He viewed a colorless world. The teenagers, the cars parked on the road, the towels, and natural surroundings were all varying shades of gray. He and his uniform, on the other hand, were rich in color and glowed against the dinginess of this human dimension.

Armada opened a scroll. Bright rays of colored light formed the three-dimensional lettering upon it. After he read it, he shook his head, sighed a slow, full breath, and then rolled-up the glowing parchment. Once closed, it disappeared from his hands. He vanished as well.

***

Sam's muscles tensed. His body seized-up like a dead motor, followed by uncontrollable convulsions.

This is it. I'm dying and I haven't even kissed her yet, Sam thought.

A vision of Hayley Goodman, the girl he'd loved since the second grade, flooded his mind. She stood next to a window in the hallway at school, where the glow of the sun backlit her blond hair. This mystical Hayley caught sight of Sam watching her. He shot her a wink. She rolled her eyes, snapping him out of the vision.

He took a breath. This should have been the end of him, but it was as if he was breathing air instead of water.

Have I sprouted gills?

He watched catfish swim by, as he breathed like a catfish himself, and wondered what to do next. For the moment, since the need for air was apparently not so crucial, his panic subsided enough to gather his wits.

Silently, eyes open, he prayed. *Father God, Help me. Please...*

Through the wet gloom, a vertical slice of light nearly blinded Sam. He squinted as it appeared to be getting closer. Amidst the glare, a figure floated before him, from which rays of light blazed.

9

Am I dead? Sam wondered.

His heart pounded so hard he could almost hear it.

"You have been chosen," the figure announced clearly.

Sam garbled through the water, "Chosen?"

He could only assume this was an angel. He reminded Sam of a linebacker. Invincible. His striking eyes were like illuminated sapphires; richer than any blue thing he'd seen on Earth.

The being then disappeared as fast as he had come. The water turned dark again.

The branches freed Sam's feet. He propelled upward. Breaking the water's surface, he coughed-up the water from his lungs, and then sucked-in air until his throat hurt.

"Sam's gonna be quarterback next year!" Garth yelled.

"Sam! Sam! Sam…" the last-day-of-school crowd chanted.

Oblivious to his classmates, and instead utterly distracted by the phenomenon he had just experienced, Sam wondered if he had hit his head on a rock or something.

If it really was an angel, what am I chosen for? Sam's thoughts circled in his brain.

He rubbed his head while the chanting continued. "Must've been a rock," he muttered to himself.

"Quarterback?! Why didn't you tell me?" Trevor shouted, throwing a football toward Sam.

It bounced in front of his face, splashing him as he treaded water. Prior to the angel's appearance,

Sam would've relished this moment of attention from the crowd, but it paled in comparison now.

"Pass it to me!" Trevor said, jogging away.

The memory of the angel's eyes burned through Sam's mind like flares on a two-lane highway at midnight. Leaving the football bobbing in the water, he trudged out of the old wash hole like a sleepwalker, right past Hayley who was clapping and smiling at him.

He didn't even notice her.

***

Armada shot straight up out of the water, past the crowd on the banks, undetected by human eyes, yet, as he flew past them, he saw everyone and everything in great detail. He slammed out of Earth's atmosphere and into the stellar heavens. Zadkiel waited for him, suspended like a star in space. Armada stopped immediately, facing him.

"Your mission was clear. You were to remain on Earth. Why do you stand before me now?" Zadkiel asked.

"My intentions were not disrespectful, Sir. Sam's character may still need seasoning. And Hayley is not even—"

"Armada, your past must not interfere with your mission." Zadkiel grew larger as his voice grew deeper. An electrical storm stirred within his eyes. "A way will be made clear to you. Return to Earth and complete your task."

In an instant the angel disappeared, and Armada found himself alone in the deafening quiet among the stars.

***

Two horn blasts from the milk delivery truck jolted Sam out of his slumber. Panic ensued.

I missed my alarm?

He looked for his clock on the nightstand, but instead found it on the floor. He vaguely remembered swatting it earlier to silence its ring.

He vaulted out of his warm bed.

There was no time for a shower or breakfast. He threw on jeans, a t-shirt, and his letterman jacket. A straw hat covered his messy light brown hair. He yawned as he began to tie his boots, wishing he hadn't stayed up so late.

The memory hit him like a sonic boom: The hypnotic blue eyes. He let the boot laces drop.

The angel. Was it real?

The engine of the milk truck started up, snapping him back to reality. He finished tying his boots and sprinted down two steps at a time to 'Spott's' their family-owned market, where he heard his mother, Deborah Wright, humming along to a tune sung by Doris Day. She liked to sing to her plants as she worked. Multi-colored spots speckled the green apron that wrapped around her small frame. And green was also the color of her thumb. Deb grew and sold so many plants in the market, some thought it was the town nursery or florist shop.

"Good morning, sweetheart. How'd you sleep?"

"Good, Mom. Gotta go," he said, and then kissed her cheek. "Bye, Pop." Sam said, running past the ice cream counter, towards the back door.

"Just a minute, Son," Hank Wright said, looking up from his desk behind the counter.

Sam stopped, one hand on the creaking screen, the only portal to escaping the upcoming lecture. He turned to face his dad. "I'm gonna be late, Pop."

"Staying out until all hours of the night is not going to be repeated. Is that clear?"

"It was just— "

"This is serious."

"Everything is serious with you."

"Life is serious, Sam. The sooner you understand that, the better."

Sam decided the fastest way to end this scolding was to stand still and nod his head. And so, he did.

"You're in a leadership position now. Being quarterback means a whole team depends on you and the choices you make."

"Yes, sir." He said it respectfully even though he hated how rigid his father could be.

"Enough said for now. I'm proud of your accomplishments, Sam, but in life sometimes you give up what you want because it's the right thing to do." He looked at his wife, and she locked eyes with him for a moment that seemed to Sam like an eternity. Hank looked back toward his son— a gaze somewhat softened by Deb. "Better hurry up."

"Bye, Pop," Sam said as he bolted out the door and into the alley.

Sam hopped on his bike and pedaled through the town square, trying to forget the reprimand. He passed Wallace's Used Motorcycles, and wished he'd saved enough to buy the Dragonfly parked on the corner. It wasn't the best motorcycle on the lot, but it would be better than his bicycle.

His attention was then drawn to a memorial erected in the square in honor of four people lost at sea during a church choir trip. It had been five years since the disaster, but he could still remember each of them:

There was Brother Rogers, the choir director whose voice was as smooth as buttered glass— not crackly and shrill like the director the church had now.

And there were the three inseparable Model A widows: Eleanor Littlejohn, her sister-in-law, Gladys Littlejohn, and Isabella Chop. Isabella's husband, the late Johnny Chop, had taught her how to drive, and until the disaster, the three widows went everywhere together in the old jalopy.

Sam thought about all the times Isabella's uncanny timing— or as she would say, her "gift of discernment"—had spoiled his childhood pranks. He could still hear her wobbly voice. "Sa-am Wright." She would stretch the 'a' in Sam until it almost snapped. "When are you *EVER* gonna grow up?"

Pedaling harder out of town, he traveled down County Road 304, and then rushed along a stretch of road lined with loblolly pine trees.

From above the trees, a demon swooped toward Sam and flew next to his bike. Its ebony wings pulsed rhythmically through the air. It soared close enough for Sam to have touched it— if he'd known of its presence.

Sam's tires kicked up dust as he rode beneath the wrought iron sign over their driveway: *The Goodman Ranch.*

The demon perched itself on the sign like a gargoyle, talons clutching the top of the word 'good'. Its tail dangled and twitched. A mohawk of crimson spikes flared on its head. Surveying the property, it considered its orders: *Follow Sam Wright.*

***

Sam found the stables, leaned his bike against a fence, and then plopped down on the bench where he'd been told to wait. He yawned and stretched, wishing he could have slept for another five hours.

A pristine, white house with black shutters and towering columns ascended two stories up. Jasmine meandered on white trellises encasing an ample, wrap-around porch. The landscaping reminded Sam of the grounds of a ritzy hotel in Dallas where he and his parents had attended a wedding a few years ago.

He scanned the upstairs windows.

Hayley's in one of those rooms… probably still sleeping, he thought.

In a flash, white light blazed before him, and again, an angel hovered in front of the bench. Sam leaned back and squinted. The angel remained silent, until a faraway voice called out his name.

"Sam? Sam?"

The sound seemed to come from the angel, but his mouth never moved. Sam rubbed his eyes, trying to make sense of it. The lights dimmed, the angel faded, and in his place was a smiling, middle-aged, black man in overalls, standing at least six-foot-four.

"Sam? You Sam? Glad to meet you, kid. Name's Ray. I'll be showin' you the ropes here," his friendly voice boomed. Ray's large, dark brown, work-worn hand shook Sam's with one firm pump.

Sam groggily realized he had fallen asleep on the bench.

It was a dream. No angel this time. Just sleeping on the job. Great. Good first impression, Sam thought, scolding himself.

"Right now, we got fourteen horses. Three of 'em are new and needin' training. I'm startin' you on simple jobs at first. See how you work out. Do yourself a good job, and I'll teach you what I know. You come highly recommended, but this is hard work— not for no lazy kids." He patted the napping-bench. "Still interested?" He wiped his brow with a tattered handkerchief before sweat could trickle into his cocoa-brown eyes.

Sam nodded. "Yes, sir."

Ray continued his rapid flow of instructions while leading Sam on a tour. "Now it ain't no picnic, but horses need clean stalls. See that shovel over there? Y'all will be good friends."

Ray's overalls were covered with patches and mud. A wide brimmed hat, that had seen better days, hung down his back by a thin leather strap around his bulky neck. As he continued to talk, he walked from stall-to-stall, stroking each horse—introducing each by name. They responded by nuzzling him, looking for the pocket containing apple slices.

As they left the stables, piano music from the main house captured Sam's attention. It poured out of an open window, spilled across the lawn, and swirled around him like a summer breeze.

Maybe that's Hayley practicing, Sam wondered.

He followed Ray to a washing pen with a concrete floor. The horse trainer stroked a palomino that had just come from the pasture. Puffs of dust escaped with each pat, and with his other hand he removed clumps of grass from its tail and mane. He rubbed petroleum jelly on her hooves.

"You know, Gracie here is an award winner. Miss Hayley rode her to win the state championship two years in a row," Ray spouted.

At the mention of Hayley's name, Sam's heart leaped. "State, huh? That's impressive." His eyebrows rose as if he didn't have the newspaper clipping at home in an old shoebox.

17

"This here jelly will keep her hooves from drying out while we bathe her. Hey, kid, fill up that bucket over there."

Fourteen horses and three hours later, Sam dumped a bucket of fresh water over his own head. He never wanted to smell another horse. He knew his friends were spending their summer days back at the old wash hole. He was tormented as he envisioned the carefree scene that he was missing. At least he might occasionally get a glimpse of Hayley here.

Ray chuckled at the sight of him dripping wet. "I'm goin' into town to have me some barbecue and pick up a load of hay. When you finish mucking-out these stalls, you can stop for your lunch."

"Yes, sir."

Sam wanted to make a good impression, so he cleaned the stalls better than he cleaned his own room— not to say that his room had piles of manure in it, but the stalls *were* very clean. And he had the blisters to prove it.

Lunch.

In his rush to get to the ranch, he'd forgotten his lunch. If he were the type of kid who cursed, colorful words would be flying left and right. Instead, he just sulked down on a bench, listening to the painful gurgles of his stomach. But then another sound captured his attention— the distant sound of laughter. He knew that laugh. He followed it.

On the other side of the stables, across a well-manicured yard, he found Hayley and another

18

classmate, Minnie, enjoying a picnic in the shade of an abundant willow.

Yes! Food!

He ventured out to the tree, tipping his hat at the picnicking girls. *She's prettier than Miss Texas.* Sam smiled his most charming smile. *She doesn't know it yet... but she loves me,* Sam thought.

"Hello, ladies. What's for lunch?"

"Whatever you brought, I s'ppose," Hayley said in perfect Scarlet O'Hara fashion.

Minnie giggled and took a bite of her fried chicken leg.

Sam's stomach growled again. "Now where's your southern hospitality, Miss Goodman?"

"Left behind... like your lunch?" Both girls giggled at that. "And Mr. Wright, don't presume your employment here has any bearing on our friendship."

"Our friendship?"

"Well... uh... if we had one— a... a friendship, I mean," she stammered. Frowning slightly, she regained her composure, sitting up taller on the blanket. "Sam Wright, you are *not* invited to this picnic."

He enjoyed watching her squirm but decided to offer a compromise. "One drumstick, and I'll leave."

"Fine. Okay. One leg." She grabbed one out of the basket and held it out for him with a huff.

He took it from her, tipped his hat again, and smiled. "Thank you for your generosity." He took a huge bite, turned and then sauntered away.

Crossing the yard, he could hear the girls' faint laughter. And then he wished the strangest wish: that he was a fly or an ant on the potato salad, so he could hear what they were saying… and so he could eat some.

***

Hayley fanned herself with a clean plate and gulped some lemonade. "I can't believe him."

"He is so sweet on you, Hayley," Minnie said.

Hayley frowned. "I know! Ugh. He's been on this one-sided flirting spree since the second grade."

"He *is* the quarterback next year."

Her singsong voice made Hayley frown more.

"That kind of stuff doesn't impress me."

"Can I have him then?"

"Be my guest. He drives me crazy. And he'll be here all summer. Help me, Minnie!"

Ray drove up with the truck full of hay for Sam to unload. The girls didn't speak much as they watched him work. He threw them a wave, which triggered more giggling, of course.

Minnie decided it was time for her to go home, but before she left, she gave Hayley some advice. "Honey, you need to open your eyes."

The words echoed in Hayley's mind long after her friend had left.

She mumbled to herself like a crazy person. "He *is* gorgeous. Minnie's right. And he *is* charming... maybe *too* charming." She fanned herself again. "But this is Sam... I've known him since... This is just insane."

Despite her better judgment, she took Sam some more fried chicken, potato salad, and a large glass of lemonade.

"Wow. This is great! Thank you," Sam said, digging-in.

"I made it myself."

"I didn't know you could do it."

"Cook?"

"No. I didn't know you could give me a chance." He gulped down a forkful of potato salad.

"Well, don't go getting the wrong idea, mister. I'm just being nice."

"Exactly."

"Honestly, Sam. Will you ever give up?"

"Nope. And I'm not asking for your hand in marriage or anything. Just talk to me."

"Talk to you?"

"Go fishing with me." He downed the last of the lemonade, and then wiped his mouth with his arm.

"Fishing?"

"Fishing or... horseback riding... that's it. Go horseback riding with me. Show me the woods or Dixie Lake. I mean, you have all these horses. Just go for a ride," he mumbled through a large bite of fried chicken.

"But you're working."

"I'm done at three. It'll give you time to change."

"Change my mind?" she smirked.

"I think you already did that." He smiled and stood up. "Thanks again for the lunch. Best potato salad I've ever had."

She was speechless, her mouth agape.

He took a few steps toward the stables, turned, and looked at her. "See you at three."

She didn't say no.

***

The mohawk demon shadowed Sam's every move, peering at each of his activities curiously, eerily.

Chapter Two
Bittersweet Evenings

Hayley could not believe the words that were about to escape her mouth.

"Mama, can Sam stay for supper tonight?"

She cringed, clipped the last of the thorns from a yellow rose, and handed it to her mother, Dottie Goodman. The flabbergasted look on her mother's face said it all. In fact, Hayley herself was bewildered at her change of heart toward Sam.

"Honey, your daddy and I are not too keen about you flitting around with that boy. And you know, I saw you two yesterday. Riding horses by the lake. I've seen how you've ignored your girlfriends since he's worked here." She arranged the roses in a crystal vase.

"He's just a friend."

"Well, he seems awfully smitten with you. You shouldn't encourage anything."

"Is it because you think he likes me, or that he isn't Nick Laird?"

Dottie paused, put the vase on the dining table, and turned, looking her daughter in the eyes. "Honestly, Nick does seem more your type."

"Because his family's wealthy?"

"Oh, speaking of Nick's family," she said, changing the subject, "the Lairds are spending a few months in Europe, so Nick will be staying here in Carthage with the Wedgeworths for the school year. It would be nice if you made him feel welcome. Oh! And, he's apparently a star football player now. A quarterback!"

"Honestly, mama, you act like we're engaged or something. And Sam's the quarterback anyway."

"I thought you'd love the news. He's like family."

"You mean you *wish* he was."

"Well, you always had fun when you were younger."

Hayley sighed. "What about Sam? Can he stay for supper?"

"Alright. He can stay, but we'll be watching this one."

Hayley kissed her on the cheek. "Give him a chance. You'll like him." She dashed for the back door.

***

Sam survived supper. He managed to win over Hayley's father, Richard Goodman, with some witty sentiments and clever jokes— which may not have been so clever had the wine not flowed so freely. Dottie Goodman was a bit tougher to reach, though. He answered her poignant questions

24

honestly, and with a smile that would have captured any woman's heart. He saw her wink at Hayley once, which he hoped (rather than believed) meant she approved.

After supper they sat in the parlor, eating warm apple pie. Sam was amused that the parlor was almost as big as his family's entire apartment.

"Hayley, does your friend here know what an accomplished musician you are? Why don't you play for him?" Mr. Goodman suggested.

"Oh, Daddy, he hears me play all the time—"

"There is nothing I would like better, sir. I'm usually out working. I can only hear her playing through the open window."

"Now, Richard, if she doesn't want to…" Dottie said.

"Go on, Darlin'. Daddy didn't pay for all those lessons for nothing," he said, lighting his pipe.

She played a Schubert piece.

Mr. Goodman leaned over and quietly spoke to Sam.

"I expect Hayley will do well in life. She will go off to college after graduation, and then marry well."

"Sounds like you've got it all planned out for her."

Without responding, Richard leaned back in the Victorian chair, and replaced his pipe between his teeth.

When the music ended, Richard and Dottie retired to the porch. Even though he'd been put in his place, Sam refused to be discouraged.

"You play like an angel," he told her as Hayley plopped down on the couch next to him.

"Thanks, but I wish Daddy wouldn't make me play for every guest we have."

"No, really, Hayley, you play the piano like it's part of you. I've never heard anything more beautiful."

She looked at him with grateful eyes and smiled.

"But enough mushy, sentimental stuff. I challenge you— no, I double-dog-dare you to a game of *Night* Horse Tag," he proposed, trying not to crack a smile.

She accepted the challenge.

They had invented the game on their first ride: Horse Tag— the ordinary, childhood game of tag…only on horseback …and this time at night.

***

"We can't be out too late. Daddy'll have my hide," she said, tightening Gracie's saddle and then hopping on top of her horse.

Sam mounted Blaze, a mustang that Ray let him name. "Since I'm a gentleman, I'll be 'it' first. Are you read—"

She disappeared into the darkness of the meadow before he could finish the question.

"Spunky move," he said to himself, spurring Blaze into action.

It took a few minutes to catch-up to her, but as he drew nearer, Hayley cut across a meadow, weaving in between a row of Cypresses, trying to shake him. When that failed, she headed for a stream, following it for a half-mile or so before leading Gracie into the water, crossing to the other side.

Sam shadowed her moves until the stream's uneven floor caused Blaze to rock. Splashing down into the water, Sam's pride hurt more than the fall. He just sat there drenched, until Gracie turned and pranced back to the water. Hayley laughed at the sight of him.

"This isn't over," he huffed, springing onto Blaze.

Gracie bolted out of the stream and back out into the meadow, but Hayley's riding form was compromised due to hysterical laughter.

Hayley's laughter gave Sam an edge. He closed the gap, leaned over (still dripping) and grabbed her wrist.

"Tag! You're it!"

"You got me. But at least I'm not all wet," she giggled. The laughter soon faded into awkwardness as she looked down to see he was still holding her wrist. "Well, it's getting pretty late. We should head back."

Sam leaned toward her.

She must be kissed, Sam told himself.

Hayley leaned toward him.

The horses suddenly whinnied and stomped their hooves. Hayley pulled away before their lips met, and they both looked toward the trees. They could hear someone approaching quickly on horseback.

The moonlight shone through the thinning edge of the woods, casting sparse backlight on the silhouette of a man with a wide brimmed hat drawing near.

"It's really late. I bet that's Daddy."

Great, thought Sam.

"Miss Hayley?" It was Ray. He pulled the reins tight, stopping next to them. "Y'all need to come on back to the house right away."

***

The horses galloped at a maddening pace toward the house. Sudden, wicked winds tossed branches onto the trail, causing the horses to weave and rear back. When they arrived, they saw a sheriff's patrol car in the driveway. Sam thought he might be grounded for the rest of his life.

Ready to apologize and beg forgiveness, they dismounted and ran through the front door. They halted when they saw Sam's mom in tears, sitting on the Goodman's couch. Dottie was next to her, holding her hand. Richard talked to an officer by the window in hushed tones.

Sam rushed to his mom. "I'm sorry. I didn't mean to worry you. We shouldn't have stayed out so late—" He stopped short, realizing he and Hayley weren't the reason for all the commotion. "What is it? What's wrong?"

She wiped away the tears, took a deep breath, and looked at Sam. "Honey, your dad has had an accident. The car skidded into the Sabine

River near Highway 79. They found our car, but they can't find him."

He blinked rapidly, his mouth open, as he processed the news. His chest ached. "I've got to look for him." He ran for the door.

"Sam, wait!" Deb shouted.

He didn't listen.

Jumping onto Blaze's saddle, he rode like a jockey toward the river. During the ride, Sam was numb. Numb, but focused on getting to his dad.

Through the whipping windstorm, at the vicious curve on Highway 79, the revolving, flashing red and blue lights of the patrol cars lined the dirt shoulder. Sam dismounted and ran to the edge of the Sabine River. Next to the steep embankment, three tires jutted out of the rushing whitewater.

Sam stood mortified. He wanted to scream. He wanted to just open his mouth and let the loudest utterance escape into the night. But he didn't make a sound. Balancing on massive roots of an ancient tree, under its lofty canopy trimmed with moss, he watched volunteer firemen in rowboats next to the muddy banks below him. They shook their heads at the sheriff as water sprayed in their faces from the winds. A lantern in one of the boats blew out. Against the strong gusts, the sheriff announced they would have to postpone the search until daylight.

Sam continued the search all night. Ray and the Denton brothers joined him.

The search lasted for three days.

Hank's body was never found.

***

Hayley found Sam slumped on a bench in front of the sheriff's station when she drove up in her mother's Cadillac. The search had officially come to an end, and it had been decided that a memorial would be held in Hank's honor in one week.

She joined him in the shade. He was twirling a pine needle back and forth. They didn't speak for a while as a slight breeze drifted through the Texas heat. His mind was engaged in a childhood memory of his parents:

Eight-year-old Sam, sitting on the market floor, building with blocks, watched his mother run into the room shrieking at such a level, Sam had to cover his ears.

"Did you get it, Hank?! Oh, I hate spiders!"

Hank joined them. "Yeah, I got it." A small grin turned into a devilish smile. "You want to see it, Deb?" He held out a scrunched-up napkin toward his wife.

"Get that thing away from me...don't you dare..."

Little Sam's eyes opened wide as he followed the flight of the napkin sailing toward his mother. She screamed and jumped out of the way just in time. It landed on the floor.

30

Deb frowned a playful frown at Hank and tried to swat his arm, but he dodged and ran up the stairs to the apartment over their market. Laughing, she followed him.

Sam heard the chase overhead, and then things got quiet. He soon realized they were probably kissing again.

"Yuck."

He went back to his blocks until movement caught his attention. Out of the crumpled napkin hobbled a seven-legged spider.

Snapping out of the memory, Sam finally spoke to Hayley; without looking at her.

"You know when I was little, my dad and I would climb trees. I mean *really* climb them. We would go so high that people would pass under us, and they wouldn't even know we were there. We'd talk about baseball or football or whatever.

"On Saturdays we would listen to baseball and eat Crackerjacks. One time he took me to a minor league game." He paused. Hayley waited.

"That was back when I was little. Lately, we've just argued. Or at least I did. I think I missed what he was trying to teach me. Now it's too late.

"He was always there for me. He prayed with me, listened to me. I know God has a reason for taking him home, but I'm not sure I'll ever understand."

Hayley reached out and held his hand. "I wish I'd known him better." She took a deep breath, stood up, pulling on his hand. "Sam, maybe you should get some rest at home. Come on. I'll walk with you."

In the town square, life went on as normal all around them. Sam watched as people went into the theater for a matinée, and as people came and left the bank. It seemed like life would never be normal again.

"The saddest thing is that he won't be there when I graduate, or when I get married. My children will never know him." He choked up on these words.

They stopped in front of the market. Hayley took both his hands in hers, and then turned to face him. "You'll tell them, Sam. And, in a way, they'll know him because they know you." She kissed his cheek. "Get some rest. I'll see you tomorrow."

*** *

The memorial left him empty; completely consumed by grief. Exhaustion overpowered even normal tasks. Later that evening he and his mother stood together in the living room, surrounded by floral arrangements and well-wishing cards.

"We'd better try to get some rest, Mom."

"You're right," she said reaching up to give him a hug. "Goodnight."

"Nite," he said, hugging her back— tighter than he had in a long time.

Sam thought he would flip-flop and stare at the ceiling all night, but he fell asleep instantly. Hours later, he awoke to an unfamiliar noise. Following the sound down the hallway, he came to his mother's room. The door was open, and her bed was still made. The sound continued, leading him to the stairs of the market. Halfway down the creaky stairway, he saw her sitting at his father's desk, praying through heart-wrenching sobs. He could only understand some of what she was saying. The market. How would she run it by herself?

Silently, he returned to his room where he didn't sleep the remainder of the night. She needed him. He knew what he had to do.

***

August

Sam found himself at the top of the visitor's bleachers, alone. The rest of the team began the routine of stretches and drills in unison on the grass below.

Rain lurked in the gray sky that matched Sam's state of mind. An oppressive gloom settled-in, suffocating all that mattered to him.

Somehow, he had survived the first day of school despite feeling numb and lost. He had felt like a stranger among people he'd known all his life. Some had offered their condolences, others looked away unsure of what to say, while most just stared at him with sad eyes.

His father's death…the crazy vision under the water— he wished he could just erase it all. He wished for his life back.

Giant raindrops suddenly pounded a spastic rhythm of thuds and pings on the wooden bleachers and metal railings as dry surfaces became scarce. The familiar smell of fresh rain on hot asphalt invaded Sam's nose.

He didn't budge. Neither did the team. Practice continued despite the rain, and despite his absence. The cadence of counting out their drills echoed in his ears like soldiers rallying before war. He wanted to be a part of it all, he wanted to be down there in the mud with his friends, but without his dad cheering from the stands, everything seemed pointless. And there was mom and the market. She needed him and he knew she would never ask him for help.

Letting the rain saturate him like an abandoned couch in an alley, the sounds finally drilled into his mind, getting the better of him. He bolted down the bleachers, unaware of his destination, just anywhere but there. As he rounded the storage shed by the edge of the track, he thought he was flying under the radar when he slammed into Coach Benson.

"Hey. We've been looking for you. Suit up."

With stringy, wet hair sticking to his face, Sam avoided eye contact with the coach. Instead, he just stared a hole through a ride-on lawn mower parked in the mud by the shed.

The coach let out a deep breath. "I know it's a hard time for you, Sam, but I need to know if you are going to play...or should we go ahead with the back-up quarterback, Nick Laird? I can only save your position for so long."

Sam couldn't believe what he was hearing.

A back-up? Nick Laird? They've already replaced me? Not Nick.

"I'll give you until tomorrow to let me know." He put a hand on Sam's shoulder. "Your dad would've wanted you to play. I do, too."

Sam thought about the last conversation he had with his dad. He looked at his coach and echoed his dad's words. "In life sometimes you give up what you want because it's the right thing to do."

Sam turned away from the coach, and the team, and from what he wanted. He walked at first, but gradually he increased his speed until he took off in a sprint for home. When he arrived in the back alley, it was still pouring.

He bent over, breathing heavily from the run. The anger inside of him magnified until he picked up a metal trashcan and threw it like a javelin several times against the brick wall. And then, raising it over his head, he brought it crashing down before him. It had nearly caved in completely.

An odd feeling prompted him to look at the back door to the market. Two figures stared at him; mouths slightly ajar at what they'd witnessed. On one side was his mother. To the left of her stood Hayley holding a plate of baked goods tied up with a bow.

He froze, unable to explain himself. She probably thought he was a monster. He was sure he must've looked like one.

Hayley gave the plate to Deb, turned and left without a word to Sam.

***

Just before the day surrendered to the night, with everything darkish pink and windows glowing, Sam ventured out to the ranch to make amends with Hayley. He hadn't seen her for weeks, but there was a glimmer of hope she would understand. The flowers he balanced on the handlebars couldn't hurt.

The long gravel driveway crackled under his tires as he passed a familiar car parked by the front walkway: Nick Laird's black, convertible corvette. Even in the dim light, the car shimmered.

He rode around back, and then leaned his bike against the steps of the service porch. With the flowers behind his back, he reached up to knock on the screen but stopped.

In the glowing light of the kitchen, he saw them. Nick chased Hayley. She was giggling. Nick grabbed her waist from behind, and then spun her around to face him. Straight out of Sam's worst nightmare, Nick kissed Hayley. Not a friendly peck on the cheek either. An end of the movie, 'boy gets girl back' kind of kiss.

Sam was mortified. A locomotive had just slammed into his chest. He wanted to break Nick's neck. She was *his* girl... or was she?

His head spun as he thought about how half the summer had slipped by while he grieved for the loss of his dad. How could he blame Hayley?

Nothing was established between them. She had tried to reach out to him, but he'd blown it.

Sam dropped the flowers, and then tore down the driveway on his bike. He never slowed his crazed pace until he threw his bike against the back wall in the alley behind the market. He attempted to escape to the sanctuary of his own bedroom, but his mom stopped him at the stairs.

"Honey, come out front. There's a surprise that you'll never believe," she said with a sweet southern drawl.

He couldn't find words to excuse himself, so he followed her in a numb trance. He walked to the front door in a defeated daze, hoping it wouldn't take long, but then stopped like a stone when he saw some friends from school, Mayor Houlihan, and a few people from church outside, looking directly at him, grinning. He stepped out on the mat. He looked from person-to-person, finally settling on the mayor in front.

"Sam, nice to see you, boy," he said, standing next to his expectant wife. "Bet you're wondering what we're all doing here."

Sam nodded, stuffing his hands in his front pockets.

"Well, I'll tell ya. We all pitched in. She's all yours."

The small crowd parted to reveal the Dragonfly. Sam was speechless as he stared at it. It would have been the happiest moment of his life if circumstances were different.

The crowd hushed, anticipating his response.

"Unbelievable. Thank you," he whispered.

"Well then, get on it. We want to see you ride it," the mayor insisted.

Sam fired it up, and then waved before he rolled away for the first time— the bittersweet wind in his face. He didn't stop until he reached the rapids of the Sabine River. With his arms folded on the handlebars, he wept.

Chapter Three
The Golden Staircase

Before school, a girl— under an enormous hat— waited at the front counter in the office. Sam rushed in, carrying an order of chalk and thumbtacks from the market. He could barely see the girl's face for all the hat, but he knew he'd never seen her before.

"Here you go, Mrs. Sisco," he said, plopping the order down on the counter, bumping the pencil cup. He tried to steady the cup, but instead caused it to crash to the floor— pencils scattering across the light green tiles.

Mrs. Sisco, the no-nonsense secretary, rolled her eyes behind her cat-eye glasses.

The mystery girl squatted down to help pick up the pencils, her long, wavy, auburn hair practically sweeping the floor.

He couldn't help staring at the large sunflower on her over-sized, straw hat. And he couldn't help noticing she was beautiful.

"Thanks," he said.

She smiled.

"Sam, would you do me a favor— well, actually two favors?" asked Mrs. Sisco from under a pair of black-rimmed glasses. She didn't wait for a reply. "Could you show our new student... uh..." She glanced at a folder. "... Miss Tallulah Ayres to P.E. class? And deliver these papers to Mrs. Weaver as well? Thanks so much, dear." The phone rang, and she got busy again.

Sam looked at Tallulah. He was still embarrassed about the pencils flying through the air.

"Hello. Nice to meet you, Sam," she said, boldly offering her hand.

Her British accent was as big as her hat.

"Hi." He shook her hand. "Great hat."

"Thanks."

As they left the office and rounded the corner, Sam's eyes were still glued to the sunflower hat, causing him to slam into Nick at the water fountain and drop Mrs. Weaver's papers. Hayley was standing next to the fountain. She helped Tallulah pick them up.

Sam leered at Nick. Nick leered back.

I can't believe this guy is gonna be quarterback... and that Hayley kissed him, Sam thought.

Nick, looking perturbed, wiped water off his black, leather jacket with a handkerchief. His blond hair was cut short and slicked back.

A bruise on the side of Nick's face caught Sam's attention. He wished he'd been the one to put it there. It looked curved, like a horseshoe. Sam wondered if Hayley's horse, Gracie, had kicked him. For a horse, she was a good judge of character.

40

Sam had spent years living in the shadow of Nick— watching him dazzle everyone with his family's money and connections. He had to admit that he was jealous of Nick, but it wasn't just that. He watched how Nick would put himself first in every situation. He wanted someone better for Hayley. Even if it wasn't himself. Anyone but Nick. But that kiss. He couldn't even look at her. He felt like he was in a pressure cooker.

Tallulah looked at Sam. "Are you going to introduce me then?"

"Tallulah, this is Hayley and Nick," Sam said.

He hated the sound of their names together. *She doesn't even know I saw them last night,* he thought.

Hayley smiled. "Nice to meet you. Oh! If you're new here... do you know about the football game tonight?"

"Football game? I wouldn't miss it. I simply adore American football."

"Well, look for me and Nick. I'm a cheerleader and he's on the football team." She glanced at Sam, and then quickly looked at the floor.

"Sounds fantastic!" Tallulah said with energetic, British flare. "Can I sit with you Sam?" she asked, touching his arm.

The question was uncomfortable. Sam didn't want any part of any of this. Nothing was working out the way it should.

No Pop. No Hayley. No football. Nick Laird. Wrong, wrong, wrong.

41

As he was trying to think of a good excuse to skip the game, he noticed a strange expression on Hayley's face. She was looking at Tallulah's hand on his arm.

Could she be jealous?

"Yep, sure. You can sit with me," Sam said.

The bell rang, summoning them to first period.

***

Sam headed for the game in Spott's delivery truck. The setting sun was hidden by ominous thunderheads. Air whistled through the cab as he wondered why he was going at all. Tallulah was gorgeous. He'd be lying to himself if he said he didn't notice. He thought about his attempt to make Hayley jealous. Big mistake. Now he would have to endure watching the game in which he would have debuted as quarterback. At least Tallulah would be good company.

He parked in the school lot, and then breathed a defeated sigh as he slammed the door shut. After buying a ticket, he scanned the growing crowd for Tallulah. He saw no sign of her or her hat, so he found a seat close to the exit for a quick escape.

The teams warmed up, the crowd grew, and the marching band performed their pre-game show. It wasn't long before Tallulah arrived with a box of popcorn. Her sunflower hat was gone, but another large sunflower was knitted on the front of her bronze-colored sweater. Binoculars that hung from her neck swayed as she sat down next to him.

"Hello, Sam."

"Hey, you made it."

"Wouldn't miss it," she said, tilting the popcorn box his direction. "Want some?"

"Thanks," he said, plunging his hand into the box. "You must like sunflowers."

"You know, I simply adore them. I'm always wearing at least one somewhere on my person. They're so cheery."

Man, she is beautiful, Sam thought, trying to find something interesting to say. "Are you an exchange student or—"

Suddenly, the crowd burst into applause. Sam stood up, whistling with his fingers, as the players rushed across the field. He was excited for his former teammates, his friends, but it was hard to think of all he'd given up. If things were different, he'd have been wearing that uniform, and his dad would've been in the stands, cheering the loudest.

Tallulah joined in the ruckus, screaming and clapping.

In their red and white uniforms, the Bulldogs took their place on the home team sideline. The marching band played the fight song, while the cheerleaders jumped and rustled their pom-poms in time to the robust tune.

Sam and Tallulah took their seats. Carthage won the coin toss. They chose to receive.

Throughout the game, Sam found himself staring at Hayley in the line of cheerleaders.

Tallulah noticed. "She's pretty, Hayley is. Does she like you?"

"Not anymore."

She aimed the binoculars at Nick, and then at Hayley. "Is she Nick's girlfriend?"

Sam's stomach knotted.

Applause suddenly exploded in the stands. The Bulldogs had scored. Everyone jumped up and cheered— except Sam.

***

Sam was one of the last to leave the stands. Tallulah had offered to walk out together, but he just wanted to be alone.

He missed playing football, but more than anything he missed how his dad used to say, 'Well done, Son,' after every game, and then slip some money into his hand. 'Get something with the team over at Charlie's Diner. We'll leave a light on for you,' he would say. It was such a simple thing, but now that his father was gone, he wished he could hear those words again.

He wondered if Hayley would be at Charlie's with Nick tonight.

The field lights turned off, so he decided to head for the truck. As he passed the restrooms, and then rounded the corner, he came face-to-face with Nick.

"Leave Hayley alone," Nick said, leaning towards Sam.

He glared at Sam for a moment, and then turned as if he was going to walk away, but instead swung around connecting his fist with Sam's jaw. Knocked against the wall, Sam's cheek collided into the cold, hard bricks.

"And don't bring her anymore flowers," Nick said.

Sam cradled his face as the pain surged, and he nearly blacked-out. Blood trickled from between his fingers to his wrist. The taste was nauseating. When he looked up, Nick was walking toward the parking lot as if nothing had happened between them.

In what seemed like one enormous leap, Sam sprung onto Nick's back, taking him down— face first onto the gravel. Nick scrambled out of the attack and tried to connect with Sam's face again, but Sam blocked and threw a counter punch to the side of Nick's face.

Nick looked dazed. Sam stood up.

"She's all yours." Sam said, coldly.

Nick was down for the count, but not completely out, just nursing his wound. Sam turned and walked towards the restrooms. Tallulah stood by the ladies' room.

"You alright?" she asked him.

He nodded, and then entered the men's room. After washing off the blood, he sat on the floor, crying into his hands. He took a deep breath. "Pull it together, Wright," he told himself, as he began to calm down.

Nick must have seen me at Hayley's house. Did she see me, too?

A fast-moving car in the dirt lot marked Nick's departure.

***

In the ladies' room, Tallulah reported to Hayley, "Well, there goes Nick."

"What? There goes my ride home, too. Although, I think I would rather walk than ride with Nick."

"He just left you stranded? Are you two quarreling?" Tallulah asked.

"I guess you could say that."

"Well, I could give you a lift."

"Thanks."

Tallulah was touching up her lipstick. Hayley glanced at her and wondered if Tallulah was usually this nice of if she was just after Sam by way of a friendship with her. She and Sam had no understanding. They weren't boyfriend-girlfriend. He was free to choose. Hayley couldn't figure Sam out. He'd been after her for years, but now he seemed so distant. He had been through a lot though…

***

Sam's wounded pride and aching face recovered enough to trudge to the truck. He drove towards home at a snail's pace that matched his mood. Tallulah's baby blue Chevy Bel Aire zoomed around him, nearly missing some bushes on the side of the road. Sam shook his head at her crazy driving.

"We drive on the right side!' he shouted as if she could hear him.

***

The delivery truck traveled down Bulldog Drive, turned on Panola Street, and headed back toward the town square. Up ahead, Sam noticed Tallulah's car on the side of the road, next to an empty lot. The 'Welcome to Carthage' sign was broken, and her car was stuck in the mud. Steam from the radiator rose, swirling around the sign. The tires were hidden in deep ruts, spinning helplessly, going nowhere fast. He sighed, slowed down, and wished his conscience would let him keep driving. As he got out of the truck and approached her car, he heard the girls laughing through the closed windows. It was a sleepover kind of laughter that ends up with someone squirting soda out her nose.

"Well, Sam," Tallulah said, rolling down her window, "we're stuck!"

More laughing.

"Yeah, I can see that," he said, not amused.

"We could use a lift," she said, trying to regain her composure.

They tumbled out of the dented car and then into the truck. With Sam at the wheel, Hayley hugging the passenger door, and Tallulah squeezed in between them on the bench seat, they journeyed on to County Road 304. The girls were still on the verge of a giggle attack, but the laughing had calmed by the time they arrived at the Goodman Ranch.

"Wow!" Tallulah craned her neck, surveying the property. "Nice place!"

"Thanks," Hayley replied.

"Okay then… how about a quick game of 'Night Tag'?" Tallulah said, patting Sam's knee.

"How do you know about that?" Sam asked, as he parked near the front walkway.

"On the way here, I was telling her about it," Hayley said, glancing at Tallulah's hand on Sam's knee.

Before he could stop it, his heart swelled, knowing he'd been in their conversation, but bitterness still masked his hope.

Hayley noticed Sam's bleeding lip and reached out toward it. "Oh! What happened?" she asked. "You're bleeding."

"It's nothing." Sam turned away.

"Well, are we going to play, or not?" Tallulah asked, crawling over Hayley and hopping out of the truck. "Which way to the stables?"

She waited, Hayley pointed, and then, half-trotting, Tallulah made her way to the horses.

"I guess we're playing?" he asked, unable to look at her.

"I guess so," she shrugged.

***

Sam was "it" first, riding Blaze. Hayley rode Gracie, and Tallulah chose a gray, speckled appaloosa: Mac, named after McIntosh apples.

"I hope Mac has some pep in his step," she said, swinging her leg over the saddle.

At a faster pace than ever, the game took them past Mrs. Jasper's house, through the town, past the market, into the woods, and then into a huge open meadow, bordered by a quaint house on the east side and a trickling creek to the west.

The game was different— not the way he and Hayley had played. The joy of it was gone.

The leather reins cut into Sam's hands with each gallop. Leaning forward and giving Blaze a good nudge in the side with his boot, he was sure he'd never ridden a horse this fast before. He closed the gap on Tallulah, leaned toward her, and reached for her arm. Mac sped up, but he and his rider could not escape. Sam grabbed Tallulah's shoulder.

"Gotcha!" he yelled.

She shrieked.

They slowed to a stop.

"Whew! That's incredible! I can see why you like that game!"

Hayley caught up to them.

"Oh, look… that's my place just over there. Why don't we rest the horses a bit?" Tallulah said, turning Mac in the direction of a picturesque gazebo in the meadow behind her house.

Tiny white lights framing the gazebo beckoned them. They dismounted, climbed the steps, and sat in over-sized wicker chairs. Light coming from Tallulah's house flickered through the windows, and smoke drifted from the chimney. The night was chilly, clear, and moonlit.

"Gazebos are so romantic. I just adore my new home." She rose from her chair and began to twirl like a four-year-old ballerina performing for her parents on a makeshift stage.

Sam chuckled at how dramatic Tallulah could be.

"How do you like Carthage so far?" Hayley asked her.

She stopped spinning, and then fell into her chair. "I like it very much. In fact, it's one of the nicest places I've been."

"Do you move around a lot?" asked Sam.

"You have no idea! I've seen the world!"

A sudden, overpowering blast of light and rushing wind knocked them to the ground— wicker chairs and all. The horses scattered in fear.

Had a bomb exploded?

Instinctively, Sam shielded his face with his arms and squeezed his eyes shut. When the shock subsided a bit, he forced his eyes open, squinted and blinked until he could see. Frozen with fear, Sam gaped at the same angel that had appeared in the pond.

The being hovered, as a hawk would, suspended on a substantial air stream. The cape of his warrior uniform billowed in the wind like swelling ocean waves. His soul-piercing, blue eyes aligned with Sam's. Sam felt the urge to flee, if only his feet would work. He couldn't breathe, let alone run.

Hayley, trembling, inched next to Sam, and clutched his arm.

Tallulah scooted closer to them, looking thrilled at this encounter. The wind whipped through her hair.

"Can you believe this?" Tallulah exclaimed, the only one that could even muster words.

A slight expression of kindness washed over the angel's face as he finally spoke, his voice commanding respect as it fell upon them.

"Do not be afraid. I am Armada. Your presence is required in the Angel Realm. Follow me."

He turned around, not waiting for a response.

Tallulah's backyard and woods— gazebo and all— had vanished, and in their place stood an enormous golden staircase, the width of each step measuring wider than a city block. It ascended for miles, disappearing into a blinding light. The stairs shone like a mirror. Bending with each step, their reflections gawked back at them. Armada floated above the stairs, rising at a majestic pace.

Finding the courage from beneath the shock, Sam stood, and then held out his hands for the girls. Standing together, facing the staircase, they watched as Armada ascended.

With jittery knees, hand-in-hand, Sam, Hayley, and Tallulah began to climb.

Chapter Four
Archai

Step after step, they followed Armada up the staircase. Light shone down on them brighter than stadium lights, drawing them in.

Hayley stopped climbing.

Sam and Tallulah stopped as well, searching her face for an explanation.

She pulled her hands away from theirs. "This is just like those crazy visions I keep having," she said as tears welled up in her eyes.

Sam's eyes widened, and goose bumps prickled his skin. "You see angels?"

She nodded. "I've never told anyone. They'd think I was crazy or something."

"You'd be surprised," Sam said sheepishly, thinking about his own angel encounter.

"Hayley, this is real." Tallulah offered her hand, grinning, wide-eyed.

With reluctance, Hayley took her hand, and they began to climb again. Their pace quickened until they were sprinting up the stairs. They struggled to keep up with Armada.

"Faster!" Sam shouted.

They finally reached the top of the stairs. The light faded, revealing the solar system all around them. Sam felt like he could float away at any moment.

"It's like the top of a skyscraper!" exclaimed Sam.

Hayley pointed to a huge mass of darkness just beyond the top stair. "What is that?!"

Suddenly, the stairs shook like a paint mixer, knocking them to their knees. They clung to the steps. Everything went dark. The shaking continued. Sam felt like he was in a vacuum, being pulled through the darkness. He could hear the girls shouting out to him, but he couldn't see them. He wondered if Armada was a fallen angel masquerading as a holy one. Sam prayed aloud, keeping his eyes open, searching for light.

The darkness disappeared, replaced with blotches of brilliant color that swirled around them in a rushing wind. The colors succumbed to a brilliant white light that forced their eyes shut. They buried their faces in their arms.

Everything halted.

They raised their heads with cautious anticipation. Rubbing their eyes, they squinted as the view became clear. Like children on Christmas morning, they exploded with excitement for what they beheld.

The brilliant light had diminished, unveiling green rolling hills, waterfalls, and countless, lush plants bursting with blooms. The trees were giants.

Sam's eyes scanned the horizon. A glittery dust trickled down from between churning, white clouds. The atmosphere appeared sunless. Light was just everywhere. A warm glow showered everything, but it didn't come from a particular light source that he could see. The sky was a rich royal blue, lined by one continuous rainbow. There seemed to be no beginning and no end to this ribbon of colors that paralleled the expanse of the horizon.

Directly above the rainbow, the blackness of space manifested a spectacular display of stars, and planets that gyrated before his eyes. It was like his eyes were telescopes, and night and day existed simultaneously. Sam wondered if night ever fell on this planet.

The heavenly globes seemed close enough to touch, and the speed of their rotations and revolutions exceeded that of the solar system. Several moons and planets propelled quickly through the darkness as if they were juggling balls. Many planets had rings that resembled the movement of atoms. They appeared to glow from within.

Sam looked down from the splendor to see that the staircase was no longer under his feet. Instead, he was knee-deep in a field of wildflowers. Their intoxicating aroma swirled around him.

He turned toward Armada. "Are we in heaven?"

"No, Sam. We are on the planet Archai of the second heaven—the stellar heaven."

Sam nodded.

"It is now time to join the others," the angel said.

It wasn't until they climbed to the peak of the hillside that Sam understood what he meant by 'others.'

"Oh, wow." Hayley gasped in awe.

In the valley below, a swarming mass of thousands of people, escorted by angels, migrated toward a massive building.

Breathtaking, Sam thought.

Armada motioned for them to follow him toward the crowd. They scurried to keep up. Tallulah was the first to break into a full gallop through the flowers, laughing with the pure joy of the moment. Sam and Hayley chased after her, the laughter having spread to them.

They slowed as they joined the crowd. A majestic bugle fanfare erupted in multiple-part harmony played by hundreds of seraphim, floating just above the perimeter of the building.

The colossal building's white marble walls glowed. It was trimmed in gold that shone like mirrors, flashing beams of light in all directions. Sam's neck stretched as he examined the massive doors that rumbled as they swung inward, allowing the crowd to pour inside. Hebrew words were etched on a gold plate above the doors. Armada told them it said: The Celestial Hall.

"Look at those exquisite windows!" Tallulah exclaimed.

The stained-glass windows were rich shades of green, blue, purple, and teal, trimmed with silver, gold and precious gems. Each window—a work of art in itself—displayed an image of angels' missions.

Armada led them to their elegant opera-style seats, positioned high above an immense arena with a glossy hardwood floor. The seats resembled thrones: white velvet, rich cherry wood, high backs, and cushioned arms. Each had fanciful stitching spelling the name of the intended occupant.

"Our names," Hayley said, caressing the velvet arm of her own chair. Her glowing expression reminded Sam of when things between them were right.

Armada motioned for them to sit. They obeyed. And then he vanished.

The music faded. Silence overcame the hall as a figure floated down to the stage. Like a kaleidoscope, bursts of colors—some that Sam had never seen before—churned inside the figure's humanly shape, while electric sparks flashed within the being. Its shape seemed to be fluid-like and transparent. Right before their eyes, the figure morphed into a man. He donned a full-length, royal blue robe.

They waited on the edge of their plush chairs for him to speak. He took a moment to survey the hushed crowd.

"Welcome! I am Zadkiel. I have assumed this human form to better communicate with you. Angels can manifest themselves in many ways. I descended in spirit form to exhibit the form in which angels were created. Angels are neither male nor female. We do not marry or reproduce. We are not souls of your departed loved ones. The Lord created us to worship and serve Him."

His face was Roman-like, statuesque and stoic, but his eyes were kind. Tight waves of long blond hair rested on his brawny shoulders. Like

Armada, Zadkiel's eyes were blue as well, but his were more of a whisper of sky-blue.

"You have, no doubt, great anticipation to learn why you have been summoned to this place. God has revealed to us an imminent demonic uprising in each of your hometowns. In His wisdom, He has chosen you and legions of angels to defeat these satanic powers."

The crowd appeared to squirm, talking amongst themselves.

Sam looked at Hayley and Tallulah. "Defeat demons? Only angels can do that, right?"

Hayley shrugged her shoulders.

"Apparently we've been chosen," Tallulah said.

Zadkiel continued. "It is perhaps not a physical battle for which you have been chosen, but a spiritual one. Your eyes have been shielded from the presence of angels, holy and fallen. Those who listen fervently to the Spirit may have detected their presence. They can also sense a demonic attack. These attacks are often accompanied by a natural disaster, bizarre weather phenomena, or unusual disturbances."

Sam thought of the strange weather they'd had lately as he glanced at Hayley. Her eyebrows were raised.

"If you choose to assist God's angels in conquering Satan's army, you will become Knights of the Angel Realm, trained in dual-dimension warfare, and given supernatural gifts not usually bestowed upon humans. Dual-dimension means you will have access to both the spiritual and human dimensions simultaneously—you will be privy to what angels see every day."

Without warning, an enormous beast—three times Zadkiel's size—landed next to the archangel in a cloud of smoke. Sam jumped back into his seat, terrified by the sight of the creature's jagged scales, ominous horns, and vacant, black eyes. The darkness of it consumed the light around it. Even though it was on the stage below, Sam estimated it would only take a few jumps for it to reach their seats.

A man in a gray suit fled at the sight of the demon. People everywhere cowered and shielded their eyes from the creature. A woman a few rows below began crying out in prayer. Next to Sam, a Japanese woman in her twenties, cringed, huddled in a ball, and rocked with her knees under her chin. He noticed the name on her chair was Katie.

Zadkiel drew his sword, and with one powerful strike, smashed the demon's sword into innumerable pieces that floated into nothingness. Zadkiel forced it to the floor, his sword pressing at its throat.

"You fools!" it screeched. "You will surely die!"

Zadkiel drew back his sword, and then struck the demon. It was sucked into a churning abyss— a turbulent black hole that opened in the floor. Applause burst from the crowd. Zadkiel merely raised a hand until the clapping and cheering subsided.

"That was a demon in its purest form. Demons usually masquerade in more appealing and attractive forms. They are masters of deceitfulness and lies. Although menacing, Christians need not fear demons; they are powerless if you are a child of God. Sin! Sin is what you should fear. Run away from it at all costs. It makes you vulnerable. Allow it into your life, and Satan will take full advantage of it. At the very least, it distracts Christians, making them ineffective for their godly mission. None of us can know the mind of God. Not even angels. If He chooses to allow a demon to take your life in battle…it may be so, but it is only according to His will."

Sam's stomach tightened as he thought of battling demons. And about dying.

"You will be defending all who live in your hometown— especially the unsaved. Usually, they are unaware of their precarious situation, and are susceptible to injury and even death from demonic attacks. They are not children of God. They are therefore unprotected."

Sam tried to wrap his mind around this information, still in disbelief that he was actually in Stellar Heaven… in the Angel Realm.

"And now, you have a choice. Your God-given free will applies to this Knighthood as well. God specifically selected you; however, He wants you to freely choose to serve Him. There will be a moment of silence now for you to make your choice. God will look into your heart to find your answer. If you wish to decline this mission, you will return home with no memory of this place."

Scanning the hall, he saw a man in a uniform vanish. He could hardly believe his eyes.

Two older ladies just in front of Tallulah also disappeared. People began to vanish throughout the hall. The sound of gasps and murmurs of disbelief rushed over the crowd as they watched those around them disappear.

More than half the crowd was gone. Those left behind looked at each other in shock, yet with a certain determination. Pride filled Sam's heart. He knew he was part of something extraordinary. But he was still terrified. Hayley's color had returned to her face, and he detected a look of boldness in her expression. Tallulah looked as if she might jump from her seat and lead them in a cheer.

Zadkiel smiled. "You have now entered the Knighthood training period." Cheers gained momentum until the entire hall rocked with shouts of praise and applause. Zadkiel waited until it was quiet to continue. "Your guide will escort you to your living quarters. Intensive training begins tomorrow as time on earth stands still. Rest well."

***

A petite angel with a fair complexion and bright red hair, named Dina, floated over the cobblestones as they followed her down the road that meandered through redwood giants. Sam had read about redwoods in geography. He found himself completely distracted by the enormous trees and scanned them to the top. The orbiting, stellar sky zoomed just beyond the redwoods as Sam found there was night on Archai after all.

"I really can't believe this is happening," Hayley whispered.

"It's incredible." Tallulah added.

Sam smiled—feeling like it was one outlandish dream.

As the trees thinned, exposing an open meadow, an illuminated castle, constructed from white marble like the Taj Mahal, debuted at the top of a hill. Smoke escaped from several chimneys, and light glowed from conspicuous windows. Dina led them to its ornate, leaded glass doors.

"Make yourself at home. The west wing is for Sam. Tallulah and Hayley will share the east wing. A meal is waiting for you in the dining room. In the morning, when the chimes ring, follow this path to begin your training." She pointed down the path ahead that led to more woods.

"Thank you," Sam said, amazed they were going to live in a castle.

Smiling, Dina ascended above the trees, and then disappeared from sight.

They ventured inside, and then explored the rooms together. There were several common rooms on the first floor; but the one they admired the most, was the sitting room next to the dining room. It was decorated with intricate tapestries and heart-warming paintings. Fresh flowers and plants, crystal vases, and silver candlesticks embellished plush furniture. Recessed ceilings framed paintings that reminded Sam of Michelangelo's works. The fireplace blazed, and the marble mantle over it displayed a spectacular blown glass horse. Hayley crossed the room to admire it more closely.

"Let's find our rooms," Tallulah suggested.

Two curved staircases framed the main entrance. They assumed one led to the west wing and one to the east, although they had no idea which was which. Massive chandeliers hung in balance with the staircases, lighting the intricate designs carved into the polished wood railings. Floral patterned runners gave the stairs a finished look. They picked the staircase on the right, raced up to the top and into a hallway the size of Carthage. Tallulah ran to the first door.

"This must be the east wing because here's my name!" Tallulah exclaimed, pointing to the nameplate on the polished wood door.

When they entered, Tallulah was amazingly speechless for the first time since Sam had met her. Every inch of the room: rugs, quilts, paintings, and curtains were adorned with—of course—sunflowers. Bunches of her favorite flowers arranged in vases dotted the room.

In her private bathroom stood an over-sized, claw-foot tub. Tallulah dashed over and jumped into the empty tub.

"I absolutely cannot wait to take a bubble bath. This is wonderful!"

She hopped out and explored the rest of her suite. Adjoining the bedroom was a private library complete with a stocked teacart.

"God knows what you like," Sam said, shaking his head.

"It couldn't be better," she said grinning. "Now let's see Hayley's room."

"Let's!" Hayley agreed.

The first thing Sam noticed when Hayley opened her door was the flickering light coming from dozens of candles. Her face was gleaming. She scanned the room to find a king-sized, lace covered canopy bed with a three-tiered step next to it. In a spacious, adjoining retreat was the best of all—a white grand piano in a room surrounded by large mirrors and windows. The scent of roses flowed from the yellow, white and pink arrangements filling the suite. Romantic paintings of horses finished the décor.

"I may never leave this room," Hayley sighed.

"Yes, you will...you haven't seen Sam's room yet," Tallulah teased.

"Race ya!" Hayley said, sprinting for the door.

Wanting to be the first to his own room, Sam bolted, passing them on the west wing's staircase. His jaw dropped when he opened his door.

An enormous, four-sided, stone fireplace was the focal point of the room. Facing one side of the fireplace there was a cozy retreat, with over-sized and over-stuffed, black leather couches. Another side could be viewed from a king-sized bed with kingly drapes hanging around it. His bathroom modeled loosely after ancient Roman bathhouses with a sauna, and an extra-large, sunken tub that had extensive patterned tile work.

But the best surprise of all was two Labrador puppies (one yellow, one black) napping by the fire. He scooped them up like a little boy, and their pink tongues licked his neck and face.

"Aaaaaw," the girls said in unison, almost squeaking.

"They're adorable," Hayley said. "Come to Auntie Hayley." She took the yellow pup.

"Now come on, you have to share, you know," Tallulah complained, reaching out for the black one. "I wonder what their names are…here's a tag… oh, it's blank."

"Let's see…" Sam said, reclaiming the black puppy. "We're here in a castle, so I think I'll call this one… Lancelot. Maybe I could get it inscribed—" He looked at the tag and it read: Lancelot. He quickly showed the girls.

"But it was blank—oh yeah, pretty much anything is possible here," Hayley said.

Scooping the yellow pup from Hayley's arms, he said "Okay, this one will be Guinevere." They all looked at the tag while the letters appeared, spelling 'Guinevere'.

Couldn't have been better if I'd designed it myself.

Playing with the puppies almost made them forget about the meal that was waiting for them, so they headed for the dining room.

It was an intimate room, not large and proper like one might assume a castle's dining room to be. The lights were low, and under silver domes their meal was still hot. It was by far the best food Sam had ever consumed: lightly seasoned steamed vegetables, prime rib, and herb bread with garlic butter. He had never been so satiated. He felt like a king.

Tallulah decided it was time for a bubble bath, so she left Sam and Hayley alone.

"This is really something, huh, Sam?" Her eyes searched his as if looking for a sign of the old Sam.

"Yeah, pinch me… I *know* I'm dreaming." An awkward silence brought to mind the vision of Hayley with Nick. "Goodnight, Hayley," he said firmly as he walked directly out of the dining room and then to the staircase.

A few steps up, he paused on the stairs, his head hung low. *What am I doing? Why can't I forgive her?* After a brief tug of war between heart and head, stubbornness won and he began to climb again at a sloth's pace.

Upstairs he got ready for bed and relaxed on the couch in front of a mammoth fire. The puppies were curled up on his chest. He fell asleep listening to the distant sounds of Hayley's piano playing.

Chapter Five
Knights in Training

Light trickled through parted curtains in Sam's room, gently waking him. As his eyes began to focus, he heard music, sung in Hebrew, coming from outside. He opened French doors that led to a large, private balcony. Stepping outside, he observed a lone angel, in spirit form, soaring through mountainous clouds, dipping in and out of the rainbow that was below the spinning stars and planets. Sam stood still, letting the warmth of a new day on Archai wash over him. The music seemed to come from that single angel.

"I could get used to waking up this way."

Lancelot and Guinevere scurried out a doggy door, yapping and bounding in circles around Sam. "Hey there," he said, patting them. They scampered off to investigate some potted plants and rose bushes.

"A doggy door in a castle? Now I've seen everything."

He could see rolling hills for miles in the north and east and oceans of redwoods in the south and west. In the distance, several other castles—some white, black, gray, and even…a pink one—graced hills of their own.

He bathed and dressed in the only clothes he found hanging in the closet: a black and gray speckled, long-sleeved uniform tunic revealing a subtle angel crest on both sleeves and sturdy, black pants and boots that told him the training would be vigorous. He hadn't seen anyone in the castle, but everything he needed appeared before him.

When he greeted the girls at breakfast, he saw their clothes matched his. He wanted to feast on the incredible meal, but then decided he should eat lightly before training—whatever that training might entail. The girls picked at their plates as well. He only looked at Hayley once.

Tallulah broke the silence. "Incredible music this morning, wouldn't you say?"

"I thought I was dreaming," Hayley said.

"Beyond spectacular," Sam said, stretching his arms.

The impending training made the three of them pensive and reserved. Through the quiet, Sam could hear the puppies yelping, so he excused himself from the table. He needed some fresh air anyway, so he took the puppies out into a side yard.

Tallulah joined him. She plopped right down in the grass and played with the labs. Rolling onto her back, she let them spring about her, licking her face, while they got lost in her voluptuous, auburn hair. She laughed until she found it hard to breathe and sat up. Sam sat next to her.

"They are adorable," she said, straightening her hair. Then she turned and looked directly at him."

"I'm so glad we're here!" She threw her arms around his neck.

His face got buried in her hair, her scent intoxicating him.

"Isn't it fantastic?" She squeezed hard in her usual exuberant way, but when Sam was silent, she pulled back slightly to look at him. "Are you alright? You seem…"

He cleared his throat. "No, I'm fine. Maybe just a little awestruck with this place?"

"Hayley told me about how you lost your pop. I'm so sorry. That must be incredibly hard for you."

"It has been rough."

He looked up, catching a glimpse of Hayley in a window, looking down at them. Before he could react, Hayley turned away and then disappeared from view. He realized his former plan to make Hayley jealous seemed really stupid now.

"How do you think Hayley's getting on?" Tallulah asked, letting him go. "I thought I heard her crying last night. Do you think she's a bit nervous?"

"No. She's stronger than you think. She's alright."

"Well, I'll just have to keep an eye on her," she said, fixing a wave of his hair, and then flitting back inside.

The chimes rang, so he put the puppies inside.

The three walked without speaking, down the path that led through the woods until they came to a large open field where dozens of others had converged, sitting on stone benches. One angel stood on a platform in the middle of the group. Sam found a bench, and the girls sat on either side of him.

An angel, with shoulder-length, dark, smooth hair, olive skin, and wild sea-green eyes, began the meeting.

"Good morning. I hope you rested well. I am Camael. It is my pleasure to present some information beneficial to your success. Let me begin by posing a question: What do you believe is the best defense against a fallen angel?"

An older man, a jokester, with buzzed hair of an army recruit, stood up and saluted. "Sir, garlic and a wooden stake, sir?"

Mild laughter eased the tension. The man belly laughed.

Camael chuckled, too. "Old Jack, you have always been a comedian," he said, still grinning. "Humor is always good for the soul, but seriously…anyone else?"

The crowd was silent. Sam knew it was prayer, but chose to keep quiet, as others were most likely doing also.

Camael continued. "The dimension in which you will soon enter differs greatly from this one. The Word says: 'For our struggle is not against flesh and blood, but against the rulers, against the authorities, against the powers of this dark world and against the spiritual forces of evil in the

69

heavenly realms.' Battles are not fought physically as much as they are spiritually; therefore, your greatest defense is prayer. The Lord can move mountains by pointing a finger or even just by a mere thought, but He wants you to *ask*. Legions of angels anticipate your request for their protection.

"And remember…Christians are children of God, and hence under His protection. Demons have no power over you unless He allows it. Dark angels may be more powerful than you, but the Great I Am is omnipotent. Trust in His strength, His plan. Be strong, have faith, and follow the Lord in everything." He let those words ruminate.

"As you know, each of you will receive a supernatural gift—an ability humans would not usually possess. These gifts will vary within your group. You need not be in the alternate dimension to use them. A personal instructor will train you daily until your gift is mastered. Remember that these gifts are designed to aid your mission, not replace prayer. Use them wisely.

"You will now meet your instructor," Camael said, vanishing.

No one spoke as they remained on their benches. Sam had that first-day-of-school feeling in his gut when, from every direction, like parachutists, dozens of angels landed gracefully on the platform. Silence still filled the air, as the angels ventured onto the field to find their students. Sam almost fell over from shock when his instructor approached.

"Ray?" Sam was shocked.

Ray chuckled. "Yep. Ray... short for Raziel."

"An angel? All this time..."

"How ya doin'? Ray asked, holding out his hand to Sam.

"Shocked out of my skin, to tell you the truth!" They shook hands like long lost friends. "Really glad to see you."

"Glad to see ya, son," he said, grinning. "But...we've got a lot to do. So, let's get busy." Raziel motioned for Sam to follow him.

Dumbfounded, Sam walked a few steps behind as they crossed the field, stopping next to the edge of the woods. Sam was too distracted by Ray to even notice where the girls had gone.

In front of Sam's eyes, Ray changed. His appearance went from work-worn to handsome elegance. Leathery, wrinkled skin disappeared. In its place shone a vibrant, smooth complexion. At the ranch, Ray had assumed the role of horse trainer. Here, he was an angel of beauty. If Sam hadn't witnessed the change himself, he may not have recognized Ray.

"You're gonna learn the basics of swordplay and combat skills." Ray explained.

For a moment, the little boy somewhere still within Sam was thrilled to hear he would have a sword, but then he realized the seriousness of it. This was not a childhood game.

"It's gonna get tough, but I know your abilities. Because of your experience and strength from sports and labor, you are physically prepared for the next stage."

71

Sam thought back to the heavy lifting and vigorous chores Ray required of him at the ranch.

"My training began this summer," Sam said.

Ray laughed. "Yep. Shore did. So, today, and the rest of this month, we'll do footwork skills, then weeks of sword control, attack exercises, and defense skills. And there'll be demon observation— learning your enemy. When ya complete all this, I 'll present the gifts the Lord has chosen for you."

Sam nodded.

Ray motioned for him to turn around. Where nothing had stood before, appeared an obstacle course. Mountains of ladders and steps told Sam that it would be a very long day.

"Warm up on this here course, and then I'll show ya stances and lunges."

***

After training, Sam trudged back to the castle and collapsed onto his bed. He thought he might stay there forever, until the aroma of supper reached his room. That was motivation enough to get moving.

He washed quickly in his swimming pool- sized tub, dressed, and flew down to see what the angels had cooked-up this time. He was surprised to see nothing in the dining room. The sound of singing in the gourmet kitchen drew him in. Tallulah and Hayley were cooking.

"Hey, what's going on?" Sam inquired.

"We thought we'd give the angels the evening off," Hayley joked, as she sautéed mushrooms.

"Aren't you exhausted from today?" he asked them.

"What do you mean? I read Bible stories and sang worship songs all day. In fact, I was thinking I should go for a walk after supper," Hayley said.

"We studied paintings of birds and worshipped all day as well," Tallulah reported. "Why? What did you do?"

"Let's just say that today was harder than all of my football games combined."

The girls looked at each other and exploded with laughter.

"Poor Sam," Tallulah mocked. "Maybe I'll join you for that walk, Hayley."

More laughing.

Sam felt a little uneasy with the girls getting along so well. After all, just this morning Hayley seemed jealous of the attention Tallulah was showing him. Suddenly he imagined them making a secret pact to laugh at him for the rest of their lives.

***

Despite achy muscles, Sam decided to join the girls on their walk. The draw of meeting their neighbors outweighed his weariness.

"Okay, Sam, you may join us, but we are visiting the pink castle first. No complaints," Hayley demanded with a smirk.

He rolled his eyes. "Pink."

73

As they walked the half-mile or so, Sam was surprised at his replenished strength, especially when they climbed the hillside elevating the pink castle.

Tallulah knocked on the grand pink door, and with a Hitchcock style squeak, it opened slowly, revealing an impressive entry of pink marble floors and pillars—a Pepto-Bismol paradise. Lace, ruffles, flowers, and pearls smothered everything.

"I'm going to be sick," he said, putting his hand over his mouth.

Tallulah jabbed him as if his comments would diminish the view. "Let's go in."

"Uninvited?" Hayley asked.

"The door invited us," Tallulah said, stepping inside.

"Hello?" Hayley said, following.

Sam followed, unimpressed.

The sound of laughter drew them to a courtyard filled with exotic plants and birds. They were expecting to see people, but realized the laughter came from multi-colored parrots. They watched the parrots, amazed at their human-like voices.

"Hello?" *This* voice came from behind them.

Sam turned, and instead of a parrot, he recognized a young Japanese woman standing in the doorway.

"Katie?" he asked.

"Do I know you?"

"Well, not exactly. I saw you in the Celestial Hall."

"Oh, yes. I remember you now."

74

Hayley spoke. "Sorry that we just let ourselves in...the door opened..."

"Don't worry. You are very welcome. Will you please sit down?"

She motioned to wicker chairs with floral-print cushions camouflaged in the mock jungle. Before their eyes, tea and dessert appeared on the matching wicker table.

Tallulah appeared delighted. "Tea! Would you like me to pour out?"

"Yes, thank you." Katie said. "Well, you know *my* name, but..."

"I'm Hayley," she said, pointing to herself.

"I'm Tallulah," She poured tea into a cup, and handed it to Katie.

"Thank you."

"My name's Sam."

"Nice to meet you. I love your accents. You two sound like you're from the south, but yours is British, right?"

"That's right...and let me guess. You're Japanese, but I detect a bit of New Yorker." Tallulah said.

"Wow, you're good," Katie said. "I've lived there since I graduated from high school, and, in those two years I have at least accomplished that."

"Let me guess...you're an aspiring actress?" Hayley inquired.

"Yes, and while I'm aspiring, I wait tables."

A knock at the front door, called her away from her guests, but she returned in a few minutes with two men and two puppies.

"Lancelot. Guinevere." Sam stood up to claim them.

"I found them sniffing around our garden…chasing rabbits, I think," the dark-haired man said, handing Lancelot to Sam. "I'm Spencer."

They shook hands. Spencer had a firm grip, was well groomed, and in his thirties; and Sam, being six feet himself, found himself looking up at Spencer who was at least six foot four.

"Nice to meet you. My name's Sam. This is Hayley, Tallulah…and y'all know Katie?"

"Now we do…we only met her at the door." He turned toward the other man, chuckling. "This is Montana Jack."

Jack was more Sam's height, but unlike Spencer, he appeared unkempt. Shaggy, brown hair and an untrimmed beard tried to hide his rugged, yet handsome, forty-something face.

"No, no, just call me Jack," he said, smirking at his friend. "I *live* in Montana, though, *usually*…" He handed Guinevere to Sam. "But for now, I'm staying in the black castle up the road, with Spencer and Old Joe."

"Nice to meet you, Jack." Sam looked at Tallulah and Hayley. "Black. Now *that* is a suitable color for a castle."

The girls started to object, but then were interrupted. A tall, attractive woman with long, blond hair entered the courtyard. "I thought I heard voices in here—that weren't parrots, I mean. You didn't tell me we were throwing a party." She smiled at her roommate.

"All of our neighbors decided to drop by at the same time! Rebecca, meet Hayley, Tallulah, Sam, and…Spencer, was it? And, uh, Jack. Whew!" Katie said, pointing towards each person, seeming relieved that she remembered.

"Too bad Old Joe didn't come along. We left him snoozing in a hammock," Spencer said.

"Tea anyone?" Katie asked, as she held up a pink teapot.

"One lump or two? One lump or two?" a parrot squawked.

Chapter Six
Gifts

"This is the day, Sam. You've worked hard. Now you'll get your gifts," Ray said with pride.

It had been nearly two months of drills and agonizing workouts, while the girls did who-knows-what. He didn't ask them anymore. It was too painful to hear about 'art appreciation' and 'craft class'.

Ray led him to a wooded area next to a cave. The sound of a creek nearby made it a serene location. Four angels stood guard at the cave's entrance. Ray and Sam sat on a fallen log by the cave.

"Son, our time on the ranch was very good. Of all the assignments I've had, I think I liked working with you best of all. You're diligent, kind, and truthful, but, frankly, you need to work on forgiving. And you need to trust the Lord."

The words slapped Sam in the face. No one had ever called him out on these things. He was unable to respond. But he knew they were true.

"I know times have been hard, but you also know He works things out for good according to His purpose. Be patient. Try to rejoice *through* challenges in life. If you are bitter, or unforgiving, then you may not hear the Lord when He calls. Understand?"

"Yes, but how do I change all that?"

"The Lord will show you." He stood up. "Are you ready for your first gift?"

"Yes!" Sam stood also, brimming with excitement.

"Now, I know you've read Ephesians 6:10-18."

"The part about putting on the full armor of God?"

"Yes. Your first gifts represent this armor: a shield and a sword. With these things you may send demons into the abyss, just as angels can."

As he spoke, the sword and the shield appeared in Sam's hands.

"One strike with the sword, one look at its own reflection in the shield and a demon is hurled into the abyss."

Sam found it hard to focus on what Ray was telling him, because the sword and shield were captivating. "The abyss," he echoed, observing the intricate details of the weapon.

The shield was mirror-like. When he looked at it, he felt as if he could see his own soul. The sword's handle had sapphires and diamonds surrounding a seemingly bottomless, fiery opal—an opal churning with a sea of colorful clouds and lightning. The shield was much the same with sapphires and diamonds around the perimeter, a matching, turbulent opal gracing the top.

"I can tell you like them." Ray grinned.

"What's not to like? Thank you."

"Thank the Lord, son, not me. Sam, they represent the Shield of Faith and the Sword of the Spirit. They are not just material weapons. They were chosen specifically for you. Remember, the Sword of the Spirit is the Word of God...the Word of God spoke the universe into existence. The universe."

"The universe," Sam echoed again.

The sword disappeared and reappeared in a sheath on a braided belt around Sam's waist. The angel's crest was on the sheath.

"Your second gift is useful and unusual. Angels cannot even do it. Unfortunately, it is not a pleasant gift, I'm afraid."

Sam held his breath as he waited to hear.

"Enter the cave, and then you'll know."

His enthusiasm faded, but he ventured into the cave anyway. The guards at the entrance didn't move as he passed by. Holding the sword and the shield improved his confidence a little as he made his way down a dark tunnel that turned to the right. It opened to a larger space where he found a cage. More angels were surrounding the cage. Sam was glad he was not alone. Without a word, they stood aside, revealing a demon.

Sam wanted to flee, but instead tightened his grip on the hilt of his sword while the creature thrashed around, crashing into the bars that appeared electrified. When it caught sight of Sam, it stopped, staring right at him.

A screeching voice, that made Sam shudder, came from somewhere in the cave, echoing off the dimly lit walls. He couldn't see who was speaking.

"Who is this?" the voice rasped. *"Maybe I could trick him into releasing me. Dull-witted, pitiful Christian. If only I could get him alone. I could tell him lies…"*

As the voice continued, Sam searched everywhere, holding his shield up higher, but could not find the owner of the voice. Then it occurred to him: *It's the demon!* He could hear it, but its mouth wasn't moving. *I hear its thoughts!* He stared at the creature, becoming more repulsed with each syllable.

That's my gift? **That's** *my gift? Sounds like more of a curse than a gift!* He searched for perspective. *I'm sure He has His reasons.*

***

After the training session, Sam hiked along the water. He came to a secluded, calm pool, fed by the creek, and went for a swim in his black shorts and matching tank undershirt. It felt like back home in the old wash hole.

When his fingers pruned, he stretched out on a large boulder—using his clothes as a pillow— watching the planets spin hypnotically above him. He fell asleep.

His clothes were almost dry when he awoke to the unforgettable sound of a demon's voice. Grabbing his clothes, sword and shield, he took cover behind the boulder. The voice seemed to come from a patch of trees a hundred yards away.

He cautiously set out to find it, secretly hoping he wouldn't.

Just like a training exercise, he crept quickly in the shadows of the trees, trying to be as stealth as possible. Instead of a demon, he found Hayley and her instructor. He didn't mean to spy on her, but he knew the demon was nearby. It needed to be found.

The demon's voice bounced around the treetops, but Sam could not see it. "I'll wait. Weak…helpless…" it snarled.

The demon was then quiet, and Sam decided that he should stay hidden and wait.

***

As Sam knelt behind dense shrubs, he noticed Hayley's instructor, Florelle, had an air of sophistication, as shown by her lean features and graceful mannerisms. Florelle's sleek, jet-black hair was pulled back taut, and braids encircled her head like a wreath.

They were sitting cross-legged, facing each other on sparse grass with a canopy of oak branches above them. Light twinkled from between rustling leaves above, exposing hazy dust as it sifted to the ground. For the moment, he forgot about the demon's voice as he peeked through the crowded bushes.

"Hayley, you are a beautiful, young woman, and so you shall be paired with a beautiful gift. I will show you how it works."

The angel took a pair of glittering, white gloves from her vest pocket and put them on. With her gloved hands, she took both of Hayley's hands. She breathed in deeply and shut her eyes. Hayley copied her. The angel sat motionless while Hayley seemed restless. A few seconds later they dropped hands, and Hayley appeared extremely excited.

"That was amazing! I cannot believe that! I *actually* saw Jesus' life! It was like watching a movie, but it also felt like I was there...*in* the movie...*with* Him! Wow! That's incredible!"

Sam had never seen her so animated—in fact, she reminded him of Tallulah.

"How long have we been sitting here?" Hayley asked.

"Just a few seconds."

"It felt like hours to me." Suddenly, she looked like she was about to cry. "I can't accept this gift. Something doesn't feel right. I can't explain it." She buried her head in her hands and sobbed.

"It is true. Currently, I am unable to bestow this gift upon you. The Lord has just revealed to me why. Do you know why, Hayley?"

She shook her head.

"Your name is not written in the Book of Life yet."

With a tear-soaked face, she froze. "You mean...I'm not a Christian? How can that be? I have gone to church my whole life. I-I believe in God!" She raised her voice as she began to panic.

"The demons also know of God's existence...and they tremble because of it. But they

83

are also not in the book." Florelle's voice was calm, but firm.

"What do I do now?"

"Search your heart. The Lord is calling you."

The look of pure epiphany flooded her face. "That's what Zadkiel was telling me. I need to choose."

"He told you this?"

"Just last week, I was walking home and came across him at the river…fishing. I was surprised to see an angel fishing."

Florelle chuckled.

"He invited me to fish with him. He didn't say much, but he did say it was time to make a choice. Before I even asked what he meant, he said it would be revealed in time."

"So… how many?"

"How many what?"

"How many fish did you catch?"

Hayley smiled. "I caught three and Zadkiel caught seven."

***

Sam was stunned beyond belief. How could she not have been a Christian all these years? She had acted more Christianly than most of the people in church—not in some pompous or righteous way—just through her warm generosity.

He watched as Hayley bowed her head, and although he couldn't hear, he knew she was praying. His eyes streamed with tears as he watched the girl he loved accept the Lord as her Savior with an angel by her side.

A multitude of perfect voices came from all directions. Hayley, still on her knees, searched the trees above for the joyful sounds. Sam watched from his hiding spot as Florelle began to sing and rise up among the trees. Dozens of angels, some in spirit form, swooped through the trees, singing joyfully in harmony. Bursts of color and a glittery light sifted to the ground like confetti.

"Beautiful," Sam whispered.

As the song came to an end, Florelle returned to her spot next to Hayley.

"That…that was amazing." Hayley spoke as if in awe.

"It was for you."

"For me?"

"Angels rejoice every time someone accepts the Lord."

Hayley smiled the largest smile he'd ever seen. She held her hand to her heart and breathed heavily, shaking her head slightly with pure amazement. Florelle produced a handkerchief and held it out to her. Hayley took it with trembling hands and dried her joyful tears. After a few deep breaths, she appeared calmer and ready to receive her gift.

"Now, it is my pleasure to give you this gift from the Lord," Florelle said, holding out the gloves. "With these, you may help many come to the Lord as you have today."

Beaming, Hayley held the gloves like a mother holding her newborn. "What can I do with a

85

gift like this?" she said, slipping them on and admiring them.

"I am glad you asked. The potential influence you could have on an unbeliever is staggering. This experience could easily help turn their heart to the Lord. However, if you were to touch a demon—"

"Whoa! That's not happening." Hayley's smile faded.

"Well, *if* you were to touch a demon, it would be electrocuted and sucked into the abyss."

"That's good…but I'm *not* touching a demon. No-o-o… thank you."

"Well, let us see where the Lord leads you. Keep your mind and heart open. Now, you still have one more gift."

It appeared instantly in Hayley's hand,

She began to laugh and covered her mouth as if embarrassed.

"What is it?" Florelle asked.

"For a moment I thought I was holding a jump rope."

Florelle smiled. "This whip can send demons into the abyss. You have handled one before, correct?"

"Well, this is a bull whip. When I helped Ray train some of the horses, we used a lunge whip. Hayley cracked it. But ours are not this beautiful."

The handle resembled a stained-glass window, illuminated from within. The lash was not constructed of leather, but of diamonds, strung together.

Florelle then pointed to show Hayley it was hanging from a belt around her waist. The belt was white leather studded with diamonds to match the whip.

***

Again, Sam heard the demon's voice behind him, and turned around, scanning the area. No one in sight. He looked back to find Hayley and her instructor had finished their time together. They had begun to walk away. He followed like a spy, trying not to crunch the leaves beneath his bare feet.

Florelle accompanied her to a path by the creek, said goodbye, and vanished. Hayley continued walking and began to hum, while Sam secretly followed.

As he began to hear the voice again, a man in his twenties that resembled Nick joined her at a fork in the path. His uniform matched the one Sam carried under his arm. She was startled at first, but he was gentlemanly, putting her more at ease. As they continued walking, they chatted enough for Sam to overhear him introduce himself as a Knight in training. It was hard to hear what he was telling her over the demonic voice nearby.

"Lies! Lies!" the demon spouted.

Sam frantically searched for the demon, when it occurred to him: it had manifested itself as the man. He zeroed in on the voice. He was sure.

Without contemplation, Sam's intense training kicked into high gear. He charged the masquerading demon, swinging his sword deep into the creature's side. It instantly shed its façade, appearing now in its grotesque, purest form: blacker than black, four pairs of jagged wings, a long, hooked snout, and spikes on its back. Hayley and Sam watched it flail and scream, as the abyss swallowed it up.

She stood speechless, looking horrified. The ground where the creature had been sucked, had returned to its original state, but she was still staring at the spot.

Bent over, catching his breath, Sam also stared at the ground, half-expecting the creature to reappear. He looked up at Hayley and noticed that she was looking at him strangely. It was only then that he realized how informally he was dressed.

"You alright?" he asked her, picking up his clothes, still amazed he'd actually slain a demon. He dressed quickly.

She sat on a boulder, appearing stunned— her face pale, eyes wide, and mouth open. Through panicked breaths, she said "I'm fine…I guess… but how did you do that?"

"My first gift," he said plunging the sword into the soft ground in front of her and handing her the shield. "You can see what they're capable of."

"Yeah, I got a pretty good look," she said, nodding. "This is breathtaking. The sword is, too," she said picking it up. "Whoa…it's heavy."

"Yes," he said sitting next to her on the rock. Sitting this close to her was a little awkward, but after what they'd just gone through, the past didn't matter as much.

"How did you know he was a demon?"

"My second gift: hearing demons' thoughts." With this information, her eyebrows raised. He continued. "I tracked this one, and then came across you and your instructor. I followed you to make sure you were okay."

"You can actually hear what they're thinking? I'm glad that's not *my* gift."

"Believe me, I would much rather have yours."

"You know about my gifts?"

"Well, like I said…"

"Right…you were hunting demons and *spying* on me," she kidded.

He took the bait. "I wasn't actually *spying* on you. I was *protecting* you—"

She smiled, letting him off the hook. "Then you must have seen me praying…and the angels rejoicing!" she said with a child-like smile.

"Yes," he said reverently. "I'm really happy for you—for your decision."

"And aren't my gifts awesome?"

Her face glowed with excitement, like it had during the early weeks of the summer.

"Here, let me try it with you," she said, putting on the gloves.

He leaned back in hesitation.

"Don't worry. You'll only be electrocuted and flung into the abyss if you're a demon."

"Ahh, man. You'll blow my cover."

She smiled.

He sat right next to her, but still felt a million miles away. She reached out for his hands and he closed his eyes, overwhelmed by the conflict inside. To love her…to love her not…

He felt a subtle tingling, and he was instantly at Jesus' side. Everything looked real, but he knew it wasn't. It was as if he had stepped back in time, into Bible times. He could reach out and touch Jesus. He could hear Jesus' soothing voice. Sam witnessed every major event in His life including His miraculous ascension, and then it was over. He wanted to do it again.

"That was…unbelievable." Sam's eyes welled up and he fought back tears from the experience. "*That* is a cool gift."

He realized they were still holding hands and let go. Feeling like it was minutes, but knowing it was only seconds of awkward silence, he said, "Well let's get going. Tallulah's probably waiting for us."

They strolled toward the castle, making small talk—carefully avoiding taboo subjects like their relationship.

***

Tallulah was in the sitting room, reading a book as she waited for them. A fire warmed the room, and Lancelot and Guinevere warmed her lap. The puppies scrambled to greet them, tails wagging.

Sam noticed Tallulah was not herself—quiet.

"Okay, spill it. Why are you so quiet?" he said, cutting to the chase.

"Is it your gift? Don't you like it?" Hayley asked.

"I have been blessed with an enormous ability."

"Well… what is it?" he asked.

"You're not going to believe this."

"Tell us!" they exclaimed in unison.

"I think I should *show* you. Come with me!" she said, running from the room.

They followed her to the east wing staircase. She scrambled to the top, and then stood on the railing.

"You'll fall!" Hayley cautioned.

"That's okay if I do…I can fly!"

And with that, she plunged toward the tiles below, pulling up at the last second. As she flew circles above their heads, Sam and Hayley stood watching her, dumbfounded.

"I can't believe this," Sam said.

"But wait… there's more!" she said, hovering.

She put her right hand out, and magically moved a vase from one table to another. Extending her left hand, she opened the front door. The chandeliers shook when she raised both together. She lowered her arms, and the lights dimmed. Giggling, she shrugged.

"How on earth are you doing that?" Hayley asked.

"It's a secret…the angels told me I can't divulge anything."

Jokingly irate, Sam said, "You mean I have to hear the creepy thoughts of nasty demons, but *you*…you get to fly? …And move stuff? I want to trade gifts!" he said, half-kidding.

Showing off, Tallulah did a loop and landed next to them. "Woohoo!"

"I wonder what gifts the others received," Sam said.

"We'll find out at Feast and Joust tomorrow." Hayley said. "I just wonder…*why* we need them."

Chapter Seven
A Final Gift

Tomorrow was to be their last day on Archai. But today they would feast. Tonight, they would dance.

Among rolling hills, wildflowers, and willow trees, the Knights, in casual, medieval dress, mingled on picnic blankets, relaxing and feasting. The group seemed never ending, blankets spanning across an enormous field. Seven magnificent waterfalls feeding several streams marked the edges of the field. The streams merged in the center—producing a massive geyser type fountain

A richly decorated and almost endless buffet of platters, baskets, tureens were complimented by fanciful ice sculptures, beverage fountains, and floral centerpieces. Meats, cheeses, breads, pastries, garden vegetables, exotic fruits, and chocolate treasures satisfied all who partook. They drank from goblets of silver; dined off plates of gold.

Their team of eight sat close on an over-sized blanket in the shade of a willow. It felt like the last day of camp—they had grown so close and now their time together was ending.

They talked in groups of twos and threes, sometimes; and laughed, all together, at other times. Hayley and Tallulah were sitting farthest away from Sam, speaking mainly to Katie, usually in hushed tones. Lancelot and Guinevere were there, too, of course, sneaking many treats from generous admirers, and receiving so much attention they had to curl up for a nap.

"Your puppies are adorable, Sam," Rebecca said.

"Thanks, I only wish they were really mine."

"I bet you'll miss them when we go back home tomorrow."

"Yeah," he said, stroking Lancelot's floppy ear. "Where is home for you?" he asked.

"California. I teach third grade in the town of Orange."

From across the blanket, Spencer set his plate down, and looked at Rebecca. "Did you say California?"

"Yes."

"Hey, I live in Corona Del Mar," he said

Her eyes lit up. "I've been there many times. I love that beach. What street do you live on?"

"Ocean Boulevard."

"Oh, yes. I park on that street and hike down an enormous hill, past a mansion to get to the beach."

"Actually…" he seemed reluctant, "I own that mansion on that enormous hill."

Sam and Rebecca's mouths dropped open.

"Are you a millionaire or something?" Sam asked.

"That's what they tell me."

They stared at him.

"I don't tell just anyone, but I trust you."

They were still staring.

"Hey, it's only money," he said waving a hand to break their trance.

"Oh… yeah…you know, I got a little saved up myself," Sam winked, straightening his collar. "Very little."

They chuckled.

"You know, we should look each other up when we get back, since we live so close. Let's find something to write with…I wonder if the angels have pens…" Spencer kidded.

He and Rebecca wandered off, searching for paper and pen, while Sam's mind was still swimming in the thought of all that money.

Tallulah addressed the group. "So, what gifts did all of you receive?" She zeroed-in on Jack. "How about you Jack?"

Jack's face was flushed from laughing. Old Joe had been entertaining him with his endless repertoire of knee-slappers.

"My gift?" he asked, wiping a tear from the corner of his eye. "It's sort of top secret. But I can say this: I've been communicating with and training supernatural… uh… 'beings'. The training will continue on my ranch in Montana."

"'Supernatural… beings'?" Tallulah asked.

"Yeah, I hope it's not too supernatural. My teenage son thinks I'm strange enough."

"You have a son? And how about a 'Mrs. Jack'?" Tallulah asked.

He looked down, and then picked up a leaf on the blanket. "I'm afraid my wife, Holly, died a couple of years ago in a rafting accident."

"Oh, Jack. I'm so sorry. I'm sure that's been difficult…especially with a son to raise," Tallulah consoled.

"It's been rough." He looked up at everyone. "But, hey, this is a picnic. We can talk about this some other time," he paused, rubbing his bearded chin.

As the sharing continued, the group was impressed with Hayley's gloves and Sam's sword, shield, and demon mind reading ability; but they were most impressed with Tallulah's gifts—which she refrained from showing off, despite the begging within the group.

"You're next, Katie. What's your gift?" Tallulah asked.

"I received a 'prayer chain'," she said, lifting a silver chain from her slender neck. "I'm officially a prayer warrior for all of us. A name is inscribed on each link. If a link glows an orange color, that person needs prayer…so, I pray for them until the link stops glowing. I'm also the communications hub for the group. If you need information about someone, call me. What's really interesting, though, is that all of your names were on my chain before I met you…not surprising…we were supposed to meet."

Each person wanted to see their name engraved on a link, so Katie leaned forward displaying her gift for them. Sure enough, each person's first and last name, and the place they lived was etched into the silver. There were other names on it as well—people Katie hadn't met yet, but thought she might meet someday.

"My instructor told me I received this gift because I pray without ceasing. It's true. Living alone in New York…it really helps me feel like He is with me."

"Where does your family live?" Hayley asked.

"My mother lives with my older brother in California with his wife and children. We only see each other every two or three years." Her eyes welled-up. "My family has really been through much hardship. I was just a little girl during the war. We were relocated, even though we were American citizens—you know, the Japanese Internment. We could only take what we could carry. For four years we were forced to endure winters in tar paper-covered barracks without plumbing, without proper clothing, and surrounded by barbed wire and armed guards.

"The worst of it wasn't being ripped out of our home, or the horrific living conditions…it was watching a guard gun down my father."

Sam's heart tightened hearing that. He knew what it was like to lose a father, but witnessing your own father's death so violently…that would be devastating. He couldn't even respond.

"The world has a lot of beauty, but sometimes it's hard to find it through the evil. But we're here in this amazing place. Let's forget the evil today, and celebrate the good," Katie said. "Tallulah, who's next?"

For once, Tallulah was speechless. An empty, long ten seconds was finally filled with words. "I'm so sorry, Katie." She hugged her for a long time; everyone else sat quietly.

Katie broke the hug. "Okay, well? Who's next?"

"Let's see…well…um…we'll have to hear from Rebecca and Spencer at the ball tonight, seeing as though they've disappeared. That means it's your turn, Old Joe Jones," she commanded.

Sam caught a glimpse of Old Joe's forearms peeking out of his rolled-up sleeves. Twenty (or so) small, tattooed crosses branded his skin, all in black ink—except one in red. Old Joe—a well-seasoned drill sergeant with a contradictory sense of humor.

The old Air Force man cleared his throat and coughed several times. Sam noticed the glimmer of a tear in the corner of the old guy's eye.

Hayley asked, "Are you—"

"I'll be…I'll be fine," he stammered, taking a drink from his goblet. He breathed a few heavy breaths and cleared his throat one last time. "In the angelic dimension, I'll be invisible. I'm going to follow reconnaissance orders—a spy for the good guys."

They all nodded in approval, but then a bugle fanfare interrupted, announcing it was time for the competitions.

First up: the hundred-yard dash. And then the relay, shot put, javelin, and, of course, arm wrestling. Old Joe, Montana Jack, and Sam competed in every competition until another bugle signaled it was time to get ready for the evening ball.

(Much to the chagrin of the younger men at the pinic, Old Joe won the Grand Champion Medal at the competition: Best overall.)

***

Torches as tall as the redwoods blazed above the steps leading to the Celestial Hall. Sam stood on the top step with Spencer, Jack, and Old Joe, waiting for the ladies of their group to arrive.

Hayley, Tallulah, Katie and Rebecca made a big entrance in a horse-drawn carriage, pulled by snowy thoroughbreds.

The Knights-in-Training dressed like royalty, donning a variety of formal, ivory-colored, medieval attire.

"Unforgettable," whispered Sam, not loud enough for anyone else to hear as he watched Hayley float up the stairs like an angel herself.

Inside the Celestial Hall, polished hardwood floors reflected the light of thousands of flickering candles. White chiffon wavered, resembling ribbons on a maypole, draping from the center toward every wall. Towering white pillars displayed dozens of white rose bouquets. The ceiling receded, exposing the sky that burst with fireworks and heavenly bodies. They entered, awestruck from the beauty around them.

Tallulah asked Old Joe for a dance, and Spencer asked Rebecca, while the rest of the group relaxed, observing from a round table decorated with white lace and roses.

Sam fiddled with the edge of the tablecloth and couldn't look at Hayley. He wanted to ask her for a dance, but every time he played it out in his mind, Nick got in the way. And he couldn't make him leave.

He looked up to see Hayley leaving the table. Escorting her to the dance floor, was Jack. Sam didn't want to watch, but found his eyes fixed on her, waltzing like a princess from a storybook.

Spencer and Rebecca returned to the table, out of breath, and crashed into their chairs.

"You can really cut a rug!" Spencer told her.

At the end of the song, Jack and Hayley returned, and the entire group sat together again.

"Okay, now that we're all here, Spencer and Rebecca, it's your turn to tell us what your gifts are," Tallulah instructed.

"Ladies first," Spencer declared, holding his hand out towards her.

Rebecca used her 'teacher's voice', as if explaining long division, as she revealed her gift. "I received a set of books that will guide me somehow."

"And she loves books. Says she has a whole library back home with thousands of them," Spencer said.

"The pages are blank now. Guess that's why I'm just sitting around with you fuddy-duddies," she kidded, fake-punching Spencer in the arm.

"Hey, now," Old Joe warned. "Don't break him!"

"Oh, I almost forgot the best part…*I'm* the only one that will see what appears on the pages, but I have to wear these spectacles, she said pulling them out of her purse and putting them on her face. "Sort of silly, don't you think?"

They agreed, smirking at the quirky spectacles that looked like a cross between 3-D glasses and old-fashioned driving goggles.

Sam wondered why she hadn't married anyone yet. He imagined that all of the boys in her class were secretly in love with her. It appeared Spencer might be in danger of that as well—his gaze never left her as the group chatted at the table. *Talk about your match-made-in-heaven, or second heaven,* Sam thought.

"Last, but not least…Spencer's turn," Tallulah said.

"Well…I got this incredible silver sword and shield with jewels—diamonds, rubies, and opals. They can send demons into the abyss. And let me tell you, after the training I had to go through, I feel like I could take them all on myself. I've never worked so hard in all my life." Spencer said.

"Same here, brother," Sam concurred, shaking his hand.

Spencer stood up, looking determined. He raised his goblet.

"A toast! This is our last night here, possibly our last moments together. I need to tell you all something." A somber expression fell across his face. "With no intention of bragging here… I am as tall as my bank account is deep. All six-foot-four of me lives in extravagance: an estate on a private

101

beach, luxury cars... you name it. I throw parties that cost more than some of you make in a year—for people I call 'friends'. I have it all." A smile grew as he looked at each of them, stopping with his gaze fixed on Rebecca. "But I have never worked so hard, learned so much, or loved so deeply until I met all of you, amidst these awesome angels, in this unbelievable place. I hold up my glass in appreciation for who you are and how you have changed my heart forever."

"Here, here!" They raised their goblets together.

***

Their training complete and gifts bestowed, it was time to leave the Angel Realm. Leaving this place was difficult, but the hardest thing for Sam was saying goodbye to new friends: human, and labrador. After a final morning together, they made their way to the Celestial Hall.

As they waited for the closing ceremonies to commence, the hall was electrified with brass instruments playing a majestic march. They sat, eager, in their elaborate chairs as their instructors filed in, forming a giant arc in front of the stage. The Knights-in-Training then stood up and faced their instructors, joining them in the arc. Zadkiel and Camael, were on the center platform.

Zadkiel addressed them. "Your training period has now concluded. It is time to make a final commitment. Kneel before your instructor, and, with the blessing of the Lord, you shall be dubbed Knights of the Angel Realm. Your instructor will then bequeath a final gift to you."

They knelt.

Ray winked at Sam. Sam answered with a smile. Ray's sword tapped Sam's head, then his shoulders. Left, then right. "I dub thee 'Sir Samuel Wright of Carthage, Loyal Knight of the Angel Realm'."

Sam glanced at the other Knights and felt their bond solidify.

Ray continued. "I'm proud of you, Sam. I believe you will accomplish great things for the Lord. Rise and receive your final gift."

Sam stood. The others did as well. Ray handed Sam a black pouch. The other trainees received the same. Sam opened his pouch and fished out a silver ring. Its band was wide with a cross shape cut out of it. Inside, there was an engraving in Hebrew.

Zadkiel spoke. "The inscription inside is a prayer: 'Lord, open my eyes.' Wearing it will allow you access into the spiritual dimension. While in this dimension, like angels, humans cannot see you unless the Lord allows it. Guard it well. Place the ring on your finger. And behold!"

The Knights put on their rings. A slight energy washed over them. Their black training uniforms changed to white battle uniforms, complete with their gifted weapons. But the most remarkable change was that they glowed.

Zadkiel continued "You are in the dimension of angels and demons— the spiritual dimension. Go back to your hometowns. Serve the Lord well."

Everything faded away except Sam, Hayley, and Tallulah. The golden staircase appeared in front of them, only this time, they stood on the top step, looking down.

Chapter Eight
Dual Dimensions

Although months had gone by on Archai,
time on earth had been suspended. It was as if they
had never left. The lights in the windows of
Tallulah's house still glowed, and smoke still rose
from the chimney. Everything seemed the same—or
so they assumed.

"We're back," Sam said hesitantly.

"Pretty wild," Tallulah added.

"Oh no! The horses… we'd better find
them," Hayley said.

Sam and Tallulah agreed, so they left the
gazebo to search. It wasn't long before they spotted
them, huddled together, next to a lamppost, on the
far edge of Tallulah's backyard.

"They can't see us in the spiritual dimension
though, right? I wonder if they'll sense our
presence," Hayley said.

"Only one way to find out," Sam said,
moving towards the horses.

They approached slowly, and the horses had
no reaction. It wasn't until Hayley reached out,
touching Gracie on the neck, that the horse
acknowledged her. Gracie turned and bobbed her
head like usual.

"She knows it's me," she said, springing into the saddle.

A brilliant light washed across the horse. Sam took off his ring, and then found that Gracie was no longer visible in the human dimension. Replacing his ring he said, "She entered the spiritual dimension!"

Sam and Tallulah then mounted their horses that followed Gracie's example.

"What do we do now? Should we go home for the night?" Hayley asked.

"Not a chance! I'm dying to explore! I mean, just look at how colorless everything is! We're actually in the spiritual realm! And humans can't see us! Let's go see what angels see!" Tallulah pressed.

"Good idea," Sam replied.

His curiosity was piqued. He wanted to know what they were up against. Looking around, he realized Tallulah was right. Even in the dark of night, everything seemed to have a gray haze over it, with only the slightest hint of color.

Hayley appeared uncomfortable. "Everything's gray, except for us. It's like someone's got a colorful spotlight on us. It's kind of creepy, but amazing."

"Better put your gloves on," Sam said to Hayley.

Without speaking, and with their horses lined-up, side-by-side, as if they were starring in an old Western, they inched across the meadow and through the woods— a shortcut into town.

Hiding behind the trees, and crouching on branches like leopards stalking their prey, evil peered at them through the darkness, camouflaged in the shadows. Any movement from these creatures caused a breeze to sift through the browning, dry leaves.

The fallen angels were stealth, and although Sam could see nothing out of place, he knew they were present. He heard them all. Every wicked, scheming thought seeped into his head like radiation, as if he'd thought it himself; and for the first time he thanked God for the gift, instead of chiding it. This gift would clearly give them an advantage. Examining the trees, his eyes strained, trying to catch a glimpse of the beasts. Hoping not to find them, he clutched the handle of his sword, shocked at how many different voices he heard.

They're everywhere.

The trees thinned and they neared the town square. He decided to conceal the beings' presence from Tallulah and Hayley for the moment

On the edge of the square, just before the paved road, they stopped, staring straight ahead.

"Let's go," Sam said.

They stepped off together. It was a somber parade. Their horses' hooves clomped on the asphalt in nearly the same beat, like a rank of marines. They sat a little taller in their saddles, on guard, finding nothing but gloomy-gray, deserted streets and buildings.

Sam heard them coming. He heard them before the girls knew of their presence. He pulled back on Blaze's reigns. Tallulah and Hayley followed his lead, stopping as well.

"What is it?" Hayley asked.

"They're coming."

He drew his sword with one deliberate yank. The demons' thoughts and growls resounded in Sam's ears to nearly the point of pain, but he did not cover his ears. He stood ready.

A thunderous, unified scream of hundreds of evil warriors flooded the square from underground, resembling a nest of cockroaches, rushing over each other, climbing on walls, and scattering in all directions. The sight of the bug-like infestation nauseated Sam.

The horses reared back.

A torrential rain suddenly gushed from the sky. Water pooled immediately due to the overwhelming amount released at once, soaking them instantly.

The demons crept over the brick walls of Lou's appliance store, and Charlie's Diner, supernaturally jumping farther than earth's laws of gravity would allow. Some flew, and some hovered. Many turned their attention toward the three of them—unmoving on horseback. The beasts made no direct attack for the moment. It seemed to Sam they were merely making their presence known— a psychological intimidation. Their thoughts told Sam they were curious about the presence of humans in the spiritual dimension.

The demons inched closer. Sam screamed a war cry. When the swarm came close enough, he started hacking away at them— one-by-one.

In the turmoil, Dean Walden, a deputy sheriff, cruised through the streets in his patrol car, his wiper blades on high. Dean appeared oblivious to the battle all around him, but he peered intensely out his side window, seemingly amazed at the unexpected heavy rain. He drove the entire square unaware that a demon was on the hood and at least two were inside the vehicle. Dean rounded the corner and drove out of sight.

Under the downpour, that was now at risk of becoming a flash flood, Sam sliced through the rain, slashing any creature that neared Blaze, sending each into the abyss. He chipped away at them as if he were clearing a path through thick, jungle vines.

His peripheral vision caught sight of Hayley's whip as the light bounced off the diamonds. He glanced quickly and saw her stand on Gracie's saddle— he assumed to get better leverage for the overhand throws she delivered in a crisscross, diagonal pattern.

She had solid balance and strength, focused straight ahead, but appeared oblivious to a demon approaching from the side.

"Hayley! On your left!" Sam yelled out.

She put her gloved left hand out, and upon contact the creature was electrified instantly and fell into the abyss.

He turned back to his own attackers, wiping out three with the reflections of his shield.

Looking over towards Tallulah, he watched how she merely raised her hands to push demons away without even touching them.

Other than the sheer number of them, the demons didn't seem to pose much of a threat. In fact, it brought to Sam's mind the idea of shooing away pests until he saw the one on his mother's bedroom window. It wasn't wild and skittering like the others. Instead, it resembled an enormous black widow, guarding its nest. Its decrepit, jagged claws clanked on the glass, producing an eerie scratching sound.

The light in her room was out. She was most likely asleep—alone and unaware of the evil surrounding her. Sam felt helpless to defend her. The creature on the window stared directly at Sam, taunting him. It gnashed its fangs, and a mohawk of red spikes fanned on its head.

A hatred grew within Sam he never knew existed.

Abruptly and inexplicably, the mohawk demon turned and shouted to the rest of the creatures, "Mission complete! Fall back!"

Mission complete? What had they accomplished? Sam wondered. Then the thought occurred to him that the hate inside of himself could have been what they had come for. But how would they know that? Sam knew only God can see what is in our hearts.

Following the orders of the higher-ranking demon, the fallen angels turned and crept back into the shadows and holes, out of sight.

As the rain eased to a light sprinkle, Sam jumped off Blaze. His legs were shaking, but he stood tall.

Hayley and Tallulah dismounted as well.

"I can't believe I touched a demon," Hayley said.

"Is it me, or did this seem too easy?" Sam asked.

"I'm not sure I'd say easy, but I imagined it would be harder." Hayley said.

"Round One," Tallulah said in a somber tone. "Let's go home. We've got school in the morning,"

"Oh, yeah, I've got a vocabulary test in second period tomorrow. Do you think the angels could come take it for me?" Hayley kidded.

Sam walked both of them home without much conversation, and then trudged towards the market, unaware of the demon with the mohawk trailing him in the distance.

* * *

Sam woke suddenly—like a bomb had detonated in his room, but now the sound was nonexistent.

Was it a dream? Maybe the whole thing was a dream?

He didn't have long to contemplate that thought. From somewhere in his room, he heard it.

"Maybe I could trick him or, better... lie to him. He'll be easy to discourage. I can always make him feel inferior. Maybe I should work on his bitterness? Make him depressed about his father?"

Sam could hear its thoughts, but couldn't see it. He'd left his ring in the bathroom the night before. He scolded himself for it.

111

He jumped out of bed and headed for the bathroom, while the demon thought on.

No wonder I feel defeated sometimes, Sam thought.

"You're a loser. And a quitter. You let everyone down: the team, Hayley... "

It followed him into the bathroom, and then stood so close that Sam thought he could almost feel its breath on his ear. Listening to the demon's thoughts was like a vice squeezing his soul. He knew the things it was saying weren't true; but they still hit home, they still slashed at his heart.

Sam grabbed for the ring, but then dropped it. It bounced three times in the sink, and he watched in horror when it began to roll towards the drain. Slapping his hand down on the cold porcelain, he trapped the ring at the drain's edge. He exhaled one huge breath, standing there frozen, with his hand still on the ring.

"Why do you want that stupid ring? You're pathetic. It can't help you. You have no power over me," it snarled.

Sam pushed the ring onto his finger. He was instantly in the angelic realm—white battle uniform on, shield in his hand. Now he could see the demon in the mirror, standing directly to his right. Jumping to the left at the sight of it, he regained his footing and turned to face it.

"You think I have no power over you?" Sam asked, confidently.

It looked confused.

"Think again!" Sam shouted, disgusted.

He put the shield directly in front of the demon's face. It screamed a desperate cry as it viewed its own reflection, and then was sucked into the abyss that opened right on the bathroom floor. Sam watched until the abyss closed, and the floor returned to its original state.

"Sam, everything okay in there?" his mom asked, knocking on the door.

"Yeah. I'm fine."

"Sam?" she knocked louder.

He then remembered she couldn't hear him in the other dimension and quickly pulled off his ring. "I'm fine, Mom."

"Breakfast is ready," she said as he heard her footsteps fading in the hall.

"Okay. Be right out."

He replaced the ring and stepped where the abyss had been—just an average floor, no trace of anything unusual, except for the floor being an unusual gray.

In fact, everything was gray. He hadn't fully experienced the colors in the spiritual dimension in daylight yet. He was enthralled.

Weird.

He looked in the mirror and noticed his skin *did* glow; but, more than that, the colors of his features were vibrant as well. His teeth shone bright white, his face was a warm tan like he'd been on vacation at the beach. Rich waves of golden highlights streamed through his light brown hair. His eyes were blue— like the sky after it rains and there's not-a-cloud-in-sight kind of blue. *Weird again.*

113

He splashed cold water on his face, and grabbed a hand towel to dry it, but as soon as he touched it, it changed from a dull gray to a bright yellow—even brighter than its original color. The color spread gradually until it filled the fabric. Amazed at this, he walked around the bathroom touching objects. Everything he touched turned from gray to a brilliant color, until he let go of it, returning it to gray. He was still holding the hand towel, so he tossed it— a cross-court-at-the-buzzer— kind of toss into the hamper. When it left his hand, it changed back to gray in mid-air.

All kinds of weird.

***

They had decided to meet early, in the alley behind shop class. Sam arrived before the girls, and then leaned up against the brick wall. A low, thick fog hung in the air, blanketing the field by the P.E. department. Pulling the ring out of his jeans pocket, he placed it on his finger.

When the girls arrived, he positioned himself directly in front of Tallulah and removed his ring, appearing instantly before her. She jumped back, startled.

"Sam! I just about had a heart attack!" she fussed.

"I was just 'avin' a li'l fun, now, come on." Sam tried to imitate Tallulah's accent.

"Now y'all better stop yer shenanigans. Weeze gots werk ta doo," she protested, attempting to speak in a southern drawl.

"Touché. Truce. Please...stop before you hurt yourself," he kidded. "You're right, we need to get going."

They put on their rings and observed the angelic dimension. Nothing seemed out of place— just shades of gray everywhere. Walking the halls proved to be a waste of time. They only saw the janitor, the principal, and a few teachers, but it was still early. Students had not arrived yet.

They ventured outside to the lunch tables. Sam sat on a table with his feet on a bench. Hayley sat next to him, and Tallulah leaned against a pillar. A few students began to arrive, walking right past them, oblivious to their presence.

"What do you think our mission *is* exactly?" Hayley asked.

"God will show us," Tallulah said.

They toured the halls again, this time digging deeper into crevices they hadn't investigated.

"The door's locked," Hayley reported, standing outside the band room.

"Who needs doors?" Tallulah asked strutting through the brick wall. She stuck her head back out, looking at them. "Are you coming?"

They stepped through the wall and through a piano inside the band room. The sound of a radio came from the director's office, and the light was on. Nothing seemed out of place. The director approached them, but passed right by, unlocking the door. A few early students strolled in, and then began warming up their instruments.

"Hey, he's pretty good," Tallulah said, referring to a trumpet player.

As they rounded the corner near the locker rooms, they discovered a dozen demons encircling the P.E. instructor, Mrs. Weaver, on the basketball court. She was talking to a Sophomore named Claudia. A dense fog crept into the court from the field, swirling slowly around them.

"Hey!" Sam shouted at the beasts.

They turned, looked at him, and went back to pacing around Mrs. Weaver and the student. One of them jumped onto Mrs. Weaver, overlapping her body. It seemed to soak into her— as if her body absorbed it. She appeared to be unaware of its presence, but then started to sway. Looking at Claudia with a suddenly different countenance. The teacher growled and her face contorted. Her eyes bulged as they glared at the girl.

Claudia jumped backwards, dropping some books to the ground.

"Go away!" screeched the teacher in an unrecognizable, guttural voice, before her eyes rolled back in her head, and she dropped to the ground in a heap.

"Mrs. Weaver? Mrs. Weaver? Somebody! Help!" Claudia screamed.

A few students and a teacher ran toward the court, as did Sam, Hayley, and Tallulah. Mrs. Weaver's body shook with convulsions, the demon still inside her.

Sam aimed his shield like a machine gun, mowing down five demons in a line that peered into its shiny surface.

From above, Tallulah engaged a standoff in the air with two more demons.

Hayley and Sam approached Mrs. Weaver and the remaining demons pacing like guards around the teacher's spastic body. Hayley's gloves zapped one unintentionally as it backed up into her. Sam cleared the rest out with his shield.

Hayley knelt beside her and placed a gloved hand on either side of the teacher's face, hanging on firmly. Mrs. Weaver's convulsions became more acute, but Hayley didn't let go.

Sam and Tallulah stood watch as energy surged from Hayley's gloves. Within a few moments, the demon emerged. As it separated from the teacher, Hayley followed it, holding *its* face instead. It was thrashing, shaking, and screeching, while electrical sparks flew from its body as she held tight to its leathery, serpent-like face. With one final, low, grumbling outcry, it was pulled from Hayley's grasp, nearly taking her with him into the abyss. Tallulah pulled her back, as she teetered on the edge. They stared into the never-ending, brewing, black pit, while the last of Satan's soldiers sunk into its depths, the eerie fog also withdrawing into the closing cracks.

A crowd of people and the Knights surrounded Mrs. Weaver as she slipped in and out of consciousness, incoherently jabbering through slurred speech about what most assumed to be mindless babble; but Sam, Hayley and Tallulah

117

knew her ramblings to be a true account of the event. A teacher shouted to a janitor for him to call for an ambulance.

"Jesus... I saw Him... mmm... demons... sword... gloves... Hayley... mmm..."

"Can she see us?" Hayley asked.

"On Archai, I learned there are occasions for people to see glimpses of this dimension." Tallulah said. "Most times, the memory of it fades as would a dream."

"I guess she got a front row seat with this glimpse," said Sam.

Mrs. Weaver's head whipped about in frantic jerks, and she continued her nonsensical jabbering until the ambulance arrived. As they loaded her inside, she still spoke in fragmented sentences about her experience, but no one took her words as fact— except the Knights.

The racing of Sam's heart had finally begun to subside. The three of them watched the ambulance leave the scene, and then breathed a little easier.

"Let's get going," Sam announced.

In the alley behind Shop class, they removed their rings. Resembling ordinary students once again, they hustled out of their hiding spot, because now they were late for class.

Chapter Nine
The Tree Lady

Wrestling with a razor blade and a large box, Sam quickly opened a new order at the market in anticipation of Hayley and Tallulah's arrival after closing.

At the register, Deb rang-up Mayor Houlihan's rainbow sherbet and sardines. His expectant wife sent him to Spott's daily with bizarre food requests. He left, whistling a shrill Sousa favorite, "Stars and Stripes," and passed Mr. And Mrs. Carver in the doorway. The Mayor tipped his gray hat without missing a note, and they smiled in response as they entered.

The Carvers, maternal grandparents of his friends Trevor and Junior Denton, had started coming in more often since Hank's passing. Sam suspected they were showing support during this difficult time.

"The usual for you two? Spoiling your supper again?" Deb asked them, winking.

They nodded as they snuggled into their favorite booth in the corner.

As Sam straightened the peanut butter jars he'd just unpacked, he glanced at his mother making their banana split—her specialty. No one he knew would pile them as high with the correct distribution of ice cream and toppings. She was especially famous in Carthage for dotting the top with extra cherries— at no extra charge. She shared the craft with Sam once, divulging all her secrets, and he tried to emulate her frozen masterpiece; but the ratio of pineapple to vanilla was too great, and the chocolate syrup oozed to one side. It didn't compare.

Even though he knew she had mountains of work waiting for her, he watched as she delivered their treat, and chatted with them. She wasn't one of those waitresses that dropped off an order, barely looking at her customers.

"Is your hip still bothering you, Freda?" Deb inquired, pulling a chair next to their booth.

"Oh, yes, it's a real pain. And now, with all this strange weather we've been having, my arthritis is flaring up again, too," Mrs. Carver said, wringing her hands as her husband wasted no time digging into the banana split.

Sam tackled the last box, wishing he were already done, when he discovered an unusual item.

"Excuse me, Mom…"

"Yes, honey?" Deb responded, walking over to him.

"The pinwheels… Where do they go?"

"Oh, good. They finally came. Mrs. Jasper has been asking about them. Could you take them out to her?"

"The Tree Lady?" Sam asked, frowning.

"I know. She is an odd bird. But she'll appreciate the delivery."

"I'll go after this last box."

***

As Sam pulled into Mrs. Jasper's driveway, he looked up to view the spectacle suspended in her trees. Thousands of shimmering, twirling, whimsical objects trickled from the branches—a lifetime collection of fancy, fluttering dust catchers: animals of all types, trains, cars, flowers, wind chimes, kites, airplanes, and many purely decorative ornaments—each representing events that occurred in her eighty-eight years of life. She could tell you about each dangling doohickey—when and why it was placed in her trees for all to enjoy.

Sam was probably her first visitor in weeks. As he parked the Dragonfly, she squealed as she popped out her front door onto her paint-peeling, wraparound porch.

"Oh, Stevie! It's so nice to see you!"

"It's Sam, Mrs. Jasper," he reminded her.

"That's what I said, didn't I?"

Sam just smiled. "I brought the pinwheels you ordered."

"Wonderful! Let me see them." Years disappeared from her face when she saw them. "They're even better than they looked in the catalog. Look how shiny they are," she said, pulling some string from the large pocket in her floral print apron. Wasting no time, she tied all six of them to nearby branches as he watched. "Now, these pinwheels, there's six of them— one for each of my great grandchildren. They love to see my trees when they come for a visit, but they live too far away to come very often. Two live all the way in California. Have you ever been there?"

"No, ma'am."

"They tell me it's nice there." She looked up at the trees, and then back at him. "Can you stay for some peach cobbler? Just made it today—in fact, it's still warm."

Sam thought about how the girls would be coming to the market soon, but also knew how much Mrs. Jasper would appreciate the company. Besides, she made the best peach cobbler in the county, with the blue ribbons to prove it.

"I guess I could stay for a few minutes." He watched her smile grow, revealing abundant smile lines.

"Come on inside, Scottie. I'll put the kettle on for some tea as well," she said as she scampered up the stairs to the porch—as much as an eighty-eight-year-old could scamper.

"It's Sam. Remember Mrs. Jasper?" he said, with respect.

She stopped at the door, scratching her head. "Didn't I say that?" And with a shrug, she scurried inside, Sam close behind.

Not many people from Carthage would venture inside her home, because of her claim that a little girl's ghost lived there. Most people thought she was just senile or crazy, but others feared it was true.

She invited Sam to sit at her pine kitchen table that was happily situated by a large window, with a view of her backyard garden.

"Wow. It got really dark all of a sudden. But I don't see any clouds. It's like an eclipse or something," Sam said.

"Oh, that happens all the time around this old house."

Sam knew what was coming.

He watched a scarecrow's ragged sleeve flutter in the breeze as she bustled around her kitchen, setting the water to boil, preparing the teapot, teacups, linen napkins, crystal bowls and her best silver spoons. Each bowl and cup so delicate, he thought they might break if he just looked at them.

The aroma of a simmering stew drifted from a large pot on the stove. It was quiet enough to hear the stew bubbling from under the lid that was slightly askew.

As she presented a serving bowl full to the brim with her award-winning cobbler, his attention was abruptly pulled from the dessert. That hair-prickling-on-the-back-of-your neck kind of feeling overcame him when a voice invaded his mind.

"I'm watching you," it hissed in an unnatural whisper.

As he turned to find the voice, he saw a shadow rush past the kitchen door, and heard the rapid cadence of small shoes clicking down the hallway. He looked at Mrs. Jasper, who was apparently aware of it too, but proceeded to spoon the cobbler into the dainty bowls, humming.

"Don't worry, that's just Elizabeth playing in the hall again. She's a little shy of strangers."

"Who's Elizabeth?"

"Well, I know some folks think I've lost my marbles, but Elizabeth, she's the ghost of a little girl who used to live here. I looked it up in the town hall records. Little Elizabeth Morgan Jasper. She was my late husband's cousin who passed away when she was only five years old. I have a picture of her in a drawer in the parlor. I'll show you," she said, as she shuffled into the next room.

Sam waited quietly, staring at the doorway. The cuckoo clock on the kitchen wall chirped once, marking quarter 'til four. It startled him, but he never moved his eyes from the hall.

"Here it is," she said, returning to her seat, giving a yellowed photograph to him. He looked at it, keeping one eye on the hall. "Wasn't she a doll? Those lovely ringlets. You know, I wish girls would still wear their hair that way, but I guess it's too old fashioned. And have you ever seen so many freckles? She was adorable. I'm sure it pained her mother greatly when the Lord took her home at such an early age. Maybe that's why she's here… searching for her mother."

Sam knew better. There were no ghosts.

The teakettle eased into a full whistle, and Mrs. Jasper rose to silence it. Sam watched her take a potholder from a hook on the wall. As she turned the knob on the stove, the whistle died, and he turned back towards the door to find the little girl from the photo in the doorway.

"Hello," the little girl said with a sweet voice that echoed into eeriness. She smiled at him, and then her ringlets bobbed as she turned and ran down the hall with a giggle.

"Uh… may I use your restroom?" Sam asked, his eyes still glued to the doorway.

"Yes, dear. Down the hall and on the right."

He ventured out of the kitchen, alert to all his surroundings. With the same feeling of being watched, he skulked down the hall with care to prohibit the wood floor from creaking. No sign of the so-called Elizabeth. He crept past a small table in the hall, just under the stairs. On the table were more framed photographs—he assumed they were Mrs. Jasper's family. He recognized a young Mr. Jasper next to a Model-T in one of the photos.

Just as his eyes left the photograph, he sensed motion on the stairs above him. He looked up to find 'Elizabeth' crouching low and peering at him under the banister. Sam, holding his breath, waited to see what she would do

"Follow me, you fool." The demon's thoughts sounded like fingernails on a blackboard.

Once again, she giggled, stood, and skipped down the stairs, her lilac cotton dress waving with each skip. Glancing back at him, as if tempting him to follow her, she pushed the screen door open, and trotted outside. The door slammed behind her, and Sam knew what he had to do.

He hurried into the restroom, locked the door, and rushed to the window. As he scanned the darkened yard, he found her standing by the clothesline, next to a large white sheet rippling in the breeze. Sam fumbled for his ring in his jacket pocket without looking away. He pushed on the ring, returning to the angelic dimension, while she simultaneously morphed into the type of creature he had expected—except much larger.

This dragon-sized demon was all red—a dark, blood red, with reptilian scales. As he stared at it, the demon spotted him through the window. It rose onto its back legs, and bellowed a screech matching one Sam had heard last summer in a Godzilla movie.

Despite his nerves, he jumped through the outer wall, and down to ground level, drawing his sword upon impact. The screeching intensified as it plodded toward him, shaking the ground with each step. Sam knew the demon had no power over him, but the sound it was making sent chills over his entire body, and the sight of it shocked him to the core—like a nightmare. He aimed his shield toward the beast, hoping it would zap itself, but the creature's eyes avoided the shield completely.

"He cannot harm me. He may know my secret, but he's helpless," it thought, still projecting its evil sound.

Just as it reached striking distance, it veered right. Sam edged left, and they paced in a circle like cats in a cat fight. Its fierce screech was the loudest sound Sam had ever heard, but he remained confident.

"He's a coward. I think I know what will really affect him."

The demon's thoughts swam through Sam's head, swirling around as he wondered, *what could be worse than this?*

It changed back into Elizabeth's form and begged through tears.

"Please, don't! Please don't!" the insidious creature screamed with a little girl's high pitch.

Towering over her juvenile frame, he swung his sword, but stopped just short of her ringlets.

I can't do it. I can't strike her.

His thoughts were interrupted when he realized his sword was pointed at nothing. She had vanished. He scanned the yard. He could find no trace of it— girl or demon.

The sound of Mrs. Jasper's voice and a knocking on the door inside made him give up the search, and then return to the bathroom.

"Are you all right, Freddy?" Mrs. Jasper called through the closed door.

He took his ring off, and returned it to the pocket in his jacket as it replaced his white battle uniform. "Just fine. Be right out. Name's Sam, Mrs. Jasper," he reminded her politely.

He heard footsteps and mumbling as she returned to the kitchen. "That's what I said... Sam."

***

The peach cobbler filling his stomach, he rode toward home with the memory of the demon's screech filling his mind. Still, he had enjoyed his visit with Mrs. Jasper despite the demonic confrontation. Her cobbler proved scrumptious, as usual, and she even called him 'Sam' once; but now his sights were set on meeting the girls at Spott's.

Just as he passed the water tower, he saw something that slammed everything to a halt. He approached a person from behind, walking on the side of the two-lane road… a figure he'd seen many times, but now he couldn't believe his eyes.

Could it be…? Could it be him?!

He sped up towards the male figure. Slowing, and rolling next to him, his suspicions were confirmed. Excitement grew within him as if he might burst. His heart overflowed with gratitude.

"You're alive!" he shouted as he jerked the Dragonfly to a stop and flew off the seat.

"Sam!" his father cried out. "I'm all right. I'm all right."

They engulfed each other in a magnetic embrace before Sam could think clearly. He wanted it to be true so badly, he disregarded the red flags waving all around him. It looked like his pop, smelled like him, hugged like him, even sounded like him. To his amazement he did not detect any thoughts from the creature. He had tuned everything else out; and for the moment, Sam was whole again. His dad was alive. The tears streamed, and arms squeezed, as the precarious bliss blinded him.

"What happened? Where have you been? We thought—"

It was only when Sam felt cold and damp that he broke the embrace, beginning to realize the horror. He pulled away from his father who was now drenched, and even dripping. Water began to pour from the top of his head, as if he were standing under a hose. There was no hose, but the water gushed over his face like a waterfall, distorting it.

"What's wrong, Son?" his father inquired, his voice now foreign to Sam's ears. He began to chuckle an eerie laugh, slashing through Sam's heart.

"I knew this would shake his very soul," the demon thought.

Sam just stood there in his grief, watching as the demon turned and then walked into the woods, still laughing.

Chapter Ten
Snow in the Square

The sun had set by the time Sam parked his motorcycle in the alley, but daylight still lingered like an eerie dream. Standing at Spott's back door, burdened with images of his dad soaking wet and cackling, he felt alone and disturbed; but amid this dark place, his mood lifted because a pleasant and familiar laughter came from inside the market, through the screen, and wrapped around his oppressed soul.

Venturing inside, he found Tallulah and Hayley lounging in a booth, sipping hot chocolate, and looking like they hadn't a care in the world.

Typical, he thought, shaking his head. *I thought I was supposed to be making Hayley jealous… now they're two peas in a pod. Girls. Go figure.*

"There you are! We were getting worried," his mother said. "Oh, you're freezing! Here sit down. I'll get you some hot chocolate."

He fell into the seat across from the girls. The encounters with the demons had left him numb, and he was only now realizing that he was cold.

"It's the coldest day I can remember," Deb reported, setting Sam's cup in front of him, and throwing a blanket around her shoulders. "The weather report on the radio said this was an all-time record low for Panola County. They'd expected warm temperatures until this surprise cold front rolled in."

Sam knew what that meant. More demons.

"It feels like twenty degrees in here," Tallulah guessed.

"The heater's on, but it's barely making a difference. Tallulah, you don't have a coat," Deb said, rubbing her shoulders. "That sweater isn't enough." Grabbing a shawl from the coat rack, she wrapped it around Tallulah. "Sam that reminds me. Why haven't I heard about your new friend here. Tallulah's been telling me about all the places she's stayed. Feels like I've known her for years." She patted her back and winked at her.

He shrugged while he sipped his cocoa. "I've been sorta busy these last couple of days, I guess." He meant that, more than she knew.

"Well, I'm glad you're here. I hope you like Carthage."

Sam caught sight of something odd out the front window. He squinted and stared in disbelief. "Is that snow?"

Deb walked to the window. "Oh, would you look at that! It is! It's snowing!" The pitch of her voice got higher with each syllable. They all got up and joined her at the window. "I don't think it's snowed here in ten years," she said with childlike amazement. "Bizarre. It's almost like..."

"Let's go outside!" Tallulah said, not waiting for their response.

Sam was excited it was snowing, but he knew a battle may be imminent. He kept his eyes open as he sprinted outside with the others.

Catching snowflakes in their mouths, Tallulah and Hayley twirled with their shawls spread, while Sam and his mother examined flakes that landed on their arms. Most of the shops had already closed for the evening, but a crowd gathered in the square from Charlie's Diner and the theater. All heads pointed up at the rare spectacle getting heavier by the second.

Tallulah stopped spinning and pointed at the bench across from the fountain. "Look! The snow's already sticking there's so much of it."

Sam's enjoyment was cut short when he heard thoughts dripping with evil nearby. He didn't want to break-up the snow fest, but he felt urged to investigate. Searching for a reason to end the fun, he noticed Mrs. Sisco had entered the market.

"Mom, I think we have a customer," he said, pointing to Spott's.

"Oh, dear. I'd better get back in there. How can Mrs. Sisco shop at a time like this?" she said, turning to run inside.

Sam stopped her. "I'll be back in a little while, Mom."

"Alright. Zip up, honey," she said zipping his letterman's jacket. She brushed some lint off his sleeve, staring at him as if she wanted to say something motherly. And then her countenance returned to normal. "I need to get this cleaned for you." Standing on her toes, she kissed him on the cheek, and then sprinted over small piles of snow to the market.

He looked at the girls. "I think we've got work to do." He motioned for them to follow, as the snow kept sifting from the night sky.

They found a secluded spot behind the closed library to put on their rings, and then lunged through powdery snowdrifts toward the town square.

Sam wondered if it was the adrenalin kicking-in, or if it was just warmer in this dimension. A strong wind had stirred, pressing accumulating snow into fluffy waves.

"It's really coming down now," Hayley said.

"Our feet are completely covered!" Tallulah shouted over the gusts.

Rounding the corner, Sam saw a dozen people still playing in the snow. A few of them were now collaborating on a six-foot snowman that glowed red. The source of the redness seemed to come from behind and his hand tightened on the handle of his sword as he turned. Pouring from every window of Carthage City Hall, a brilliant red light illuminated the entire town square. It was as if the building was on fire, but smoke did not escape any window or door. There were no flames, but it was obvious where they needed to go.

"Let's check it out," Sam said, stepping out first, the girls close behind.

"Through the front doors?" Hayley asked.

"Why not?" Sam said, wanting to slaughter all the demons he saw.

They jogged up the steps, and walked through the locked door, past the snoozing security guard. It was quiet, being after hours. The windy spurts of snow— now knee-high— pressed and stacked against the windows.

"This way. To the second floor," Sam directed, brushing flakes off his head and chest.

They climbed to the top of the stairs, but then halted like a military squad when they reached the landing.

Every inch of the long hallway was lined with them. Like royal guards, demons wearing crimson robes with hoods pulled low, held staves. Their backs against the walls, standing shoulder to shoulder, they looked straight ahead, unmoving. Both sides of the hall were saturated with this evil sentry.

"There must be fifty of them," Sam whispered.

"There are voices coming from the room down the hall," Hayley said.

"The mayor's office." Sam took a deep breath. "Let's go."

"Past these demons? Are you crazy?" Hayley asked.

"It'll be all right. Come on," Sam said.

With his sword drawn and shield in place, he was hoping to get a shot at the demon that appeared as his father. They walked slowly past the hooded beasts that never moved except to follow them with their black eyes.

"This is a very long hallway," Tallulah reported in a whisper.

Sam heard each demon's thoughts. Most were in a trance, repeating their orders. Sam peeked at the last demon on the right, and then wished he hadn't made eye contact with it. Its face was disgusting: a pig's snout, squinted rodent eyes, large dagger-like bottom teeth, and scabby skin. As Sam looked away, the pig-faced demon's thoughts screeched in his ears.

"Don't look at me, you little man. I will destroy you. I'll rip right through you before you can even blink."

The thoughts of this demon faded as they reached the waiting room of the mayor's office. Sam tried not to focus on what it had said, but on what was ahead of them. They heard two distinct voices coming from the office. One was the mayor's, and the other was Charlie, the owner of Charlie's Diner. They crept toward the double doors of his office that were slightly open, and then remained stealth behind some potted plants.

The mayor was seated at his desk leaning forward. Sam noticed the absence of his usual jovial disposition. His eyes were round and fierce, his mouth clamped, and his hands were in fists, steadying himself in a rigid pose as he listened to Charlie.

"We must have approval today, Michael." Charlie, being a large man shook the floor as he paced in front of the desk.

Sam was used to seeing Charlie wearing a burger-stained apron and a smile to match his size, but tonight he wasn't smiling.

135

"The counsel voted against your proposal," the mayor defended.

"But *you're* the mayor. Veto it. Pass it through. We'll start building before they can do anything. You have the power. Use it. Sign the request." With each word his cold eyes squinted more.

"I'm afraid I just can't do that," he said, standing his ground. He leaned back in his brown leather chair, folding his arms as if to finalize the conversation.

"Can't?" the man said, picking up a photo of Michael's wife from the desk. "Or won't?"

The mayor froze. His eyes were unblinking and fixed on the photo. His gaze followed it as the man shifted the picture from side to side as if admiring it.

"I want this request approved." He paused, still staring at the picture. "She's lovely." He looked up at the mayor. "I hear she's expecting your first child."

"What are you doing, Charlie? I've known you for years. Are… are you actually threatening my family?" As the mayor spoke his curly brown hair shook from the force of his words.

"I *will* get this request approved and begin phase one of this project." As heated as his words were, the man never raised his monotone voice.

Michael stared at the photo in the man's grasp. "Excuse me for a moment." He rose and edged out of the room, past Sam and the girls crouched behind the plants.

Sam followed him out into the hall, while the girls stayed behind. Unaware of the demonic guards, Michael sprinted to the men's room, with Sam close behind.

Slamming the restroom door shut, he locked it as Sam slipped through the wall. The mayor rushed to a toilet and the repulsive sound of vomit hitting water, echoed against the tiles. After a few heavy breaths and spitting, Michael flushed the toilet, and rose to his feet like he carried the town on his back. Instead of his normal springy step, his gait reminded Sam of a lame animal as the mayor slunk to the sink to wash his hands and face. He let the water drip from his face as he stood looking into the mirror, unaware that Sam was just a few feet away, praying.

With a sudden look of panic, his face turned bright red. He bent at the waist, hiding his face in his hands, and began to sob. Sam wanted to leave, but felt the need to stay, even despite the awkwardness. Sam prayed with more fervor. He prayed for wisdom and strength for the mayor, and for himself.

The mayor's sobs lessened, and he wiped his eyes. Dropping to his knees, he also began to pray. "Lord, you've put me in this position of authority, but I see your hand in everything. Help me to be strong, to do the right thing. But most of all, Lord, protect my family from harm. I humbly ask for you to cause Charlie to go away... specifically, to run out of my office and never return. I know this is a far-fetched request, but I'm desperate. My only hope lies with forces unseen, forces more powerful that any powers of man. I know that you honor the petitions of your children, according to your purpose, so I beseech you to send your holy angels to this building to cleanse it of all evil. In Jesus' precious name I pray. Amen."

He then stood in front of the mirror, straightened his tie, and took a deep breath, looking himself dead in the eyes. An air of determination seemed to come over him, as he stood a little taller. He left the restroom, and Sam followed.

There was no change in the hallway. The beasts in red were still on duty. However, when the mayor and Sam entered the waiting room, it was packed with ten or so angels, waiting in formation for their orders. The only one he recognized was Armada.

As Mayor Houlihan entered his office, they surrounded him, as would the secret service men for the president.

Sam joined the girls at their look out, not wanting to miss the impending confrontation.

'What happened?"

"Our prayers are working," Sam smiled, pointing at the cavalry.

The mayor settled into his leather chair, and then leaned back. His countenance appeared determined and confident. The angels filed in, stationing themselves all around the room, and in front of his desk.

Charlie spoke. "Have you had a chance to—"

It looked like he gagged on his words. Sam leaned closer to get a better view of his mouth.

Something looked out of place. He squinted to focus on an object protruding from between the man's lips. The object grew. It wiggled and grew even longer. Sam then identified it as a tongue. Not a human tongue, though. This one was long, dark, and forked, surging in and out like a serpent.

The man's body jerked every few seconds. Then it quivered until it ramped-up into a full seizure of shaking jolts.

As a snake peels off a layer of skin, a demon emerged from within Charlie, leaving his body in crumpled heap on the floor, unconscious. The forked-tongue demon lashed out with its claws in protest, but the angels didn't move an inch.

The beast then filled his lungs with air like the wolf from the fairy tale, aiming his venomous wind at the angels. A toxic black smoke rushed out of the snake-demon's mouth causing Sam to hold his breath. Through burning eyes, he witnessed every angel, except Armada, fly helplessly backwards and through the wall.

It turned toward Sam, Hayley and Tallulah and puffed a misty cloud of blackness in their direction. Sam raised his shield in time to block himself, but the girls flew back to the wall, knocking over the potted plants.

Sam charged the creature from behind as Armada attacked from the front. It merely put out his hand, and Armada flew back.

Turning to face Sam, its tongue slithered in and out of a growing, evil smile. Sam stood in shock, but then raised his sword to the demon in vain. Its mouth opened, revealing four enormous

139

fangs that pierced Sam's arm, causing him to scream and drop his sword.

Before the sword hit the ground, the demon screeched in pain and fell to the ground. Armada stood victorious behind it and withdrew his sword from its back. This particular demon wasn't pulled into the abyss, but instead, with a screech toward Sam, slithered violently out of the room and into the hall. On the floor, Sam inched to the hall in time to see it and its red-robed guards fly toward the window at the end of the hall together, smashing it as they flew through it, and then out of sight.

As Sam sat holding his arm in disbelief, the mayor watched with wide eyes from his seat, looking unsure of what to do next. Of course, he had not seen the demons retreating, but Charlie had collapsed on his floor in front of his eyes.

"A miracle," the mayor whispered to himself.

Charlie began to stir and sit upright. Disoriented and moaning he stood. "What... what am I doing here?" He looked at the mayor, but only received a blank expression from him as well.

He stumbled and swayed, upsetting a fichus, dumping soil on the carpet as he rushed out of the room. Once again Mayor Houlihan dropped to his knees, trembling, this time thanking God for answering his prayer.

Hayley and Tallulah examined Sam's wound.

"Why?" Sam asked Armada. "Why did He allow this?"

"I have no answer for you Sam. Not everything He allows is explained, but it all works for good according to His purpose."

In a flicker, Armada was gone.

Mayor Houlihan exhaled in relief, picked up the phone and dialed. "Hi, Honey. I'm on my way home now…"

Sam got to his feet. The Knights trudged out into the hall.

"They all flew out this window? Why did they break it? They were in the spiritual dimension. They could have flown through it." Hayley said, examining the jagged glass.

They stood at the ruptured window, watching the snow surge to the ground in swollen gusts.

"It was a reminder for us," Sam said, enduring the surges of pain from his wounds.

"The snow must be knee-high now…maybe higher," Hayley said.

"Look at that police car down there," Tallulah said, pointing to a patrol car in the side parking lot, its tires submerged in snow. "It's almost—"

Before she could finish, demons sprouted out of the snow, crawling over and around the vehicle like a pack of starving wolves. Sam saw a man's figure inside the vehicle.

"Dean is in that car. Let's go," he said, making his way downstairs to the snowy parking lot. The girls were close behind.

"Tallulah, attack from the air. Hayley, I'll clear a path for you to enter the car. Ready?" Sam asked, and in that brief moment he felt like a quarterback.

The girls nodded, and they were off.

Tallulah got to the car first and deliberately brushed past a few demons positioned on the hood as she rocketed skyward, drawing their attention, causing them to fly toward her. She merely put her hand out, sending them spinning out of sight.

From out of the snow came more creatures, and Tallulah easily repelled all but one—an enormous, bat-like demon that extended its wings, sending a wave of power measuring greater than Tallulah could handle. The shock wave flung her one hundred yards away, sinking her deep into a snowbank.

Sam arrived at the patrol car next, and aimed his shield at each demon, frying them into oblivion, allowing Hayley to slip into the passenger seat next to Dean.

Sam's attention was then drawn to the only remaining creature—an orange-eyed demon with long, coarse hair, that stood perfectly still on top of the car. When their eyes met, the demon cracked a grin that steadily grew into a smile and then a full chuckle, like it knew something Sam didn't.

Sam jumped onto the hood, never allowing his gaze to leave its orange eyes until he braved a glance at Hayley's progress through the windshield dusted with snow.

The demon, still chuckling, sunk through the roof of the car into the backseat. Hayley turned toward the demon with her gloved hands extended in defense against the beast. Sam watched through the glass as the creature first smiled at Sam, and then, made his presence known to Dean. Dean spun around, screamed out in horror at the sight of the beast and fired at it six times, emptying his gun. The demon just smirked. Dean scrambled to reload, dropping several bullets, only some making it into the chambers.

Despite its own fate, the orange-eyed creature grabbed one of her gloves, and then yanked it off. It shook, and the glove dropped to the floor. The grins of the now electrified demon faded as it sizzled into the churning abyss, but before it disappeared completely, it pounced forward, ripping Hayley's ring from her finger and onto the floor in the back of the patrol car, leaving her exposed— visible to the deputy.

Dean slammed against his door with a look of confusion and disbelief. "How'd you...?" Dean yelled. His gun was now pointed at her. "What do you want? How'd you get in here?" he shouted in her face. His hand was shaking.

"I... I..." Hayley stammered, staring at the gun and then into Dean's raging eyes. She closed her own eyes.

In a desperate move, Sam blew his own cover by taking off his ring, bringing him clearly into Dean's sight.

"Hey hey hey hey... Don't shoot!" Sam bellowed, the words scratching his throat like broken glass.

Dean jumped back in his seat at Sam's appearance, but his gun was still aimed at Hayley.

She slowly edged her hand toward her whip, but he was far too close for it to be effective.

"Where'd you come from?" His breathing was labored. "Back off, Sam!" His face turned a shade of purple with every syllable, his veins bulging. He aimed his gun toward Sam, then back at Hayley.

Hayley tried to pull away.

"Freeze! I *will* shoot you!" Dean screamed.

"No!" Sam shouted.

"Sam!" Hayley shrieked.

The deputy suddenly screamed out in pain, grabbing his chest. He yelled out once more, and collapsed, slumping forward onto the steering wheel.

Heart attack? Sam thought.

As Tallulah floated down to the car, the three stared at Dean. Sam wondered what to do next.

"Is he dead?" Tallulah asked in the meekest voice with which Sam had ever heard her speak. She retrieved Hayley's ring and glove for her.

Sam heard their rejoicing before he could see them. He slipped on his ring just in time to witness five or six demons pouring into the car shouting a celebratory chant of victory. The girls also appeared in the supernatural dimension.

They watched the chanting demons pull at the deputy's body until they grasped what they came for.

His soul.

Sam shuddered as he realized Dean Walden's soul, coherent, kicking and shouting out in

144

horror, now belonged to Satan. He watched horrified as the demons dragged him into the abyss. The officer's last screams echoed in Sam's mind, a sound he would never forget. Dean's body remained crumpled over the steering wheel, silent and still.

Sam jumped off the hood and, with his hands, shoveled the accumulated snow next to the passenger door. Helping Hayley out of the car, he could feel she was trembling. Tallulah joined them, putting her arms around them both.

Hayley sobbed into her hands. "Why did they take him? He was a good man."

Tallulah stood up and let go of them. She stared out at the gentle white drifts blanketing the square. "I guess his name wasn't in the book," she whispered.

***

They stayed until Dean's body was discovered, and the scene investigated. Then the three trudged through the square, still in the spiritual dimension, without speaking. The snow had stopped falling, but white covered everything.

The only thing that brightened their moods was the sight of the mayor and his wife approaching The Calico Rose, the best cafe in Carthage. Sam, Hayley, and Tallulah stopped walking to watch as the mayor took his arm from around his expectant wife and opened the door for her. The Houlihans were unaware of their angel escort.

145

***

The lights from the closed market spilled from the windows and out into the square as Sam returned home. Stepping across the porch and reaching for the door handle, he realized he was still in the supernatural dimension. He began to take off his ring, but then stopped.

From the front porch he could hear his mother singing "It Is Well," her favorite hymn; however, hers was not the only voice he heard, so he decided to take a closer look before removing his ring. As he walked through the closed front door, his eyes welled up with tears for what he saw and heard.

She was wiping down the ice cream counter with a dishtowel. Her voice filled the room, and it was pretty, but it was, by far, not the best voice in the room. Three angels completed the hymn's missing harmony parts, singing right along with her. One of the angels was Florelle, Hayley's instructor. She looked at him and smiled.

If only she knew there are angels singing with her, Sam thought. *I wonder if angels always sing along with hymns.* He decided to investigate that some time, but, for now, he returned to the porch, and took off his ring. He stomped the clumps of snow off his boots before he re-entered the market.

"Hi, honey. Did you have fun with the girls?" she asked, cutting the hymn short.

"Mmhm," he said, wondering if the angels were still in the room with them.

"Did y'all build a snowman in all that snow? We must have set some major weather records today," she chattered on, helping him take off his jacket. "Sure is strange." She hung the letterman's jacket on the coat rack, looked at him, and sighed. "Are you all right, Sam? You don't seem yourself."

"There's just been a lot of changes lately, that's all."

"Okay," she said, not looking convinced. "I'm always here if you need to talk."

"I know," he said, giving her a hug. "What's for dinner? I'm starving!"

"Now you sound more like the Sam I know. Come on upstairs. There's a meatloaf waiting for us."

Climbing the stairs, she turned back towards him. "Tallulah seems like a nice girl. Tell me all about her. She sure is pretty. And her British accent is so fun..."

Sam nodded.

Over dinner, he proceeded to tell her about Tallulah's crazy driving, fear of little, and love of sunflowers. They filled the mealtime with idle chitchat, careful not to mention the empty chair at the table or his Knighthood.

Sam slept well that night. The challenges of the day left him so exhausted he could think no more about demons and evil. Sleep came quickly, and he barely moved at all during the night.

Chapter Eleven
A Knight and His Sword

December

It was December, but all was not merry.

Kicking a pinecone along the cracked, paved street, Sam approached the church on his route home from school. Under a bare maple tree, on the bench just outside the chapel, a newspaper fluttered in the breeze, beaconing Sam to catch up on current events before working at the market.

Abandoning the pinecone, and taking a seat on the bench, he scanned the paper's headlines: *CRIME AT AN ALL TIME HIGH... UNUSUAL DISTURBANCES... CHURCHES CLOSING THEIR DOORS... BIZZARE WEATHER...*

Sam was not surprised by any of these headlines. Three months of demon slashing had brought the town of Carthage no closer to ridding itself of Satan's counterparts.

Feeling frustrated, he quickly moved on to his favorite section: Sports. He was stunned by what he read: *NORTHERN TEAM DISQUALIFIED;*

*CARTHAGE WILL GO TO STATE
CHAMPIONSHIP GAME.*

He couldn't believe what he was reading. Excitement washed over him as he realized his team was headed for the game of a lifetime. Unable to utter a word, his mouth ajar, he barely drew breath as the exhilaration surged through his veins. But just as suddenly as it arrived, the joy was replaced with familiar bitterness as he realized what could have been. He clamped his mouth shut tight, and then fought back tears of regret for all he'd given up.

I would've been quarterback in this game.

His stomach ached. His head felt light, and there were so many of his own negative thoughts rushing through his mind, he almost didn't hear the voice.

"Quitter," it whispered.

As he shifted his focus from the paper toward the sound, a forceful gust of wind pushed against him, and he watched the pinecone suddenly roll ten feet and into a ditch.

"Quitter," the voice rang again through winds that increased into a dirt devil. This time he heard it clearly.

He turned his head toward the eerie voice as he fished for his ring in his pocket. Slipping it on just in time to see the sanctuary doors fly open, he saw Pastor Tim kneeling before the cross, weeping. He wondered if the pastor could sense their presence, but Sam's attention was drawn to something even more disturbing.

149

Standing outside, shoulder-to-shoulder, the red-robed demons that lined the hallway at city hall, surrounded the church, their robes whipping in the turbulent winds.

Like a ravenous wolf pack, dozens of demons paced aimlessly on the sparse grass around a magnolia tree that shaded the area.

It's worse than ever, he thought as he turned to face the demon wolf trying to torment him.

*"**You** should be quarterback in that game."* It sputtered the suggestion with a deep growl.

The words were a tornado of bitterness in his heart as the winds rushed past him. He stood and aimed his shield at its face, screaming at it, as if the mere intensity of his voice could erase all his regret.

But shock flooded his mind when, instead of succumbing to the abyss, the unaffected demon grabbed the shield with its teeth, and then easily flung it fifty yards away.

The wolf smirked. *"Pitiful toy."*

The vulnerability Sam felt at that moment made him freeze. None of his training prepared him for this. Why was this demon immune to the power of his shield?

Sam turned his panic into action. He drew his sword, but before he could use it, the demon grabbed it with his fang filled mouth. It bit hard enough to break it in half, the pieces then clanked to the ground like thrift store silverware. Sam stared at the broken sword, realizing his defenseless position. A few of the sapphires had fallen out of the handle, and the fiery opal was now black.

Edging his way backward, he wanted to run, but his legs felt stiff and numb. Shooting glances left and right, he looked for an escape.

The creature's claws pierced Sam's chest as it pushed him to the ground. Everything spun as the hard earth met his head. The pain radiated like a strike to a church bell. The ache overpowered all his senses. Even his sight faded briefly, but returned as tiny pin pricks of sparkling light, falling like rain.

With everything spinning, he managed to look down towards his aching chest. Pinned like prey, blood now soaked his uniform. He could smell its steamy breath on his face— like a toxic gas.

Sam waited for the worst.

But instead, light suddenly overpowered the scene.

Ray.

With one hand encircling the creature's neck, Ray lifted it to eye-level.

In his groggy state, Sam saw the demon wolf dangling over him. Although Ray seemed to outrank this demon, it didn't appear afraid.

"You may not take his life," Ray said through gritted teeth, eye-to-eye with the creature.

The demon vanished.

Ray lowered his arm, as if he knew it would disappear, and looked down at Sam. "Looks like you were in a pickle," he said with a slight chuckle.

Sam didn't feel like laughing or speaking.

"Let's get you fixed-up," Ray said.

All went black.

***

The next instant, Sam was no longer on the ground, but lying on a leather reclining chair in what seemed to be a private airplane. He assumed it was Spencer's plane.

Disoriented, he tried to sit up. His bandaged head throbbed.

"Just rest," Hayley said.

He lay back, but then sat up again. Hayley, Tallulah, Rebecca, Katie, and Spencer were crowded around him.

"Ready for an adventure, kid?" Spencer asked with a toothy smile.

"Where are we going?" Sam mumbled.

The captain's voice told them all to get buckled for take-off. They obeyed. The plane taxied, gained speed, and then lifted off.

Sam's entire body ached, but even so, he was determined to look out the window. He'd never been on a plane before. The take-off forced him back against the cushion.

"Ouch."

Touching his aching head, he raised up again to get his peek at a miniature Carthage below. It was overrun with demons and darkness on every street, every building. An enormous line of red-robed demons completely encircled the town.

He thought about his mom.

"Why are we leaving? We can't go. Look! They're everywhere."

"Oh, my," said Tallulah.

"My parents are down there," Hayley whispered.

The town became a speck as they climbed and then began to level off.

Over the deep-toned hum of the plane's propellers, Sam heard their thoughts. Far away at first, but they grew closer quickly.

Sam put on his ring. The others followed.

With great force, an army of shadows landed on the plane.

The Knights watched as the vaporous beings did their damage. The bolts that secured Katie's window frame were dislodged one bolt at a time. The flaps were pried from their wings. The outer panels of the craft peeled like an orange and were jettisoned to the ground. The landing gear was obliterated before it retracted.

These spiritual terrorists would have been bad enough, but along with them came a nasty electrical storm. Relentless bolts zapped every section of the plane.

"Won't we be electrocuted?" Katie asked.

"No, we're safe from the lightning in here," Rebecca said.

"It's not the lightning I'm worried about," said Hayley.

"Pray." Tallulah told them.

"Already on it," said Katie.

"Pray harder!" Tallulah yelled.

The plane started losing altitude and control. It shuddered so hard items toppled from their storage bins. A briefcase hit Spencer in the face. A nosebleed ensued. He took off his ring, and then staggered to the front of the plane. Once in the cockpit, he found his pilot desperately trying to regain control.

"What's wrong, Clark?" he asked, easing into the co-pilot seat.

"We're crashing, sir," he said without looking at Spencer who was nursing his bloody face with a cloth from the stewardess cart.

"This wasn't on our itinerary," Spencer said with a strained tongue-in-cheek tone.

"Last minute change of plans, I guess. Heck of a storm, Sir. Plane's gone haywire!"

"Clark, I'm sure you're aware of it, but the ground *is* getting closer."

"I'm on it, Boss," he said, struggling with the controls.

Leaving his trusted pilot in the cockpit, he stumbled toward the rest, replacing his ring. Sitting next to Rebecca, he looked out the window, finding their predicament much the same as when he left.

A demonic shadow, like a toxic gas, seeped through the damage by Sam's window and swirled around in front of him. Sam heard its evil celebration.

It thought *"The master will be proud. We're bringing this plane down."*

This chilled Sam to the bones. The only weapon he had left, the only strength he had in him, he found in his prayer, "Lord, send help."

Suddenly, the shadow was sucked back out of the tiny hole and off the plane, its vaporous trail fading in the distance. One by one, the evil forces were blown away from the airplane by an unseen force.

"Look! There's an angel under the wing!" Sam exclaimed.

"On this side, too!" Rebecca reported.

Spencer made his way to the front once more.

Spencer removed his ring and then sat next to Clark. "Looks like you've got things under control."

"Hey, boss. We're back in business. Just don't ask me how."

"Good work, Clark. I knew you had it covered."

"I'll prepare for an emergency landing. Looks like we could make it to Longview. Or maybe we should turn back to Carthage—"

"Negative on that, Clark. Stick to the original flight plan."

"Sir, after what we've just been through, I—"

Spencer put a hand firmly on the pilot's shoulder. "You're gonna have to trust me on this one, Clark. Consider your salary doubled."

He paused at the sound of that and then muttered, "I hope I live to spend it."

Spencer patted him once on the back and left the cockpit. He replaced his ring and returned to the group.

With the demons eradicated, the Knights gawked at the damage.

Katie prayed "Thank you, Father, for sending us the help we needed."

Amens echoed.

"With angels doing the flying, we might just land early," Spencer joked, relieved.

"Where *are* we going?" Sam asked.

"Armada appeared to me and told me to pick you guys up and then go to Montana Jack's," Spencer said.

"What about Old Joe?" Tallulah asked.

"We go to his place last."

"And then…?" Rebecca inquired.

"I have no idea."

"Armada didn't say?" Hayley asked.

"He said Old Joe will tell us." Spencer clapped his hands together, rubbing them back and forth. "Okay… so, who's ready for some lemonade?"

With a unanimous show of hands, he and Rebecca first served a very deserving pilot, and then the Knights. They drank lemonade while angels escorted them to Montana.

Chapter Twelve
Montana Jack's

Sam paused at the top of the plane's stairs to take in the Montana view. *Majestic*, he thought. He was the last one to exit the damaged aircraft. He noticed Katie squatting, touching the ground.

"Are you going to kiss it, too?" Spencer kidded.

She replied with a smirk.

"There's a van waiting for us just through the terminal over there," Spencer said.

"That's a terminal?" Katie asked, pointing to the building.

"Smaller than New York, huh?"

"Just a little."

Sam asked, "What about the plane? How will we get to Old Joe's?"

"The plane is pretty much toast. And Jack tells me we have transportation waiting for us," Spencer replied. "Knowing him, it'll be an old clunker school bus from his personal junkyard."

Clark and an aviation mechanic surveyed the damage. One wing rested on the ground and the landing gear was nonexistent. Gouges covered the sides and belly. Large sections of the siding were gone. The propellers were warped. It looked like it had been through a world war.

The mechanic shook his head. "How in the world did you fly this, let alone land it?"

"I can give you no explanation," Clark said, not looking at him, but instead watching the Knights walk away.

***

"Hey! You made it," Jack yelled out toward the van, wiping his hands on a rag. He hugged each one as snow fluttered around them. "Great to see you guys."

"Looks like you're getting some snow," Rebecca said.

"What? This? This is just a little dusting. The barn isn't even buried yet."

Her eyes widened a little looking at the huge, rusty colored barn.

"Come on in out of the cold."

Wiping their shoes on the mat, they entered his dark cabin that had been decorated at one time, but without a woman's touch, had succumbed to dust, clutter, and a motorcycle engine on a milk crate in the living room.

"Sorry, I haven't found time to clean up," Jack muttered as he ran around grabbing old newspapers off the couches, and dirty coffee cups off tables. "Jeremiah!?" he yelled in the direction of the hallway.

No answer.

"It's been hard since his mother passed away. He was only ten at the time. Being a Knight sure hasn't made it any easier—all this secretive work I've been doing." Looking down the hall, he yelled again. "Jeremiah!?"

Still no answer.

"Must be over at his friend's house already. He'll be staying there while we're gone." Piling the papers onto an already overloaded desk, he turned and said "You guys hungry? I'll throw on some steaks. And then I'll show you what I've been working on."

"What is it?" Sam asked.

"Well, this something you just gotta see for yourselves."

***

The massive doors of the barn swung out, revealing stalls containing fantastical, vaporous, vividly colorful horses.

"My heart! I may die!" Hayley squealed.

"Coolest things I've ever seen!" said Sam.

"So… you trained them? These are the 'top secret beings'?" Tallulah asked.

"Well, yes. With help from my instructor."

"How many are there?" Spencer asked.

"Eight. One for each of us. They're called Chargers."

"They are amazing. One small problem. I've never been on a horse in my life." Katie said.

"I'll teach you. It's easy. Right, Jack?

159

"Well, yes and no. These aren't usual horses. Similar, but supernatural remember. They can fly. And travel at high speeds. They can also read your thoughts. Where you want to go. If you tie them to a post or fence or something, they go into this sort of invisible hibernation. But all you have to do is pray when you need them and they are visible again."

"When do we have our first lesson?" Rebecca asked.

"After those steaks I promised you. Come on back to the cabin and we'll get the grill going."

They left the barn and headed toward the house just as a pickup truck arrived.

"Oh, good. It's my son." Jack said.

A young man, about thirteen, who could have passed for a hobo with a stuffed backpack and worn jacket, got out of the truck. It sped away.

"Jeremiah, I'd like you to meet my team."

"I want to be called Jeremy, Dad."

"We'll talk about that later. You hungry? I'm gonna—"

A scroll appeared in Jack's hand. "What's this?"

"Maybe it's our mission details…" Tallulah suggested.

He opened it. "It says you're coming with us, Jeremiah."

"Where? I was supposed to hang out with Chuck."

"Leave it to my teenager to argue with a scroll delivered from God."

Everyone laughed. Except for Jeremiah.

"If it says you go, you go. Besides, I wasn't that thrilled about you spending time with Chuck anyway."

Jerimiah skulked into the house.

"How can he go with us? He doesn't have a ring. He's not a Knight." Katie said.

"You don't need a ring if you're on a Charger. He can ride Old Joe's Charger for now.. And I guess double-up with me later? Well, I'm sure it'll work out…" Jack said.

"Guess we'll just have to trust it will," said Tallulah.

***

With Sam's belly now full of steak, baked potato, and garlic bread, he and the group ventured out to the barn where eight Chargers waited for them in their stalls.

"So, find the stall with your name on it. Each Charger has been chosen especially for you. Open the door and take the reins," instructed Jack. "Don't worry, they are very tame."

The Knights obeyed.

"I don't know… they look pretty wild," Katie said, cautiously opening her door.

"They're gorgeous!" Tallulah said, already stroking her Charger's mane that floated and billowed as if in water and wind.

"They're like misty rainbows," Hayley cooed.

"Alright, lead your Charger out of its stall and follow me to the corral."

Sam had to keep the reins taut because his Charger had a bit more spirit than the rest. Once in the corral, Sam let go of the reins. His horse literally ran circles around the others. He was mostly cloudy white with streaks of royal blue and silver sparks pulsing though him.

"What are their names?" Spencer asked.

"Oh yeah, that's the cool part. You get to name yours," Jack said.

All eight Chargers trotted freely in the corral, mostly in the same direction, as a herd would.

"Who has that white one?" Rebecca asked.

"He's mine," Sam answered.

"Maybe you should call him 'Speedy'?" Spencer suggested.

"Hmmm... Maybe something a bit more powerful..." Sam said.

"Yeah, he's fast!" Hayley exclaimed.

"I got it... Lightning," Sam announced.

"Perfect," Hayley said.

"Of course, mine will be Sunflower," said Tallulah.

"Of course," said Hayley. "And since I play the piano. I think I'll call mine Harmony."

"Nice," Rebecca said.

"How about yours, Rebecca?" Hayley asked.

"I always have the hardest time naming things. I'll have to think it over," she answered.

Katie reported "Mine will be Ruby. As in ruby slippers. After the classic movie prop. Plus, her coloring reminds me of a ruby."

"Figures, since you're an actress… or at least a wanna be… or soon to be…" Jack winked at Katie.

Katie asked, "What about yours, Jack?"

"I named mine months ago, while I was training them. He's 'Cadillac' because his ride is so smooth."

They nodded at his choice.

"And speaking of riding, it's time to mount up. But first, there are some things you should know."

The Knights moved in close to Jack as he spoke.

"These spirit horses are connected to you… in a way. If you need them, all you need to do is pray and ask for them, and they will come to you. Also, if you are riding one, you are automatically in the spiritual realm. Just like your rings, they can transport you to that dimension, no ring required. They also cannot be seen by humans or demons unless God allows it."

"Do we need to feed them or give them water? Brush them?" Hayley asked.

"No, because they're in spirit form. They don't need that kind of thing."

Jack then spoke a few words to the Chargers in Hebrew. The herd slowed their trotting to a stop. He opened the gate and the Knights entered.

"You've all ridden a horse before, right?"

They all nodded, except Katie.

"I'll help you, Katie. Does everyone know how to mount a horse? How to use the reins?"

More nodding.

"When you want to lift off the ground, say 'Skyward'. If you want to land, say 'Down'. They respond to those words in any language. It's pretty straight forward. Okay, go ahead and saddle up. I'll be here in case you need help."

Sam mounted Lightning easily. His summer job on the Goodman Ranch had given him loads of experience.

They mounted their Chargers as Jack showed Katie how as well. He mentioned a few tips to her, and then he mounted Cadillac. "Okay, follow me around the corral."

They trotted at an easy pace, and then he led them out of the corral where they increased their speed.

Jack yelled, "Skyward!"

Cadillac rose a few feet above the ground, trotting through the air. One by one the rest of the Chargers followed.

Being the second in line behind Jack, Sam glanced back at the rest of the Knights. They appeared elated as they sailed along in the colorful flying parade. Sam felt like he was riding a cloud that had the power of a motorcycle. He thought Jack was right. It was a smooth ride. The rushing wind was exhilarating.

After the training session, the Knights, plus Jeremiah, traveled to Old Joe's house in Arizona... in just minutes.

Chapter Thirteen
Old Joe's Place

"That was fast," Hayley said, stroking her Charger, Harmony. "And amazing."

"Like something from a dream," said Rebecca. "Maybe that's what I should call her? Dream."

"I like it," Hayley agreed.

"Me too." Katie said. "Yeah, that would've taken hours by plane. I ought to know. I've flown to New York too many times." She rolled her eyes on the word 'too'. "Takes me all year to save up for my ticket to California where my family lives." she said, securing Ruby to the post.

"Is it scary living alone in New York City?" Hayley asked. "I've been there a few times with my parents."

"You get used to it. It's actually quite exciting. Besides, I'm so busy waiting tables and auditioning, I hardly have time to worry about anything except scrounging up enough rent money."

With the Chargers secured, the Knights approached a small, pueblo style home. Sam rang the doorbell. A few moments later, a petite, white-haired lady opened the creaky door, haunted house style.

"Hello, ma'am. We're looking for Joe Jones. Does he live here?" Sam asked.

"I'm Julia, his wife. Please come in."

They all filed into the modest, flower-filled living room. Ten or so large arrangements crowded the room, making it hard for them to squeeze in, but the fragrance was divine.

"Please have a seat," Julia said.

Tallulah, Hayley, Rebecca, and Katie sat close on the couch, while the guys sat on chairs and an organ bench. The air-conditioned room was quiet and still as they waited for their hostess to speak.

Julia sat in a rocking chair. "He didn't tell me there would be so many of you."

"You knew we were coming?" Spencer asked.

"Well, I wasn't sure when, but He told me."

"Joe told you?"

"Yes. And the Lord did, too. In a dream."

The room was muffled with quiet.

"I'm sorry to have to tell you. Joe passed away last week. His funeral was yesterday."

Sam felt like the floor beneath him had just disappeared.

The room filled with gasps. The Knights looked at each other with disbelief.

"He suffered a heart attack." She paused, the wrinkles on her face becoming more acute as she fought back tears. "As he lay there, dying, he of course told me he loved me, but then he divulged his greatest secret ever. My husband kept every

166

military secret to which he was privy from World War I and II. But this one he told me about because he thought you might show up sometime. I thought he was talking nonsense until I had the vision in my dream. I know you are Knights. I know where you've been and what you can do."

They sat stunned listening to her shaking voice.

"I realize this must be a shock to you, as it was to me. He gave me instructions...I'll be right back," she said, scuffling down the hall.

As the sound of her shoes on the tile floor faded, Hayley turned to Sam. "I can't believe he's gone."

Sam nodded.

"He was so full of life," Rebecca said, sniffling

"I'll bet he's as lively as ever in Heaven!" said Tallulah.

Jack cleared the lump in his throat. "She's right. But why was his time now?"

Everyone fought back tears as Julia returned holding a small, leather bound book the size of a paperback. Holding it close, like it was Joe himself, she asked, "Which of you is Rebecca?"

"I'm Rebecca," she said, looking surprised at being singled out.

"Joe told me to give this book to the Knights. In my dream, the Lord told me to give it to you specifically. I haven't looked inside it out of respect for Joe. That part was hard, as I am a very curious person," she said, handing the book to Rebecca.

She held it like she would hold the original Ten Commandments. "Should I open it?" Rebecca asked as a tear rolled down her cheek.

"Yes. Definitely," Sam said.

Without hesitation, they all agreed.

It was worn, and the cracked leather cover was rubbed smooth. There was no title on the front. And when she opened it, she appeared confused.

"The pages are blank," Rebecca reported.

"Hmm," Jack said.

Curious looks from the others flashed around the room.

"Well, I guess I could have had a peek then, couldn't I?" Julia mused, rocking again.

But then a look of pure epiphany washed over Rebecca's face. "*This* is the book," she realized. "This is one of my gifts. I didn't think Old Joe would be the one to give it to me. But why is it blank?"

"I'm sure it has great significance to your mission." Julia said, rocking at a slow pace. "Let the Lord reveal it in His time." From her pocket, she pulled an object. "Which of you is Jack?"

"I'm Jack," he said, looking perplexed.

"Just this morning, an angel came to me and told me where to find this. And that I should give it to you."

She dropped the object into his outreached hand, causing great confusion in the group. The shiny, silver ring lay there, seemingly unimportant, dwarfed by Jack's work-worn palm. Only he was close enough to see the cross-shaped hole in the band and Joseph Jones written inside.

Glances from Knight to Knight bounced around the floral-scented room as Jack continued to look at it.

"Well, I can see it is important to you," Julia said.

Jack nodded, wondering what it meant. Tucking it deep into his pants pocket, he smiled at Julia. "Thank you."

She smiled.

Quietly, Tallulah suggested "Maybe it's for Jeremiah?"

Jack nodded.

An awkward lull prompted Hayley to rise and walk to the mantel where photos of Old Joe were displayed. "Oh, wow. This is Joe, isn't it?" she asked, looking at a photo of a man in his thirties.

"He was really proud of that picture by his plane. You knew he was a Flying Ace in World War I, didn't you?"

"He didn't say a word about it," Spencer said, impressed.

"His duty was, of course, to shoot down as many enemy planes as possible. Although every plane he shot down was considered a victory, he never forgot each of those planes had a pilot, and each of those pilots had a family. That's why he had tattoos on his forearm—one cross for every pilot."

Sam remembered those crosses. "Ma'am would you mind me asking why one of the crosses was red?"

"That was the most tragic of them all. He saved a newspaper clipping..." She picked up a box from the coffee table and opened it. "Here it is," she

169

said, handing it to Sam. "In World War II he was too old to fly and still wanted to serve, so he was a guard at a Japanese internment camp."

Sam straightened, looked at Katie, and handed the clipping to her.

"What is it? Is everything alright?" Julia inquired.

Katie's mouth was open, her eyes wide and fixed on the photo. She couldn't speak for what seemed like minutes, but then she blurted out, "This man in the photo was my father." With her hands covering her face, she sobbed intensely, her body shaking with each cry.

Tallulah and Hayley put their arms around her.

The photo showed a man lying face down in the dirt as a girl knelt beside his body, crying. The girl was Katie.

Julia rose wearily from her rocker and sat down on the coffee table in front of Katie, holding both of her hands. "Katie. I know your name is Katie. Joe told me about you. He never forgot a single fact about that day and your family. It was the most devastating day of his life. In all these years, he always remembered to pray for you, little Katie. He prayed for you to grow up strong, not bitter. He prayed God would use this tragedy for good somehow. But most of all he prayed you would forgive him someday. I hope you can and will. I am so sorry for your loss." She put her head down, crying now, too.

Minutes seemed like hours as the two women consoled each other.

Through aching sobs Katie said, "I'm sorry for your loss too, Julia. Joe was a good man."

Chapter Fourteen
The Secret's Out

Southern California was famous for its orange trees which were plentiful on the school grounds. They tied-off their Chargers near the grove. Then the Knights walked together toward the main building of Rebecca's school. Not an ordinary school though. A classical, project-oriented, private school located in a turn-of-the-century yellow Victorian, framed by jasmine draped trellises.

Here they hoped to find out about Old Joe's book and what their mission was.

Rebecca led them on a quick tour of the campus.

"Over there we have the garden where the students will grow their own food. We also have the barn for raising livestock and a workshop where they will learn old-fashioned basic skills. You know, things we take for granted... how to make soap, candles, woodworking, even blacksmith skills. Auto mechanics in that garage there. And there's a science building for hands-on labs. In the main house, small classes will study mathematics, history, literature, government, and languages. And then that's the student dormitory down that way."

"This is a one-of-a-kind school. I'm impressed." Jack said.

All of them agreed.

"Thanks. It's only possible because of a very generous donor here," Rebecca said, patting Spencer's shoulder.

"I know a good investment when I see it," Spencer said.

"Do you have many students yet?" Sam asked.

"We haven't opened yet. We're about to start hiring staff.
This is a rural area, so it may take some time.
Follow me and I'll show you inside the main house."

The interior was spacious, polished, and bright. A grand entry debuted a large, curved staircase. Their shoes echoed on the shiny, checkerboard tiles. Oak trim, copper ceilings, and lace adorned picture windows welcomed the group.

"This... is... amazing!" Hayley said.

"Thank you," Rebecca said, beaming. "The classrooms are upstairs, but this is my favorite room."

She opened double doors, and they were greeted by the scent of old books in a well-stocked library. Victorian floor lamps with dangling fringes stood guard over plush leather chairs and couches. The room had a back-home, cozy feeling, an escape from the real world, a place where you could curl up and relax in quiet privacy. But the best thing about the room was not the feelings it evoked, and not the comfortable furniture, but the plethora of books lining every inch of wall space available.

Hayley was the first to reach the shelves.

Tallulah plopped down on a couch. "Very comfortable," she told Rebecca as she thumbed through a copy of *The Saturday Evening Post* she found on an end table.

The rest of the Knights wandered off, scanning titles for an old favorite or a new adventure. Jeremy sulked down next to the sports section with a huff.

Rebecca watched them for a moment like a wise librarian, as they searched through her collection. Then she sat down at a roll top desk, placing Old Joe's book in front of her. Pulling a drawer on the right side of the desk completely out, she placed it on the floor and reached into the vacant space where the drawer usually rested. With her whole arm inside, she fished around until she found the object she wanted. She eased it out of its secret spot, and then set it on the desk.

An ancient-looking, wooden box lay before her. She ran her finger over the intricate carved designs before she opened the lid, exposing an unusual pair of spectacles. Lifting them out as if they were a precious heirloom, she then placed them on her face. They resembled a cross between 3-D glasses and old-fashioned goggles.

Blinking several times, her eyes slowly adjusted to the lenses. Looking back towards the rest of the group, she found they were still absorbed in their books. Her attention turned back to the desk. She picked up Old Joe's book and opened it. "

With her spectacles, she could see what Joe wrote and drew.

"Hey! They work!" she exclaimed to the group. "There's a map on this page. And now I can look for its match in my reference books."

The Knights gathered around her desk.

Rebecca moved her finger across seven books lined up, stopping at the red one. She opened it and began flipping through pages.

"Here it is," she said, turning the book toward the group. "This gives us coordinates, facts and details to piece together with Joe's information. The red book is all maps. The yellow one is for notes. Green is sketches, blue is languages, and there's a timeline in the purple book."

"So, everything is color coded," Katie said.

"Yeah. Most of my training on Archai was researching these books."

"Okay, Bookworm," Spencer said, "I think we all know how much you love books, but I don't know about the rest of you, but I'm starving. We have some steaks waiting for us back at my place, so let's hit the beach!"

"Wait. We're going to the beach?" Sam asked.

Spencer nodded. "We'll have dinner at my house and try to make sense of all this."

"I've never been to the ocean," Sam said with excitement in his eyes.

"I guess I'll have to throw you in then!" Spencer said.

"I'd be glad to help you with that," said Jack.

Tallulah chimed in. "Me too!"

***

The coastline zoomed below the Chargers as they galloped through the ocean mist in the air. The sunset reminded Sam of the vivid sky on Archai.

Peaceful, he thought. *Better enjoy this while it lasts.*

Losing his weapons and being wounded were reminders of how dangerous this all was, how vulnerable he was. How vulnerable they all were.

Spencer directed the group past a jetty on one side and a rocky cliff. They landed their Chargers a half-mile down the shore on a private beach.

They tied-off their spirit horses to palm trees. Then the Chargers vanished to their hibernation mode. The Knights removed their rings.

A cabana with a dried-grass roof, lounge chairs, and a bar, welcomed the group; but when Sam's feet hit the sand, he threw off his letterman's jacket and shoes, and sprinted for the waves, jumping in with his clothes still on. Hayley and Tallulah followed, high-stepping over the waves while all three laughed like little kids on a trampoline.

Under the cabana, Katie and Rebecca posed like movie stars on lounge chairs, while Jack took a seat at the bar. Jeremiah sulked down on the sand under a palm tree, poking at the sand with a stick. Spencer got busy behind the bar.

"A glass of my famous lemonade?"

"Sure, thanks." Admiring the posh surroundings, Jack shook his head. "Your own private paradise, huh?"

"My favorite place in the world." He handed him a tall glass garnished with a slice of lemon and a miniature, paper umbrella—a green one.

"Thanks." Looking at the umbrella, Jack grinned. "Nice touch."

"What? It makes the drink taste better," he said, grinning back.

Taking a sip, he looked surprised. "That *is* good." He gulped down some more.

Sauntering over to Katie and Rebecca, Spencer delivered their drinks on a tray, each glass topped with umbrellas, of course.

"All you two need is some sunglasses and you'd be celebrities, don't you think, Jack?" Spencer said.

Jack raised his glass to the girls in agreement. They smiled and waved.

Ducking under the eaves of the grassy roof, Spencer swished his way through the sand to Jeremiah.

"Lemonade?"

"Thank you," he said, taking the glass, immediately drinking from the bendable straw.

"Aren't you going in the water?"

He shook his head while still drinking.

"Since Sam jumped in on his own, we'll just have to throw you in later," he said with a wink.

Jeremiah smirked behind his straw, still drinking.

177

Spencer turned and headed toward the cabana. Behind the bar again, he heard the unmistakable sound of a straw sucking the air at the bottom of a glass. Looking back, he saw Jeremiah fishing with the straw for every, last drop.

Jack looked up the steep, rocky incline behind the cabana. A long, wooden staircase, led to a massive building proudly perched at the top that resembled a modern art museum.

"That's your house?"

"Yep."

"Nice," he said, thinking about his ramshackle cabin back home.

The gurgling straw noise stopped, and Jack looked over at his son. Jeremiah put his glass by the edge of the palm tree and resumed poking the sand with the stick.

"He's still having a hard time with all this. I'll go talk to him."

Sam, Hayley and Tallulah returned from the waves.

"That's incredible!" Sam said, out of breath, shaking water from his hair onto Katie and Rebecca who shrieked from the freezing drops. Sam laughed at his prank.

"Stop! Stop! That's cold!" Rebecca yelled, shielding her face.

Spencer threw towels at Sam, Hayley and Tallulah, and they began drying off.

"You all look like drowned rats," Katie joked.

With eyebrows raised, Sam looked at Tallulah and Hayley. "Are you thinking what I'm thinking?"

Hayley and Tallulah nodded as they all dropped their towels and surrounded Katie's chair.

"No," she said adamantly. "No. You better not."

Kicking and twisting, trying to free herself, she pleaded with the others for help, but with no success. Sam grabbed her from behind and the girls each took a leg, carrying her over the sand and through the shallow water like the catch-of-the-day.

"One, two, three!" Sam said as they released her into a breaking wave.

When she surfaced, she stood up, taking deep breaths.

"Now who's the drowned rat?" Tallulah joked.

Katie stood there dripping, finally breaking into laughter. A splashing fight broke out between all of them, while Spencer, Rebecca and Jack watched from the cabana.

"Can't take 'em anywhere," Spencer said, shaking his head.

***

Sucking in air between words, Jack said, "If you… could add… more stairs… before we come over… next time… that would be… great."

As they climbed together like an uphill parade, Sam double-timed it past Jack. "It's a great work-out, don't you think?"

"Well, some of us… trained on obstacle… courses on… Archai, and others… uh… not so much," he huffed the broken sentence as Sam passed him to take the spot behind Spencer who was leading the parade.

When they reached the deck at the top, they all stopped to catch their breath—even Sam—before Spencer opened double French doors that led to an atrium filled with exotic plants and a parrot and a cockatoo.

"This reminds me of our castle on Archai," Katie said, looking around.

"Complete with parrot," Rebecca said.

"I'm a parrot," said the bird.

"See what I mean?"

"Yeah. Wow. Talented bird."

"The cockatoo over there can whistle the piccolo part from 'The Stars and Stripes Forever,'" Rebecca said, pointing to the cage by the philodendron.

"Really?" Katie asked.

"Yeah. But it's spoiled. You have to give it a treat first. But for now, let's get cookin' ladies."

The girls relocated to the kitchen. The guys manned the grill on the deck. Typical.

Following Rebecca down a marble hallway, the Sister Knights passed under a gray stone archway into a gourmet kitchen fit for an ambassador's staff.

"Cooking will not be a chore in this room," Tallulah said, admiring copper pots hanging over the island.

180

"Let's see what Lola bought at the store today," Rebecca said.

"Who's Lola?" Hayley asked.

"She's Spencer's housekeeper. He called ahead and told her there would be house guests tonight," Rebecca explained.

With only her legs visible from behind the refrigerator doors, Rebecca reported, "Looks like we've got salmon and filet mignon." She poked her head out. "It's a special occasion. Why don't we have both?"

"Both it is," Tallulah proclaimed. "I'll just run this meat out to the guys."

"What should we make to go with it?" Hayley asked.

"I have a great recipe for asparagus with a lemon vinaigrette sauce," Rebecca said, opening a cabinet and taking out a recipe box.

"Sounds good." Tallulah said. "And how about rice—?" Stopping short, she froze with a look like she'd forgotten her purse at a gas station. She nearly dropped the plate of meat. Her eyes widened as she sucked-in air at an alarming rate. And then, without moving, her mouth slightly ajar, she just stared straight at Rebecca.

"Are you alright?" Hayley asked.

No response.

"Tallulah?" Katie said, walking towards her.

"What is it? What'd I say? Is there a spider on me or something?" Rebecca asked, looking at both shoulders, uncomfortable with the sudden scrutiny.

Slowly coming out of her staring trance, Tallulah said, "Wait a minute." A smile emerged from her shock. "What's going on here?" She squinted as she stared at Rebecca.

"What do you mean?" Rebecca asked uneasily.

"Let me see that recipe box." She took it from Rebecca's hands and finger-walked through it. "Uh, huh," she said like she was in an Agatha Christie mystery novel.

"'Uh, huh' what?" Rebecca asked.

"What is it Tallulah?" Katie asked.

Tallulah put her hand to her chin and looked around the room as the others watched her. "Hmmm." Darting over to the counter by the telephone, she picked up a stack of envelopes and looked at them like flashcards. "Aha! I knew it! I can't believe it!"

Hayley, and Katie asked together in rather loud voices, "What?"

Rebecca stood quietly, waiting for her reply. She was grinning now.

"Do you want to know why Rebecca's recipe box is here... in that cabinet... in Spencer's house?" she asked, looking only at Katie and Hayley.

Their eyes widened as it dawned on them, too.

"They're married! Look! Look at the mail!" She shuffled through the stack of mail, shouting out the recipient's name. "Spencer Wetherholt. *Rebecca Wetherholt*. Mr. And Mrs. Spencer Wetherholt."

The kitchen was stone quiet as their eyes turned toward Rebecca and stopped. The hum of the refrigerator was the only thing you could hear. She just stood there, smiling like the new bride she was.

"I told him you'd figure it out. We wanted to wait and tell you after the mission… so we wouldn't distract from it."

"So, it's true then!" Tallulah screeched happily.

"Yes. We eloped last month."

Hayley grabbed Rebecca's left hand. "It's gorgeous! I don't know how I missed this clue," she said, admiring the two-carat diamond.

They flooded her with hugs and congratulations, and the high-pitched girly noises echoed off the tiled walls, making the guys come to investigate.

"What's wrong?" Spencer asked, rushing through the doorway with Jack and Sam close behind him.

Of course, the hugs and squeals were then transferred to Spencer.

"What's all this?" Spencer asked.

Tallulah showed him the envelopes.

"They know," Rebecca said, smiling at him.

Chapter Fifteen
Unwelcome Visitors

"You're the best cook ever," said Spencer, now free to put his arm around his wife.

"We *all* pitched in." she said as they relaxed on the patio, overlooking the sea.

"It's hypnotic," Sam said, following each wave as it hit the shoreline.

Taking some of them by surprise, Lola, Spencer's longtime housekeeper, came out the door humming the wedding march slightly off-pitch. Setting a wedding cake on the table, she then handed a small Macy's shopping bag to Tallulah, flashing her a grin. She scuttled back inside, still humming.

"What in the world?" Rebecca asked.

"We figured you didn't have a reception—or at least not with *us*, so we decided to surprise you with one." Tallulah stood up and opened the bag, pulling out a corsage, and a boutonnière. "Put these on, you two love birds." Out of the bag came a guest book, and a silver cake knife and server.

Lola returned with a serving cart toting chilled champagne, sparkling apple cider and fluted crystal glasses. As she turned to leave, Spencer stopped her.

"Lola, you're part of our family, too. Please stay for the toast and some cake."

She smiled, putting her head down shyly. "Si', Mr. Wetherholt."

"Don't let her shyness fool you. She's as spicy as the food she makes. The minute she met Rebecca, she told me not to let this one get away."

"I knew she was the right girl for you," she said with a heavy Latin accent. "God has blessed you, Mr. Wetherholt."

Looking directly at Rebecca, his face grew serious. "Si'."

***

Sitting around the formal dining room table, they began deciphering Old Joe's notes using Rebecca's glasses and books.

"Where's Jeremiah?" Sam asked.

"Poor kid's exhausted. I told him to rest for a while," Jack said.

"Shouldn't he be part of the planning? Or at least know what's going on? I mean, he's going with us, right?" Sam asked.

"I don't know about that," said Jack. "It might be too dangerous. He's only thirteen."

"Well, I'm not much older than he is."

"Maybe you're right, but he hasn't had any training, not to mention gifts."

"I think Sam's right. Jeremiah is here for a reason. He should stay with us—even on the mission," Spencer said.

"Why don't you go talk to him, Sam. Maybe he'll listen to another teenager," Jack suggested and then pointed down the hall. "It's the third bedroom on the left."

Sam agreed and walked down the hall, stopping at a door that was opened only a crack while the group waited for him to return. Jeremiah's voice drifted into the hall, and when Sam knocked, he heard a phone returning to its receiver.

"Jeremiah?" Sam inquired, pushing the door open more.

"Come in," he said, shifting position on the bed.

"How are you doing?"

"I'm okay."

"I'm Sam, by the way," he said, turning the desk chair around backwards and straddling it.

"So, you're a 'Knight', too?"

"Yes." He paused. "You should be out there with us."

"No way. I think you guys, including my dad, have totally lost your minds. Or you're mixed up in something evil. Or I don't know... illegal," he said, punching a pillow.

"I know it's hard to believe, but you just need to trust us. Your dad would never get you involved in something bad."

"He doesn't care about me. He works. That's what he cares about."

"Listen to me. You've flown on a supernatural wild spirit horse! Isn't that enough proof for you?"

"I don't know what to believe anymore. Maybe I was drugged and those horses are just hallucinations?"

"If you come out here with us, maybe we can help you see the big picture."

He sat silent for a full minute while Sam waited.

"Alright."

"You won't regret it."

When Sam sat at the dining table, he saw Jeremiah had chosen a seat in the adjoining living room, as far away as possible.

At least it's a start, Sam thought as he shrugged at the rest of the Knights.

They investigated each entry in Old Joe's book, finding only vague ideas as to where to start and no real idea of what the purpose of their mission was.

"It' just a bunch of maps. I mean the notes are great, but where do we start?" Sam asked.

"I know." Tallulah said.

They all looked her direction.

"We need to pray."

"You're right." Sam said.

With their heads bowed, each of them took turns in prayer as Jeremiah watched from the edge of his seat, like he was going to bolt for the door.

Glancing out the window occasionally, as if he was planning his escape, he squirmed in his chair.

As their prayer ended, the lights in the house went out. They gasped from the shock of it.

"This can't be a good sign," Sam said.

"I'll get some candles," Rebecca said.

As she finished her sentence, a brilliant flash of light from outside caused them to shield their faces. Sitting completely still, they waited for what would come next, ready for just about anything.

From the bright light, figures approached: Armada and Ray. They stood in front of Sam.

"The Lord has heard your prayers and has sent direction," Armada spoke calmly. "These will assist you in your missions."

A satchel of scrolls appeared in Sam's hand.

"Good to see you, kid."

"Same here," Sam said to his mentor.

"You'll be needing these." Instantly, a sword and shield appeared in Sam's hands. "Hold onto them this time."

With mixed emotions, Sam stared at his sword and shield. He was glad to have them back, but he knew this meant he was going to need them. "Aren't you coming with us?"

"I've got another assignment now. Just remember what I taught you."

From the next room they heard a voice—a whisper at first, and then they heard it clearly as it grew louder. "I'm sorry. I'm so sorry."

The words came from Jeremiah who was kneeling and holding a scroll as well.

"It is time for you to leave this place," Armada said, disappearing with Ray.

The lights, however, did not disappear. In fact, they were growing brighter and moving around like spotlights.

"Time to go." Jack said, tossing Old Joe's ring to Jeremiah. "Put it on." He said it with forcefulness his son knew not to question.

"Dad, I'm really sorry," he said, placing the ring on his finger.

"Why? What did you do?" Jack asked, putting his own ring on.

Once in the spiritual dimension, Jack grabbed his son's arm and started sprinting down the endless, wooden stairs, as did the rest of the Knights, with their scrolls, books, and spectacles in tow.

***

Running down two steps at a time, Sam set the pace for the Knights as they trekked down the dimly lit, wooden stairs. He could hear nothing but the darkened surf ahead and hurried feet on the creaking wood until everyone stopped at the sound of a board snapping. Turning, he looked up the stairs and saw Rebecca and Spencer trying to free Hayley's foot.

Flashlight beams at the darkened house caught his attention. Police searched from room to room.

Silhouetted against the swirling lights inside, an unusually tall officer stood on the patio, looking out toward the sea. He stood completely still, oblivious that the Knights were just down the steps.

Another officer joined the tall one. "Chief St. James, the initial search tells us they were here less than an hour ago. We've sealed off a mile perimeter. We found a few items you may want to see."

St. James never looked at the reporting officer. His eyes stared straight—as straight as his perfect posture. "Yes. Be there in a moment."

Hayley winced from the pain while balancing on the uneven surfaces. Kneeling beside her, Sam saw that one of the boards had her ankle wedged and was piercing her skin—her uniform now stained with blood. Shifting his position to the opposite side of her, he plunged his hands down between the broken boards. With the jagged wood digging into his skin, and through a muted weightlifter growl, he pried the board back until it broke free of the staircase, allowing Spencer and Rebecca to lift Hayley's leg out from the fragmented wood.

He looked down at his palms smeared with blood and pierced by splinters. His attention was then drawn to the patio above.

St. James now had company but didn't seem aware of their presence. On either side of him were what appeared to be men dressed in the same fashion as the chief, but they had disfigured, sunburned faces that would cause most who saw them to turn away. One had brown, shoulder length dreadlocks shooting out from under his red fedora.

The other wore no hat, but his bald head shone like a chrome helmet— even in the dim light. They both looked directly at Sam.

"*There's the boy,*" one of them thought, causing Sam to draw his sword. Spencer did the same.

Without taking his eyes off the men, Sam, in a surprisingly calm voice, said, "Get to the horses. They're coming."

Jack picked up Hayley, hoisting her over his shoulder like a wounded soldier, and Katie followed behind, holding her now glowing chain and praying aloud. Jeremiah and Rebecca brought up the rear.

As the ghastly-faced demons floated down like skydivers, Tallulah flew up toward them. Sam and Spencer stood their ground, causing the creatures to slow their pace and produce swords of their own.

"Up here!" Tallulah called, drawing their attention briefly.

"I'll take the boy," the bald one said.

With one giant leap, he landed smoothly right in front of Sam, its sword in strike position. Sam merely aimed his shield at its face. Like an explosive charge had been placed inside a large brick of charcoal, the beast exploded into a black cloud of tiny black dust particles that sifted down into a newly formed abyss portal.

Viewing the disintegration of his associate, the dreadlock demon stopped in flight and hovered, astonished.

Tallulah flew down to the Chargers. "Come on!"

One down, Sam thought as he and Spencer mounted their steeds, disappearing with the rest of the Knights.

The demon looked around, frantic and perplexed. Sam and Spencer were just five feet away from it, breathing heavy, watching from atop their Chargers with the group.

The demon's red fedora faded to gray.

"He's in the human dimension now," Sam said.

Chief St. James joined the remaining demon on the sand. "Well?"

"I lost them."

"You lost them. And your counterpart?"

"Banished."

St. James looked out over the dark sea as a wave crashed against a rock formation on the coast. Sam watched as moist breath escaped the man's mouth, traveling like tiny clouds into the December air. It was only then he realized how cold it had become.

"Find them."

The demon lifted its sword and plunged it into the sand. "I will."

St. James turned around like a general and climbed the stairs to the house.

The dreadlock demon stood still for what seemed like minutes. Then its ill-shaped mouth widened, producing a roar that rolled over the waves like a foghorn. Sam could only assume it was upset about losing them or maybe for his demonic partner being sent to the abyss. When the noise diminished, it snorted like a bull, and then retrieved its sword from the sand, replacing it into its sheath. It made its way up the stairs, pausing at the broken step. Stooping down, he examined it more closely, inspecting the trail of Hayley's blood. The next moment it was gone.

"You guys alright?" Jack asked from atop his Charger.

"Yeah. Nasty little thing, wasn't it?" Sam said.

Spencer nodded his head in agreement. "Looks like Chief St. James is tapping into some demonic power."

"Yeah, but what I want to know is how they found us," Jack said.

"I called them."

The group turned toward Jeremiah, waiting for an explanation.

"I'm sorry. I thought you all were possessed or something. Until I heard your prayers... and saw the angels."

Jack exhaled, ran his fingers through his mop top and moved his horse closer to Jeremiah's. "You're an honorary Knight now."

"Okay, but this is really weird. I know I'm dreaming and I'm gonna wake up any minute."

"It's about to get a bit weirder," Spencer said. "Sam, you gonna pass out those scrolls?"

Sam concurred and passed the satchel around and they opened their scrolls.

"They're glowing! And the letters dance over the page!" Rebecca said.

"It says 'Catalina, The Casino'. What does that mean?" Sam asked.

"Mine does, too," Hayley said. "Look how the letters light up—beautiful!"

"Mine says 'Catalina', as well," Tallulah said.

"Isn't that a girl's name?" Katie asked. No one seemed to hear the question as they opened their scrolls.

Rebecca raised her eyebrows as if she approved of her own scroll. "Wow, mine says 'Hollywood, The Knickerbocker'."

"Looks like I'm with you, honey," Spencer said. "Are we actually supposed to go there?"

"Mine says 'San Diego'. What about yours, Jeremiah?" Jack inquired.

"'San Diego, Zoo'."

"That's what mine says," Katie said.

"Catalina *is* a girl's name, but it's also an island off the coast—not too far from here. It's a hot spot for the rich and famous," Spencer reported.

"San Diego has that big zoo, right?" Katie asked. "My family went there when I was little."

With her spectacles on, Rebecca said, "Old Joe's notes confirm there's recent and heavy demonic activity at these three locations and the maps correspond."

"Where should we go first?" Rebecca asked. "And what are we going to do there?"

"Maybe we should divide and conquer," Jack said.

A few moments of silence darkened the room's excitement.

"Yeah, I guess that's the best. Smaller teams," Hayley said.

194

"But what do we do when we get there?" Jeremiah asked.

"I think the way will be made known to us," Tallulah said.

"Just like my favorite verse… Proverbs 3:5-6," Katie said.

"I was never very good at memorizing verses. Which one is that?" asked Jack.

"Trust in the Lord with all your heart…" Hayley began.

"And lean not on your own understanding…" Katie continued.

In unison they finished, "In all your ways acknowledge Him, and He will direct your paths!"

"You two look very proud of yourselves. I wish I had a sticker or something for you," Spencer teased.

"He's just jealous that we knew it and he didn't," Hayley said to Katie.

"Okay, so where should we meet up?" Sam asked.

"How about back at Rebecca's school?" Tallulah suggested.

The Knights agreed with the plan but looked at each other a bit forlornly. The idea of smaller groups seemed more vulnerable, but it made sense.

Spencer led them in prayer before they left the coastal paradise.

Chapter Sixteen
The Casino

Catalina

Zooming along on their Chargers, they could barely see the coast for the fog. Sam prayed silently that the spirit horses would take them where they needed to go.

"I've never seen fog so thick," Hayley said over the rushing wind.

Sam and Tallulah nodded in agreement.

Visibility returned enough and just in time for them to get a view of the approaching harbor.

"Hello, Avalon Harbor!" Sam announced.

Lights dotted the shoreline, and boats, that were anchored for the night, speckled the water.

"What's that down there?" Hayley asked, pointing to a round, 12-story building, guarded by palm trees.

"It's 'The Casino'. Maybe we'll get rich?"

They eased the Chargers down near the building.

Tallulah chuckled. "There's no gambling here. 'Casino' is Italian for 'gathering place'. The top floor is a ballroom and underneath there's a theater."

"How do you know all that?" Hayley asked.

"I was here two years ago. I told you… I've been all over the world, remember?"

The massive building stood before them, illuminated against the dark sky while formally dressed patrons milled around the entrance and balcony, some arriving by limousine.

"Looks like a black-tie event. What'll we wear?"

"We don't have much choice," Sam said, dismounting Lightning and then taking off his ring.

"Wow!" Hayley exclaimed.

Tallulah whistled.

Sam looked down at himself, realizing his uniform had not been replaced by his regular clothes as usual, but rather a tuxedo.

"Gotta try that!" Tallulah jumped off Sunflower, and then removed her ring.

Her dress was taffeta— a deep royal blue, off-the-shoulder, with a large bow at her lower back. She spun around to show-off.

"Do you like it?" she asked them.

"What's not to like?" Sam asked.

"So pretty! My turn!" Hayley exclaimed.

Her dress was sleek and long, snug to her figure. The light blue silky material was accented with rhinestones. Her hair was up in a sophisticated twist, exposing her ivory shoulders. Sam thought she seemed much older than seventeen.

"I could wear this every day!" Tallulah said.

"It might be a little out of place in chemistry class," said Sam.

***

With the girls' high heels clicking behind him, Sam led them up to the ballroom level.

"This place is crawling with celebrities," Hayley observed. "And it appears to be invitation only."

"Not a problem," Sam said with finesse as he pulled out three invitations from the tux coat pocket. "Angels think of everything."

Lined with windows and topped with a cathedral sized dome, the massive room dwarfed them. The modern, geometric lines of the art deco interior reminded Sam of a roaring twenties movie he'd seen. The crystalline wall sconces, framed by mirrors, gave the room a warm glow. Looking like they belonged, they found elbowroom within the crowd, and moved toward the dance floor.

"I'd forgotten it's almost Christmas," Hayley said, admiring the wreaths, tinsel, and giant Christmas tree by the live band.

A jazzy rendition of *The Christmas Song* was crooned by a smooth lead singer, backed-up by a twenty-piece stage band. Sam and Hayley were so mesmerized by the room they didn't move at all, taking it all in.

Tallulah was already dancing in place. "How can you two just stand there? I've gotta go find a dance partner." In a flash she was absorbed by the crowd, only her wavy auburn hair could be seen, bobbing this way and that.

"Is it wise to split up?" Hayley asked. "Wait! Is that Doris Day? Oh, wow. I think it is," she said, answering her own question, scanning the crowd for more celebrities.

It wasn't long until Tallulah scooted by them on the dance floor, giving a little wave.

"Sinatra. She's dancing with Sinatra," Sam said in disbelief.

"No! Really?" Hayley asked, stretching and jumping all around Sam trying to get a better peek at the star.

"Trust me. It was definitely him. I'm not surprised, though. If anyone could get Sinatra to dance with her, it would be Tallulah."

A hand from within the dancing crowd pulled Hayley into the action, leaving Sam standing alone. The hand belonged to Tallulah, and the partner she'd found for Hayley was none other than Gene Kelly.

Great, Sam thought, leaning against the pillar with his arms crossed. Watching the dance floor, he realized this would be the second time he would merely watch Hayley dance.

As he looked down at his shoes, wishing he were in Gene Kelly's shoes, unwanted thoughts invaded his mind like bamboo torture. From all around him, the thoughts oozed of vanity, selfishness, lies and deceit. The enemies were right in front of him… everywhere, masquerading and dancing right before his eyes, thinking evil, but looking picture-perfect.

As if watching Hayley spin around the floor with a dancing legend wasn't enough, the evil thoughts suffocated him. He had to get out of there.

A few strides toward the French doors and he found peace and solitude outside on the balcony. Leaning on the railing, he looked down at the shoreline to the right. He could barely see the waves for the thick covering of fog.

As he turned back to the left, he realized he was no longer alone. Two strong hands on the railing caused Sam to jump back slightly. His eyes followed brawny arms up to a familiar face.

"Hello, Sam," Ray's deep voice chuckled. "You clean up pretty good."

Grinning, Sam looked down at his borrowed, altered tux and nodded. "Yeah. That's why I'm out here—too many girls begging for a dance, ya know."

"You and I both know there's only one girl that you want to dance with, but that's not why I'm here." He said it and moved on quickly so Sam couldn't object. "I'm here to deliver a message. You must delay the mission. Wait for further instructions from me."

"Okay. We'll just keep dancing then." His voice dripped with sarcasm.

"My presence is required elsewhere. You must wait until I return."

Sam glanced out over the misty waters. "Isn't it something that *I* can handle?" He turned to find he was standing alone again.

Stuffing his hands into his pockets he felt the seemingly insignificant ring inside, and then debated whether he should put it on now— just to check things out. But before he could decide, he realized the balcony was completely engulfed by a fast-moving fog. As it accumulated at the French doors, they began to rattle from the force.

Sam felt his body being pulled toward the doors with the fog. He dug his heels in at first, but then decided to go with the flow; to see where it went.

The doors on every side of the round room instantly swung open in unison. The song was cut short as the mood of the room drastically changed. Everyone, including the band, froze from the shock of it, except Sam who was pushed through the crowd and right into Hayley. He grabbed her, nearly knocking her over. Tallulah stabilized them both. The fog now hung in the room like sheer curtains, distorting the view of anything more than three feet away.

They waited. Nothing. Not even a small breeze to explain the phenomenon. A few people started to move about and talk excitedly among themselves. A few people shouted out, trying to locate each other.

"My guess is that it's not usually this foggy in here," Tallulah said.

Sam's mind was crowded by a mudslide of poisonous thoughts from the demons and possessed celebrities that surrounded them:

"They do not belong here."

Although Sam could not see them, he could feel the oppression, the weight of evil pressing on him from all sides. The thoughts turned into a

201

smothering chant with an ominous rhythm. The chant pulled at him, challenging him like a bully in an alley. Waiting for Ray was not an option.

"Let's go," he said, leading the girls through the panicked crowd.

He had that sinking feeling in his gut— like when you know you've chosen the wrong path, but you keep traveling anyway. It gnawed at him, but he pushed it aside as they entered the lobby.

Ray didn't know about the fog, he rationalized. Or was that a voice he'd heard? There were so many voices it was hard to pick out his own thoughts.

Sam directed, "Let's see where the staircase leads. It's mentioned several times in Old Joe's notes."

They put their rings on and made their way slowly down each foggy step. A show had just let out, and a steady stream of theater guests walked past them, unaware of their presence and showing concern about the fog.

Inside the emptying theater, Sam stopped in amazement. "This sure beats the theater back home."

As they walked down the center aisle between fancy red seats and plush red carpet, the domed, glowing ceiling captured their attention. They craned their necks to get a panoramic view.

"Look at the curtains and the murals," Hayley said, impressed.

"Nice," Tallulah said.

Suddenly, two red robed demons holding spears emerged from the colorful murals and stood like statues in front of an odd-looking door.

"Okay, not so nice," Tallulah added.

"We've seen these guys before. They're just guards," Sam said, ignoring the warning in his gut, screaming at him like an air-raid siren. "According to what I remember from Joe's notes, what we want is behind that door."

"And behind those guards," Tallulah warned, her voice dropped in an ominous tone.

He knew he could handle these guys. *Tallulah's just paranoid.* Tightening his grip on his sword, he stared at the beasts' faces shaded by their hoods. Their eyes glowed red and were fixed on him.

Drawing his sword, he rushed the guards, swinging with all his strength. The guards didn't move, and as Sam's sword made contact with the one on the right, they both simply vanished, leaving Sam facing the door.

"That was too easy," Hayley said. "Something's wrong."

Sam reached for the doorknob.

"Are you sure, Sam?" Tallulah asked, her voice drenched in worry.

He didn't respond as his hand tightened around the knob.

Chapter Seventeen
The Knickerbocker

Hollywood

Spencer and Rebecca tied off their Chargers at a car dealership around the corner from The Knickerbocker Hotel.

"What are we doing here?" Rebecca asked her husband.

"Buying a car."

"What?!"

"We have to show up in style."

"I keep forgetting you're rich," Rebecca said, stroking Dream. "Hey, have you decided yet? What are you going to name your Charger?"

"I was thinking… since I like Johnny Cash and since you keep forgetting I'm rich, I'll call him Cash."

"Perfect. But while you're busy buying stuff, we'll have to buy some clothes too, because— " She took off her ring and realized she was already in formal attire. "Nevermind!"

"The Lord always provides, doesn't He?" Spencer took off his ring and admired his tuxedo.

"Amen!" Rebecca said, agreeing with what he said and how he looked.

***

As the valet opened Rebecca's door, a strong, hot wind blew past the hotel's entrance. Spencer came around his newly purchased convertible Roadster and took her arm in his.

"Looks like the Santa Ana winds are kicking up," he said, glancing up eleven stories at the Knickerbocker sign on the roof withstanding each warm gust. "Keep your eyes open."

Walking the red carpet toward the grand entrance, Rebecca felt like a movie star among the spinning spotlights and lush potted plants and trees almost uprooted by the wind. Blending well with the other Hollywood hobnobbers, she wore a white cocktail dress and long white gloves, while a snow-white mink wrap hugged her shoulders. Spencer wore a black suit and fedora. He carried a briefcase.

The stout doorman tipped his hat. "Hello, Mr. Wetherholt."

"Hey, how are you tonight, Buddy."

"Just fine, sir."

Rebecca removed her wrap once inside. "Been here before?"

"I've met business associates in the lounge, shot some pool…"

"Seen any famous people?"

"You'll have to keep your eyes open and find out," he teased, running his fingers through his wind tossed hair.

Rebecca stopped walking and stared at the ceiling. "Now *that's* a chandelier."

205

"Good eye. I've heard it cost $120,000 in the 1920's."

Her mouth fell open.

"Let's get a drink," he said, leading her into a lively lounge with standing room only.

"A table is available, Mr. Wetherholt. Follow me, please." A small-framed man with a heavy Cuban accent turned and walked quickly through the crowd. Arriving at a cozy booth, he removed a sign from the table that read *Reserved*.

"You're a good man, Ricardo." Spencer slipped him a bill.

"Your wife, she is very beautiful. Congratulations, sir."

"Gracias," he said looking at Rebecca.

"Having the usual tonight?"

"Yes. Make it two, please."

"Right away." He hurried towards the bar, tux tails flapping behind him.

Rebecca leaned forward across the small table so Spencer could hear her over the crowd. "This place is amazing."

"I'm glad we got to come here—even under the circumstances."

"Well, we're here. Now what? What are we looking for?"

Ricardo returned and winked at Rebecca as he placed two drinks on the table and then scurried away.

Looking down at the drinks, she asked, "Your usual?"

"A Roy Rogers, of course. Gotta keep our wits about us," he said, taking a sip.

Rebecca's face turned a little pale. "Don't look now, but over there, the booth in the corner...Elvis!"

Spencer casually looked towards the corner and back again. "Yeah, I should have warned you he might be here. One time we shot pool together. He's pretty good, too." He gulped his drink.

She shook her head in disbelief, took a drink, and then spoke like a schoolgirl with a crush. "We'll have to invite him to the house sometime."

He chuckled. "Tell me the day and time, and we'll make it happen."

"Really?"

"Anything for you. But for now, I think we should check-in and find a starting point."

"Sounds good."

Without finishing their drinks, they scooted out of the booth and walked through the lobby, Rebecca hypnotized again by the chandelier.

'We'd like to check-in please," Spencer said to a woman at the front desk.

"Your name please?" She had a pointy nose and dark hair pulled back in a bun.

"Wetherholt."

With an air of snootiness she said, "I'm sorry, Mr. Wetherholt, you don't seem to have a reservation, and I'm afraid we're completely booked."

A white haired, older man rushed up to the counter. "Mr. Wetherholt, I'm sorry. Miss Walters is new. Of course we can accommodate you, although your usual top floor suite is unavailable due to construction. I can offer you suite 1017, one floor down."

"That will be fine, thank you."

Miss Walters frowned and signaled a young bellhop who came to the counter immediately. "Take care of the Wetherholts, please. Show them to 1017."

The bellhop's nametag read Bobby. He was almost as tall as Spencer, but thin enough to blow away in the Santa Ana winds. Looking down at the key he said, "1017! You have the suite next to Elvis. He always gets suite 1016 when he's in town. I've heard if you put your ear to the wall in your bathroom, you can hear him singing in the shower."

"We'll have to remember that," Spencer said, poking Rebecca in her side with his elbow.

Once in the suite, Spencer tipped him generously.

"Thanks, mister," he said, counting the bills as he left.

"What an incredible view!" Rebecca exclaimed, hanging out the window.

Spencer pulled her back inside, wrapping his arms tight around her. "We don't want you falling out like some distraught, out-of-work actress." He kissed her forehead, and then led her to the dining area, placing the briefcase on the table from which he removed the books and spectacles.

With her spectacles, Rebecca studied the hotel's floor plan noted in the map book, and then cross referenced the map with the notes. "According to Joe's notes, the top floor is heavily guarded," she said.

"The man at the front desk said it was under construction," Spencer added.

A knock at the door startled them.

"I'll get it. Maybe it's Elvis," he said, smirking as he jogged to the door around the corner.

Rebecca heard the bellhop's voice at the door.

"Honey, did you drop a glove?" Spencer asked, walking back around the corner with Bobby.

Catching sight of Bobby through her spectacles, she screamed. He was not the boy-next-door bellhop he had pretended to be. A moment later, streams of red light like lasers shot out from the glasses, piercing Bobby in the chest. Within a few seconds, he vanished into a cloud of gray smoke.

Spencer stared at his wife in disbelief. "What—"

"He was a demon. I saw it through the spectacles." She stood frozen.

Staring at the spectacles, he said, "I didn't know they could do that."

"I-I forgot they could do that!"

"Weren't you trained…?"

She nodded, her skin pale from the shock.

"Well, now we know. Good job, sweetie. Let's keep those handy."

Chapter Eighteen
A Walk in the Zoo

San Diego

Jack's Charger landed next to a picnic bench just outside the zoo. Tourists headed toward the ticket booth, but didn't notice him or any of the Knights as they gathered around him. They dismounted.

"It's such a rush to ride them!" Katie said.

"Smooth as a Cadillac," Jack said. "A-ha! I finally found his name. I'll call him Cadillac!"

"I like it," said Katie. "And mine is Ruby. Like the famous ruby slippers. How about yours, Jeremiah?"

"I don't care. This whole thing is nuts!"

"Nuts or no nuts, you're here, so you might as well make the best of it," Jack told his son. "Oh, and I thought of a good name idea for yours... how about Ol' Joe?"

"Yes. That's just right," Katie said.

"Whatever," Jeremiah mumbled.

"You know, Jeremiah, it may not be my place to say, but you've got a lot of growing up to do," Katie chastised. "Joe was an amazing man."

Jeremiah looked at her with his mouth ajar. Coming from her the comment stung a little.

She turned away from him and patted Ruby.

Jeremiah stared at her, realizing she was the amazing one. His teenaged heart had come out of its grouchy hole and fixated on this older woman. Not that much older, he told himself. He put his hand on hers. "Sorry. Ol' Joe it its."

"I knew you'd come around," she said with a friendly smile, unaware of his newly acquired devotion toward her.

"Okay, break up this love-fest and let's get our tickets," Jack said.

Katie rubbed her arms. "Is it me, or is it freezing?"

"Yeah, it's colder than Montana!" Jeremiah said, hiding his hands deep in his uniform tunic for warmth.

Jack blew into his hands and then rubbed them together. "Yeah, it's pretty unusual weather here in 'sunny' Southern California. I guess the weather's telling us we're in the right place."

"Look there's even some frost on that window over there," Katie noticed.

Jack opened his satchel.

"What's in there?" Katie asked.

"An angel gave me these on Archai. He said they would hide us from evil and keep us warm."

Reaching into the satchel, he then pulled out some white cloth that looked like a bridal veil; only this cloth shimmered like glitter and had the consistency of a shadow.

Handing some of it to Katie, she unfurled it. "Oh, it's a cloak."

Taking the garment from his father, Jeremiah asked, "Will these hide us from demons?"

"I believe they will."

"I hope you're right." Jeremiah said.

Slipping it over her head, Katie said, "Feels like a heavy coat."

With doubt in his voice, Jack questioned her. "Really?"

"I'm not cold in the least. Come on, try it."

Jack and Jeremiah slipped their cloaks on. The material draped over them like a whisper.

"Totally warm!" Jeremiah said, relieved.

"Looks like we can still see each other," Jack said.

"That's good, but the real question is if the demons can see us," Jeremiah said.

"Only one way to find out," Jack said. "Let's go."

As they walked through the frosty, darkened front entrance, they noticed light coming from a window of a zookeeper's hut. Peering inside they saw several men in khaki jumpsuits huddled around an electric heater, drinking coffee and discussing the cold.

A man wearing a baseball hat spoke the loudest. "The lions wouldn't even eat. They're just huddled together."

"The chimps have gone berserk. They don't know what to make of it."

"We do," Jack said to Katie and Jeremiah. Let's find those chimps."

212

With the lights off, it was hard to see the signs. And an eerie quiet, absent of any animal sounds, gave them no clues.

"Katie, you've been here. Do you remember where the chimps are?"

"That was years ago. I was only four or so."

"What about this building?" Jeremiah said, walking through the closed gate. Inside, dark windows surrounded them as if in a tunnel.

"Are these offices or a ticket window or something?" Katie asked.

Before either could answer her, a distant sound sifted through the quiet. It grew louder and more numerous as it approached—a sort of crackling.

Jeremiah looked down. "Ice. The floor was wet when we came in, and now it's freezing. Look, it's even climbing up the walls."

"Someone's coming," Jack said.

The first thing they saw in the dim light was its head as it merged through the wall next to Jeremiah. A large, scaled creature with a pit bull sort of face looked around as if on a night watchman's patrol. Jeremiah jumped away from it, not trusting the cloak.

After it made its rounds, it sniffed the ice and left—unaware of the room's occupants.

"It didn't see us. The cloaks worked," Jack said as crackling ice spread across the windows." This can't be good. Let's get out—"

An explosive crashing sound rattled the building, sending broken glass flying in every direction. Instinctively, they dropped, covering their heads as glass shot right through them.

"What was that?" Jeremiah asked.

Jack stood up, crunching glass beneath his work boots. Squinting his eyes, he could see something moving.

"What is that?" Katie asked. "It sounds like a loud teakettle before it whistles."

"That's not a teakettle. That's hissing," Jack said, not moving.

A zookeeper unlocked the door and flicked on the lights. "Whoa!" he yelled, jumping back and slamming the door shut. A sign on the door read 'Reptile House'.

In the now lighted space, they observed snakes— dozens of them, slithering and twining all around and through them.

Katie screamed and then jumped off the floor and into Jeremiah's arms. He stepped back to balance her weight while trying to avoid the snakes as well.

"Wait. Look. They're sliding right through our feet. They can't hurt us," Jack said.

"I don't care. I'm still getting out of this place." Katie said, jumping down and sprinting through the nearest wall.

Running to catch up with her, they made their way down a concrete path lined with rain forest plants and trees.

Jack grabbed her arm. "Hold on. I think I hear chimps in this exhibit."

Walking through the caretaker's door, they entered the open, rocky terrain, well-lit by the moon, making their search a bit easier. They inched along a level slab of rock.

"What's up ahead? In that dark area?" Jeremiah inquired.

"Maybe where they feed them?" Katie replied. "The chimps are going wild, but where are they?"

"I think they may actually be in the next exhibit." Jack said.

Katie stopped walking. "Then what lives in here?"

As the question escaped her mouth, the shaggy resident jumped right in front of her, teeth bared and mane waving around its massive head. Swiping right through her with four-inch claws, it let out two heart-stopping roars.

Screaming from the shock, she froze, forgetting the lion could not touch her.

"Just back away. He can't see you." Jack directed.

Still frozen, she said, "Well, he sure can sense me. Look at him. He's almost staring in my eyes."

Two pit bull-faced demons dropped in from above, landing on either side of the lion, watching it curiously, and looking around. They scanned the horizon, oblivious that Katie was two feet away.

She wanted to run, but her legs wouldn't budge. Out of the corner of her eye, she saw a light. Glancing down, she noticed a chain on her prayer necklace was glowing. It was her own chain.

Upon the demons' arrival, Jack raced toward Katie, but was taken back when the demons pulled their swords and started swinging in the air like blind men.

Just as Katie found the ability to move, one of the swords caught the cloak's fabric, slicing it open. Freezing once again, she looked down at her now exposed, uniform sleeve.

"They can see me!"

The demons looked curiously at her arm for a moment, but then resumed swinging their swords as Katie fled backwards. Tripping over her cloak, she fell straight back into a sitting position on the rocks.

Ripping off the rest of the cloak, the demons stood over her like executioners, swords pointed at her neck and stomach. One moved its sword to poke at her necklace. It rattled something in Latin to its partner. When the sword touched the glowing chain, a hole burned through its metal. The beast jumped back and screeched more Latin.

Jack watched helplessly as he tried to think of a way out.

Jeremiah darted away to the far corner of the lion exhibit. Pulling off his cloak, he began shouting at the demons. Without lowering their swords, the demons looked his direction and spoke again in Latin. One of them charged Jeremiah just as he covered himself again with his cloak, vanishing from sight. The lion sensed his presence as well and trotted toward his last position, but Jeremiah had already found a new spot to hide.

Jack was stunned. *This bravery from the kid who didn't want to come?*

Following his son's lead, he ran to the opposite side, taking off his own cloak, confusing the demons and drawing their attention. When they charged him, he simply covered himself and changed position as Jeremiah had done, like a dark game of Marco Polo.

Jeremiah moved next to Katie and threw his own cloak over both of them, and they rushed to a stealth location near Jack. They clung to each other, trying to keep all extremities covered by the fabric.

Jack searched for an exit strategy for all three of them, but he was then more than surprised when Jeremiah left the security of his cloak, and sprinted up behind a demon, plunging Katie's necklace over its head. Jeremiah ran and dove under the fabric as the creature drained like dirty motor oil into the abyss. The other demon paced, growled, and slashed at the air with its sword.

"It worked," Jeremiah whispered to himself.

Staying undercover this time, he and Katie slunk together to the edge of the now shrinking abyss. Once close enough, Jeremiah grabbed for her necklace, reaching out from the protection of the cloak again.

Ice-cold pain shot through his forearm as he closed his fist around the necklace and withdrew to safety.

The cloaked Knights retreated in the direction of the wild chimps while the demon jumped toward Jeremiah's last known location, fiercely swinging at the air.

The three sprinted together toward an outer wall with the lion right on their heels, compromising their position. Slipping through the wall, they began their hasty search for the chimpanzee cage.

The demon emerged where they had exited and inspected a trail of blood, following each tiny drop.

Chapter Nineteen
Danakrius

Catalina

The sound of clapping on stage grabbed their attention.

"Bravo! You found us," Chief St. James said with a spotlight only on him. "Or should I say, we found you?"

With him, appeared more red-robed demons, encircling the room. From his position on stage, St. James pointed at the Knights—a signal for the creatures to close in. As they glided through the seats, Sam took his hand off the doorknob and drew his sword. He wondered how he'd found them, and how he had access to the spiritual dimension.

"I'm really starting to dislike this guy," Sam muttered to the girls.

From out of nowhere dropped a dozen or so gargoyle-demons that manifested as if they'd been perched on some ancient cathedral for the last century. They formed an even tighter formation around the Knights.

Tallulah attempted to fly up above them, but a gargoyle-demon with three large horns wrapped its, skeleton-like fingers around her right ankle. She stopped abruptly which forced air from her lungs. She tried to free herself, resulting in a muffled laugh from the beast. It suspended her like a lion playing with its lunch. She wasn't used to losing a fight. She tried hurling a large speaker at it, but smirked while it merely bumped it away like a moth. The smirk turned serious as it yanked her down to eye level. It grasped her head in its gnarled hands and spoke only inches from her face.

"You are nothing."

Tallulah stopped fighting, and took a breath, looking the beast in the eye. Her grimace turned to a smirk. She spoke with complete control.

"I may be nothing to you, but one day you'll be banished to Hell."

Fury flashed in its eyes. "Be gone with you," it growled.

It flung her through the ceiling. She traveled at such a high speed that Sam thought he may have only imagined it. His gut churning with rage. He envisioned himself slaughtering every one of the beasts personally.

Rushing at the demons, his voice uttered a sound he didn't recognize— a sound like a war cry the ancient Spartans might have uttered. Just the wild look in his eyes intimidated some of the beasts. He slashed at every creature his sword could reach, until one with red splotches on its leathery, dark skin motioned for the rest to fall back.

A challenge. A one-on-one.

With a deliberately slow motion, it unsheathed its sword, never moving its fixed glare at Sam.

Pacing in circles, they both took a low, guarded stance as the energy compounded. Sam held his shield defensively, his other hand clamped tightly on the handle of his sword. The challenging demon approached Sam first, like he had something to prove. A gleam in its eyes told Sam the first attack was coming.

Raising his sword to block it, the steel sparked, as their swords connected for the first time, the clash echoing through the theater. The remaining demons watched, chanting like savages.

Sam's skills matched those of his opponent. Its approach was flawless, just as Sam had been taught—a calm demeanor, regulated breathing, a good stance for balance. Like Sam, it used no fancy maneuvers, just solid, precise energy for more powerful strikes, grunting with each blow, producing room-jolting clashes of metal. Sam pulled techniques from every training session.

Hayley faced a swarming brood of rodent creatures near the door. Standing on two theater seats, she cracked her whip at everything that moved. She seemed to be doing well until an evil martyr grabbed the end of her whip and wrapped it around his front leg several times. It shook uncontrollably. Two of them leaped onto her arms from behind. They pried the gloves off her hands as they sizzled.

Hayley screamed.

Sam glanced away from his fight toward her.

The red-splotched demon took advantage of the distraction by knocking his sword out of his hand and him to the ground. Sam observed Hayley from there.

Even though the vermin were writhing in pain from the stolen gloves, they found the energy to fling them across the room. The gargoyle-demons sniffed and poked at them with their swords.

The demon still wrapped in her whip, yanked it out of her hand with one final effort before it exploded into a burst of soot, then sucked like a vacuum into the abyss.

Sam saw her whip slide under some seats a few rows down, out of her reach.

She winced and clutched her hands that were streaked with claw marks and blood. With a look of defeat, she faced dozens of demons pressing toward her, encircling her. No whip. No gloves.

Sam knew it was his fault. He was defeated. Tallulah was gone. Hayley needed help. But he couldn't help. And help would not be coming. He had been told to delay.

It was then the familiar voice came again from the stage.

"You are quite the travelers, Sam and Hayley," St. James spoke with a calm, even voice. "Let's find out what you know."

A moment later, Sam sat at a formal table. Hayley sat beside him.

"They are ready for you, Prince Danakrius," St, James said, bowing his head and pulling out an empty chair.

Sam didn't know it, but he was about to meet the mastermind behind the fall of every failed civilization since the beginning of Earth's history, answering only to Satan himself.

From behind the curtain came what appeared to be a distinguished man in a tailored black suit. His slicked back black hair made him look successful and powerful. Its appeal disturbed Sam but intrigued him as well. He moved like royalty, and when he walked, his shoes made no sound.

Its flawless face seemed non-threatening, almost friendly. He joined them at the table. A lovely tea also appeared before them.

"Please, help yourself," Danakrius said, gesturing to the table.

Sam and Hayley grasped hands under the table.

Danakrius leaned back in his seat. "Tell me, what do you seek?"

They said nothing.

Danakrius waited patiently as the silence flowed through the theater.

Then he focused on Hayley. *"She is his weakness."* The demon's thoughts traveled freely in Sam's mind.

"How is it that humans have access to our realm? Danakrius asked calmly.

"We will tell you nothing," Sam finally replied.

"We shall see."

Two red robed demon guards grabbed Hayley's arms and pulled her from her chair.

"This is your chance to save her, Sam. You might not get another."

"She is not my weakness. She is my strength," Sam announced.

Danakrius turned sharply and squinted at Sam, not hiding its shock. "What did you say?"

"You heard me."

"Tell me how you know my thoughts."

Neither Sam nor Hayley replied.

A strange and sickening smile formed across the evil prince's face. Danakrius spoke in Latin and the two red robed demons that were detaining Hayley transformed into giant crow-like demons.

"This is a much better idea," Danakrius declared.

The crow-demons flapped their ebony wings in unison as they carried her to an emergency exit. The doors to the exit burst open as they flew out into the night. The fog had receded enough for Sam to see their landing spot: a bell tower at the top of a hill.

"Now, with your 'strength' gone, you will tell me how you know my thoughts and how you have come to be in my dimension."

A sudden, powerful light blasted through the room. When Sam's eyes adjusted, he could see Ray standing in the middle of the theater. Tallulah was with him. Sam was relieved to see her.

The light that glowed from Ray caused the demons to shrink inward and hiss, covering their faces. Danakrius spoke again in Latin, and then instantly, the demons disappeared.

Without a word, Sam rushed for the emergency exit. The fog was completely gone. He could see the silhouette of one of the crow-demons sitting on top of the bell tower. Having no time to waste, he ran across the parking lot and behind some trees. Staying hidden behind the line of trees, he crept up the hill as silently as he could. Near the bell tower he crouched behind some shrubs and tried to catch his breath without making a sound.

He could see the crow-demon on top of the tower, and the other inside with its talons still grasping Hayley. She sat on the ground, looking down, her mussed hair hiding her face.

Without his sword and shield he was no match for the demons. But he'd hoped to hear their plans. As Sam concentrated on their every thought, he deduced they were waiting for direction from a higher-ranking demon.

A ragged, gray scroll appeared in the talons of the demon perched on the bell tower. With its mangled beak, it opened the scroll and read the instructions:

Bring the girl to Carthage. No mistakes.

The scroll vanished and the demon screeched something at its counterpart. Within seconds they plucked Hayley off the ground and flew up into the dark sky. Sam watched helplessly as they disappeared, Hayley's sobs floating down and cutting his heart into pieces.

Tearing down the hill, he was stopped by Ray and Tallulah.

"They're taking her to Carthage," Sam sputtered the words through heavy breaths as if she

225

was on her way to the gallows. "We've gotta go get her," he shouted as he continued down the hill, heading for their Chargers.

"Sam, stop." Ray spoke in a calm but serious tone. "We *will* find her."

Slamming to a defeated halt, he struck a tree with his fist. "This is all my fault. I should have waited for you. I just thought…" Sam looked at Ray and then down at the ground. "I'm so sorry."

Ray patted Sam on the back. "You'll get it right one of these days," he said with one of his famous chuckles. "But I think you're forgetting there's another matter that needs closure."

Sam looked at Ray blankly. Hayley's disappearance had completely derailed his thinking.

"The mission," Tallulah said.

"We can't continue the mission now. We've gotta find Hayley," Sam said.

"She would want you to keep going. They won't harm her. She's a bargaining chip." Ray said. "We'll find her."

Sam nodded slowly and, with his head lowered, trudged toward the theater. He walked numbly inside until a spark in his memory quickened his step.

"Wait!" he exclaimed.

Running to the seats near the door, he then fell to his hands and knees, scrambling about like a three-year-old hyped up on sugar.

"Sam?" Tallulah asked upon seeing his irrational behavior.

Ignoring her and the others, he frantically searched under and around a few rows of seats until

226

he produced Hayley's whip and gloves. Without explanation or fanfare, he quickly tied the whip to his belt and shoved the gloves into his pocket.

Sam then joined Ray and Tallulah who waited patiently near the once-guarded door.

"Complete your mission," Ray said.

Chapter Twenty
Demons at Work

Hollywood

Stunned but not shaken, Rebecca took her spectacles off and placed them in her pocket.

"The bellhop? You know, you just don't know whom to trust anymore," she said shaking her head. "I bet that snippy lady at the front desk is one, too."

"Could be," Spencer said, replacing the notes and book into the briefcase. He stood and took her hand. "You ready?"

"As much as I can be."

They left the room like spies, finding temporary cover in the elevator. The wrought iron bars on the elaborate door rattled as they rose without talking. They put their rings on, entering the other dimension. Stopping short at only the fourteenth floor, Spencer hit the fifteenth button, but it would not light up.

"I guess they've closed it because of the construction. It's probably better if we take the stairs anyway," he said as the door opened. They stepped out.

The hallway was empty and deadly quiet as they found the door to the stairwell. Turning the knob, Rebecca stopped. "If Bobby knew who we were, then do they all know we're coming?"

"Could be. But we're ready for them, right?"

"Ri-i-ight," she said, unconvincingly.

Creeping up the concrete stairwell, they saw the door to the fifteenth floor was off its hinges. A plastic sheet hung in its place. As they got closer, it fluttered, making Rebecca gasp and Spencer's stomach tighten a little.

"It's just the wind," he said.

Rebecca nodded.

Easing past the plastic, they found the top floor dark and littered with tools, and scraps of wood and metal. The smell of sawdust overpowered all other scents. Inching along, they navigated through broken glass, nails and cords from the heavy equipment. Several other doorways had plastic sheets instead of their doors. The only lighting came from moonlight through the window, a glowing neon sign outside and a flickering bulb next to the stairwell entrance.

They searched everywhere on floor fifteen, finding only more of the same.

"Looks like the coast is clear," she said.

Spencer merely raised his eyebrows as if to say, 'We'll see.'

Walking toward the south side of the top floor, Rebecca suddenly stopped, standing still on a busted piece of plaster. "Why isn't that door removed, too?" she asked, pointing at an ordinary door in the corner.

Spencer came right to her side and they approached the door together.

"Joe's notes didn't mention a door, but we should probably check it out," he said, reaching out and turning the knob a quarter turn.

A warm gust of moist air filled the room. It was accompanied by the sound of an enormous exhale. Spencer released the doorknob, and both he and Rebecca seemed to be frozen for a moment. Turning in unison, they found that peering in at them through an unfinished window opening was only the massive nose and one eye of what looked like a giant gorilla—a live rendition of the classic beast named Kong.

"You've *got* to be kidding me," Spencer said as he drew his sword.

Rebecca fumbled in her pocket for the spectacles.

"Whoa!" Spencer exclaimed, amazed at the size of the beast.

Before either could use their gifts, three siren demons in shredded, black dresses, pointed hats, and ratted hair, attacked from behind, knocking them to the ground. They resembled super-models in scant Halloween costumes.

Two of them held Spencer flat on the floor, reciting a spell in unison, their crooked wands shooting gold sparks that filtered to the floor. As he struggled to free himself, he found he was drawn to their beauty, unable to look away.

One jumped on Rebecca and ripped the cape from around her shoulders. Rebecca looked for the spectacles, but she found they had been knocked from her pocket and had slid a few yards away. Eying them, she attempted to reach for them, but the witch-demon slashed her arm with jagged claws. Rebecca cried out and automatically grabbed her injured arm with her other hand.

Curiously, the witch-demon took notice of something, postponing a further attack. It grabbed Rebecca's left hand, bringing it up close to its face.

As it examined her wedding ring, it whispered in a smooth voice, "Pretty."

Outside, the alpha-male bellows of a giant gorilla-demon and the pounding of its chest rattled the entire floor.

The next moment, Rebecca's wedding ring was no longer on her own finger, but on the finger of the witch-demon instead.

Mortified, she instinctively grabbed the witch-demon's hair with one hand and grasped for the ring with the other.

With one fluid motion, the witch-demon flew backwards, landing next to the other two, showing-off its new, shiny treasure with a little celebratory dance. Spencer was still immobile due to the spell they were casting.

Rebecca sat up, nursing her injured arm, glaring at the thief. She stood up. It was personal now. "Give me my ring," she said through her clenched teeth.

The witch-demons all laughed as Rebecca held her ground.

"Give. Me. My. Ring!"

"I'll get you a new one," Spencer shouted as he thrashed left and right, trying to free himself from the spell.

"That's not the point. Give me my ring."

"Come and get it," it taunted, coyly.

"Fine."

With unexpected determination, in one swift, diving roll, Rebecca retrieved and replaced the spectacles, planted herself for stable aim, and took great pleasure piercing the thief with the laser beams. Before it vanished, it watched as the ring dropped off its finger and rolled over to Rebecca's feet.

Rebecca smiled.

With an astonished look, it vanished into a small, smoky cloud.

"Next?" she said with attitude, looking at the second witch-demon who looked surprised and then vanished into a gray puff of smoke.

The last witch-demon released Spencer from the spell and attempted to aim its wand at her. The red laser from the spectacles entwined with the golden sparks of the wand, and they seemed to be equal forces—at an impasse.

What the witch-demon didn't see coming soon enough was Spencer's sword. When it pierced its side, it dropped the wand, allowing the laser to pierce its chest. It shook in convulsions, and before it vanished into a smoky cloud, a glimpse of an old hag proved to Spencer and Rebecca that beauty is sometimes only skin deep.

With no time to breathe from that encounter, Rebecca found herself being hoisted up and out the window by an enormous, hairy black hand. The force of it sent the spectacles flying and caused Rebecca to kick and scream, unable to free herself. Before she knew it, she was dangling outside the window, right in front of the gorilla-demon's face. It looked at her much like a child would examine a hamster. It opened its hand, exposing Rebecca on its leathery palm. Trying to find her footing, she teetered as if on a high wire, the Hollywood night-scene exposed below.

From out of the darkened window, Spencer, in desperation, leaped onto the beast's shoulder, thrusting his sword into its throat, causing it to vanish.

Spencer and Rebecca plummeted together. Her shrill scream echoed against the face of the hotel. They kicked their legs and flailed their arms as they fell at least ten stories. Rebecca was close to passing out when they felt themselves being lifted. They turned to find Armada and Ray at their rescue. Their moods improved dramatically.

Back on the unfinished fifteenth floor, they landed as gently as feathers falling from a bird.

"Thank you," Spencer said humbly.

"Yes," Rebecca said, still shaking. She reached up and kissed Armada on the cheek. "Thanks."

Armada touched his cheek with an amazed expression. It was the first kiss he'd ever received.

Rebecca then jumped into her husband's arms, grateful to have survived.

After a few moments, he broke their hug and said, "Hold on." He bent down and picked up her ring. Placing it on her finger he asked, "Marry me again?"

"Name the date," she said, hugging him tighter this time.

Ray leaned over to Armada and said quietly, "Humans can get so sidetracked. Have they forgotten the mission completely?"

"The mission. Right," Spencer said, releasing his wife. "We were about to open this door over here. That's as far as we got when they attacked."

The angels gave each other a knowing look.

"Sounds like a good place to begin," Armada said.

Their feet crunched through piles of debris as they made their way back to the door. Spencer reached out for the knob and began to turn it.

Chapter Twenty-One
The Rusty Door

San Diego

Jeremiah's pounding heart sounded louder to him than his own rapid footsteps as he pushed toward the sound of the chimpanzees. With one arm wrapped tightly around Katie's shoulder as they shared a cloak, he clutched the other arm to his chest, keeping the wound stable. The pain in his hand burned like it'd been hit by lightning. The flow of blood felt warm as it trickled off the back of his cold hand.

Jack was not far ahead of them when he turned back and breathlessly said, "This way."

As they slowed to a walking pace on the path of the chimpanzee exhibit, they found the chimps gathered at the west sides of all their cages, heads turned—straining to view something in that direction. Katie covered her ears to block the screeching calls and hoots they bellowed as they jumped and moved erratically.

The Knights eased past each cage. A few chimps appeared to sense their presence, breaking away from the others to look in their direction, while most of them remained focused on whatever was west of them.

Jack ducked to avoid being struck by an object hurled from the cage. On closer inspection he was glad it missed as it turned out to be feces. Katie and Jeremiah were unaware of more dung heading their way. They had no time to dodge. It traveled straight through them, hitting the cages on the other side of the path.

"That's disgusting," Katie shuddered, trying to put it out of her mind.

Despite his throbbing hand, Jeremiah laughed like any 13-year-old boy would at feces-flinging chimps. Katie rolled her eyes in response.

They inched to the end of the exhibit. Rounding the corner of the last row, they encountered what the chimps couldn't see, but could sense.

A neighboring tropical exhibit, home to an unknown animal, proudly displayed a waterfall so large they could feel the mist from where they'd stopped. In fact, the waterfall ran the entire length of the exhibit, forming a fluid wall.

In front of the display's fence was a row of red-robed demons, holding staves and staring straight ahead.

Jack was the first to step out from the protection of the chimp exhibit, into the demon's line of sight. Feeling like he was in front of a firing squad each step of the way, he led the group to the opposite edge of the exhibit. The demons didn't move at all.

They entered the exhibit by passing through a sturdy, wooden fence next to eucalyptus trees on the far side of the gushing water. Once inside, they found themselves edging past the backside of the waterfall on a six-foot ledge next to a concrete wall. Jeremiah felt as if he'd stepped into a shower from the light mist spraying off the waterfall. When he looked down at his boots, he noticed the concrete path had deep grooves in it to prevent slipping. The way the water poured out and over to the left side of them reminded Jeremiah of the gigantic waves that surfers ride. The sound of the rushing water overpowered every other sound and was only magnified by the echo factor off the concrete wall to their right. The potent aroma of chlorine in the water masked all other smells—even the naturally pungent odors of the wildlife.

As they made their way deeper into the misty tunnel, they felt a sense of protection under the canopy of water, but they hadn't seen the pit bull-faced demon hiding in a nearby eucalyptus tree. It had followed the trail of Jeremiah's blood and anticipated their next move to be in this direction. Without detection, it jumped from the tree and into the waterfall, being completely absorbed by the whitewater.

Katie grabbed Jeremiah's arm. "You're bleeding!"

"Whoa. We'd better stop the bleeding," his dad said, reaching into his satchel.

"What? That's just a scra—"

As soon as Jeremiah looked at the wound, his face turned pale. Every memory of scrapes and gashes from his childhood flooded his mind. The smell and the sticky feeling of his blood on his skin set the world spinning in a wave of nausea. His eyelids fluttered, his eyes rolled back, and he went limp.

Jack grabbed him before he hit the concrete "I knew this was coming," he chuckled. "He never could take the sight of blood. Especially his own." He eased him down to the path.

"Will he be all right?"

"Yeah. Look. He's already coming around."

Jack took off his cloak and began to fan his son with it. Katie slid hers off as well, setting it on the path. With every breeze, Jeremiah seemed to stir more.

Katie held his undamaged hand, patting it firmly. "Jeremiah, open your eyes. Jeremiah?"

With the freezing cold to wake him, he shivered as he regained consciousness. He opened his eyes and sat up, looking more embarrassed than hurt.

Jack put the cloak around his son's shoulders.

"I fainted? Great."

Katie looked away toward the concrete wall to hide her grin.

"Well, you did lose a lot of blood." Jack muffled a laugh as he secured a bandage on the wound.

Katie stood frozen, staring at the wall.

"What?" Jeremiah asked.

The rushing water was the only sound as they waited.

"That door."

She pointed at a metal door next to them. Gawking at the pattern of the faded blue paint mixing with splotches of rust, she knew it was the same door. It was distinct, unmistakable. The blues, browns, and reds that swirled into a distorted web-like design had haunted her mind for months.

They waited for an explanation.

"I've seen it before."

"When you were here as a child?"

"No. In a dream."

The worn appearance of the door was not what bothered her, but the sounds that had come from behind it in the reoccurring dream. Her shoulders tensed and she squinted her eyes as if she expected to hear the sounds at any moment.

"A *bad* dream," she added.

Jack and Jeremiah shot each other a sideways glance, but before either could comment on the door, Jeremiah caught site of an enormous bulge of water protruding from the waterfall. He pointed and they all backed-up slowly against the concrete wall.

It reminded Jeremiah of the odd-shaped bubbles he would make with a large circular wand as a child, only this bubble seemed to have more substance—although plainly devoid of any other substance but water—and appeared to be completely autonomous and mobile. For a moment, Jeremiah stared as if still a young child as it contorted and swirled its shape into various forms before settling on a large face—larger than the three of them put together. He had seen that watery face before; the one who had given him the wound on his hand.

Katie— although her eyes were still trained on the water-creature—had the presence of mind to drop to her knees and reach for the cloak she had left on the path. Before she could pick it up, a wave of water, sprayed directly from the demon's mouth, knocked her back against the wall. It hit her with such a large amount of water that she struggled to find air for a moment longer than she'd been comfortable with. It was like being hit with a fire hose and having no escape from its path. The water gradually lessened, as she tried to catch her breath. She sat by the wall, soaked, trembling, and coughing.

She looked down at her necklace, and then she gasped. Every link—representing all the Knights on the team—was glowing. "I need to pray. For *everyone*."

Without warning, a familiar fabric sailed above her, landing over her head. Jeremiah had claimed the cloak without her noticing. He whisked her from the ground to her feet and pulled her thirty yards deeper into the tunnel of water and concrete. She felt like *he* was the Knight, and *she* was the teenager needing help.

Jack followed, under his own cloak now, too.

The expression of the water/pit bull-demon was one of question and fury as it lashed out with watery teeth at their last known location. With no blood trail to follow, it knew it was just shooting in the dark, but still it made its disapproval of the situation known by randomly spraying water up and down the path, growling.

240

Jack, realizing that the path ended twenty yards from their current position, considered their options: jump into the waterfall, rush past the demon undetected, or wait for a miracle. He decided not to decide.

The demon appeared frustrated as it jerked its head around looking for them up and down the path until it caught sight of Jeremiah's boot, exposed from under the shared cloak. The growling ceased and instead it formed a knowing grin, focusing on the boot.

"I think we've been made," Jack said.

As Jack's words ended, the creature inhaled to the point of almost bursting. It then projected the water like a tidal wave directly at them with such severity that it knocked them five feet back and to the ground.

Jack struggled to hang onto to his cloak, but the force of the water made it a hopeless endeavor. He grabbed for Jeremiah's cloak as it slipped out of sight, and then had no other option but to merely sit in a six-inch deep puddle, trapped by the water demon.

Katie huddled next to Jeremiah, shaking from the cold and the fear, waiting for and fearing the worst. With the tidal wave past them now, the only sounds she could hear besides the flowing waterfall were the droplets plopping into the receding puddle. Softer than the drips was a prayer that she uttered. Katie kept reminding herself the demon could only have power over them if God allowed it. She hoped this time He wouldn't.

What is it waiting for? she wondered.

With its eyes still locked with Jack's, it neither blinked nor breathed. It stared rapaciously at him like he was lunch until it turned its head slowly toward the other end of the tunnel, its eyes squinting slightly.

Still sitting in the puddle, Jack scanned the far end of the tunnel as well, but he could see no change. It reminded him of how animals could hear things humans couldn't. Jack wondered if he'd brought more friends.

More drips echoed through the mist as they waited what seemed to be minutes until an odd greenish glow illuminated the waterfall. The green faded exposing a brilliant aqua-blue of the water, while soft white light appeared at the end of the tunnel, getting closer and brighter.

"Well, it's either the cavalry or we've died," Jack joked.

The water-demon turned to fully face the slowly approaching light with a bold stance of rebellion. The light glided closer, traveling through the tunnel. Midway down the concrete wall, the colors of the rusty door appeared to move and swell as the angle of the light changed.

Katie glanced at Jack and Jeremiah and found the light on their faces danced from the reflective glimmer of the illuminated water. Their faces were hopeful, but still guarded.

The light advanced no further, retracting now and intensifying into the familiar shape of an angel in spirit form that then changed into the more human-like image of Armada.

With one sharp inhale, Armada produced a gust of breath like a sandblaster, erasing the existence of the water–demon, molecule-by-molecule. Tiny droplets fiercely sprayed off its edges and evaporated into nothing by the time it reached the Knights.

In a few moments, the path was dry, the demon gone. Armada stood calmly before them as they rose to their feet. Through the mist his appearance seemed almost projected.

Armada spoke in an unusually quiet voice. They strained to hear him. "Abort the mission. Return to your team."

In a flash, he was gone. The tunnel was dark.

Left alone in the dimmer light, the Knights were processing the news.

"Abort the mission?" Jeremiah asked.

"That's what he said," Jack replied.

"But we didn't find anything. Have we failed?" Katie asked.

"Let's get to the rendezvous location and we'll find out," Jack said.

They found and replaced their cloaks, and then headed toward the end of the tunnel.

Although she felt slightly relieved, Katie was also a little disappointed as if all their efforts were in vain. She continued walking, sharing a cloak with Jeremiah, reminding herself she was not the one in charge. When they passed the rusty door, she looked at it intently, comparing it to the one in her memory. Not a speck was out of place.

Why would I dream of it if it weren't important? She took two more steps and then stopped dead in her tracks. "Do you hear that?" she asked Jeremiah, who was having a hard time walking next to her for all the stopping and starting.

"Uh, I don't hear anything, except the water and you."

"You don't hear those voices?"

"You're hearing voices? Have you gone schizophrenic on us now?" asked Jack

"Wait. Something is definitely not right here," Jeremiah spoke.

"Actually. I'm feeling it, too," Jack said, now serious.

Katie looked at the door again, the voices faint but still there.

The next instant, she was staring at Armada, suddenly blocking her view of the door.

The Knights gave each other confused looks.

Armada addressed Katie. "I was sent when you prayed, but I was delayed by Prince Danakrius in the second heaven."

"Delayed?" Jeremiah asked. "Then who..."

"It appeared as an angel of light," Jack said, nodding his head as if bamboozled out of his life savings by a con artist.

The Knights looked at the ground, contemplating what they'd observed.

Looking annoyed, Jeremiah asked, "How do we tell the difference?"

Armada looked specifically at him with kind eyes. "You did. You knew."

Jeremiah squinted his eyes and nodded.

"Is this door from my dream what we seek?" Katie asked Armada.

"Yes."

Chapter Twenty-Two
Them

Catalina

Ray put his hand on Sam's shoulder. "Let me know what you find in there."

Sam's hand retracted like the knob was on fire. "You're not coming?"

"You and Tallulah must enter on your own."

"Is this place off-limits to angels or something?"

"No," Ray said with a grin. "It's just the way it has to be."

"What if we need your help?"

"You have everything you need."

Sam took a deep breath and then turned toward the door. His hand felt numb, like it wore a welding glove— bulky, lacking coordination as he turned and pushed.

For being an ordinary door, it was unusually heavy. Sam had to dig his heels in more than he'd expected. *Probably hasn't been opened in a while,* he thought as it scraped against what sounded like overgrown earth and not a floor as he'd imagined. The hinges groaned open.

*Didn't expect **this**,* he thought.

He had expected a room. Maybe a room with secret files or weapons? Or maybe hidden treasure? He'd even entertained the idea of finding Satan himself—not that he *wanted* to, but the thought *had* occurred to him.

But it wasn't even a room at all. It was an entrance to another world, like a portal in a fantasy book. They were clearly leaving Earth as he knew it. The terrain filled his eyes with remnants of a bad fairy tale set in a swamp.

Spilling out of the unknown, an abundant fog lingered in the doorway, taunting Sam. With Tallulah close behind, he stepped through, his feet partially submerged into soft ground.

The fog consumed a sparse grove of ancient cypress trees protruding like abandoned Greek columns out of the shallow, murky water. Although it was daytime in this place, the canopy cover of the trees blocked the light almost completely. Vines hung like last year's decorations. The air was earthy and stale. Sam detected a slight hint of sulfur.

There was no doubt in his mind. They were not alone. Thousands of living creatures, hidden among the shrubs, trees, and fog, trumpeted their songs: a full chorus of frogs, birds, reptiles and insects—more insects than Sam wanted to think about.

"So much for these boots," Tallulah griped, looking down at her formerly white uniform boots, now five inches deep in mud.

They trudged across the pasty ground while it smacked back at their feet.

Sam, being first to reach a black willow tree, grabbed its trunk for stability. He turned to watch Tallulah, several yards behind him, struggle with each step, her arms flailing in large circles as she attempted to stay upright in the mud.

Less than a whisper brushed against Sam's ear. It was a thought so faint he wasn't sure if he'd heard it audibly, or if he'd thought it himself. "*She's beautiful.*"

The sound lingered as Sam stood frozen, considering what it meant. It wasn't a lie. She *was* beautiful. Her smile and flowing hair were like a poem that you'd read again and again or a song you'd play endlessly. He *could* have thought it. He tried to convince himself that thinking it, if he actually did, didn't mean he loved Hayley less. But if his mind hadn't been the origin of the thought, they must have company.

A sudden, loud popping sound drew his attention toward Tallulah. The mud had opened and devoured her legs. She was now up to her waist in the mud and sinking fast.

She screamed and dug her hands into the surrounding area, grabbing nothing but handfuls of soggy earth. She extended her arm to recruit a greenbrier vine from a tangled collection. The mossy ropes responded to her telekinesis gift immediately by moving toward her outreached hand, but they remained in a tangled mess. As they pulled toward her, they only created more of a rat's nest.

Sam fought the urge to jump in to free her. He knew if he did, they'd *both* need rescuing. He could help her better from more stable ground.

Painfully close, the tangled vine mocked her outreached hand still yards away. The attempt seemed futile until Sam drew his sword and sliced a strategic vine allowing the gnarled mess to unravel and stretch far enough for Tallulah to grab.

Pulling with all her strength, her hands only slid down the vine, stripping it of piggyback moss and soupy earth, exposing the rubbery plant beneath, her precarious position unchanged. A hand-over-hand approach produced the same slippery results as she sunk deeper into the sludge until she wrapped the vine around her hand several times finally stopping the downward momentum.

The mud seemed to be more than a natural element, but rather a living entity. It wanted Tallulah and it was fighting hard against their efforts to free her. Either it was alive or something living controlled it.

Sam grabbed the end closer to the tree and helped pull her out, staying clear of the muddy vacuum.

Once her feet were free, she flew up to the nearest branch and sat straddling it. Still holding the vine, she pulled it tight again helping Sam scale up the side of the tree trunk, until he could reach the branch himself. Swinging his foot over the limb, he sat next to Tallulah, facing her.

"Wow. You're a mess," he said, catching his breath.

She looked down and sighed—a sigh of relief and frustration.

Below them the mud hole gurgled as it filled itself in, returning to its original state as if nothing had happened, waiting for its next victim.

Sam began to assess their situation on their gloomy perch. Through a musical medley of swamp creatures, one particular voice grew louder than the rest. As the sound came closer it reminded Sam of a jackhammer. An insect the size of a Doberman with wings, zoomed right up between them; however, this creature had no other dog-like characteristics. The shining, metallic, multi-colors of its armored exoskeleton made their eyes squint.

"It's huge," Tallulah whispered, frozen by the appearance of the three-foot wasp.

It dared Sam to move, staring with cold, seemingly vacant insect eyes while hovering just inches from his face. The oscillation of its wings, with a ten-foot wingspan, caused a strong enough wind to knock him off the branch. Sam wondered if wasps were carnivorous, because he felt like he was on the lunch menu.

Reaching for his sword, he pulled it halfway out, trying only to move his arm, but the wasp was not fooled. Darting sharply toward Sam's face and then toward the sword, it slammed a warning against the sword twice, a grating exoskeleton against metal.

And then it flew up into the tree, out of sight.

"Is it gone?" Tallulah asked.

"Can't see it."

Searching in silence, they scanned the looming branches. Through the draped willow leaves, shadows lurked, but none seemed to belong to the wasp.

"Don't hear it eith—" He stopped short due to her expression.

Tallulah's eyes grew big, looking just to the right of Sam's head.

He didn't have to ask. He knew. He could feel the wind on his neck. Its spiny feet had landed on his back. Sam slowly craned his neck until he was eye-to-eye with its shiny, alien face. The position of the creature made his defense difficult; pretty much non-existent.

Its wings stopped. It didn't move. Neither did Sam.

The wasp's lack of activity reminded Sam of those macabre collections that display insects stuck to cardboard with straight pins and labeled with hard-to-pronounce Latin words. But this bug was twenty times the size of the collected ones, making him wonder if this bug had a *people* collection.

Tallulah raised her hands and from where she sat on the branch, attempted to push the wasp off his back. There was no evidence it moved at all.

Sam detected the smallest shadow of a grin form on the insect's hard face. Its mouth parted slightly exposing thorny fangs. He didn't even have time to breathe before the pain struck his right shoulder. Feeling like two four-inch screws had just been drilled into him, he belted out a peculiar, muffled groan. The sound seemed so unnatural— like it wasn't even his voice.

251

It was impossible to unsheathe his sword. The pain in his shoulder pulsated from the wound, down his arm, and out his fingertips. Reality slowed as if he'd just been in a car accident. Every moment felt like minutes as his heartbeat echoed in his head. Symptoms of shock crept through his body, but he fought them off, determined to defeat this bug.

The wasp launched off Sam's back. He watched it dart from limb to limb until it disappeared into the highest reaches of the tree.

He found the strength to stand on the limb and pull his sword, keeping his eyes trained on the foggy branches.

Tallulah stood as well.

They waited and watched.

Instead of finding the wasp, they found the branch on which they stood began to crack. They locked eyes and held still, but nothing could save them from the limb's surrender to gravity.

Fortunately, Tallulah was able to fly away during the drop, but Sam had not been so gifted.

His eyes automatically shut for impact as the sludgy water rushed around him. He quickly sank to the bottom, finding himself sitting in a substance that reminded him of wet peanut butter. Scrambling to his feet, he pushed off.

When he surfaced, he surveyed the scummy swamp. Through the ghostly haze of the fog, he found it littered with floating duckweed, driftwood, and objects he would rather not identify.

The splash caused quite a stir with the wildlife. At first, they went dead quiet. A few seconds later, their noises were at full roar as if they were revving up the gossip chain, laughing at the human.

The water was just deep enough that he couldn't touch the bottom without putting his head under. Dog paddling it would be.

From opposite directions he felt two unidentified things brush forcefully past his leg. He looked but couldn't see anything but murk.

Grabbing onto a large piece of driftwood, he kept his sword unsheathed as they scanned for enemies above, below and on the horizon.

Tallulah looked down the swamp's path, back in the direction of The Casino door and squinted.

The faint sound of whistling cut through the fog and grew louder, accompanied by a rhythmic swishing of water. They stared in the direction of these sounds, waiting.

He was not attractive. The more he came into focus the more unattractive he became. But the only concern for Sam was to know if he was friend or foe. The 'whistling while rowing a rowboat thing' made him seem trustworthy, but Sam knew better than to trust so blindly, especially in a place like this.

The overall physique and facial features of the small-framed man spelled out 'troll'. *The Three Billy Goats Gruff* kind of troll. In the boat he sat hunched forward and twisted slightly to the left. His straggly, thinning hair was jet black which did not compliment his pale complexion. His sizable nose overwhelmed his face, but apparently was not functioning properly or it had become immune to

253

the stench of his body. But the thing that made him uglier than sin, was his sour expression.

"You expect me to give you a ride, don't you?" The question dripped with sarcasm as the troll rowed up to Sam.

"We don't expect anything."

"It's always the same… 'Nehcterg, save us. Give us a ride in your boat. Please help us…'"

As the troll jabbered on about people's expectations, something caught Sam's eye. On the side of the boat was the word *Nehcterg.*

It sounded sort of German. *A German troll in the middle of a supernatural swamp. Anything is possible.* But then it dawned on Sam that Rebecca had mentioned the word Nehcterg before from Old Joe's notes. Although he had not imagined it referred to a troll-like, unattractive owner of a boat with the same name, he was fairly certain this was who they needed to guide them.

Sam interrupted the troll's ramblings. "Sir, could we please have a ride in your boat?"

"Here we go. They always ask for a ride," he mumbled. "For you and the flying girl?" Apparently, the fact that Tallulah could fly didn't bother him. He'd probably 'seen it all' in this swamp. "Fine. Get in."

With a little pulling by Tallulah, Sam sloshed over the side and into the boat. She sat next to him, the mud now drying and cracking on her uniform.

"Look at the two of you. You look like something the cat dragged in," the troll said under his breath.

Talk about the 'pot' and the 'kettle', Sam thought.

Being glad to be out of the water, Sam relaxed—as much as he could relax in a boat piloted by a troll in a swamp crawling with ravenous beasts.

A burning sensation on the back of his wrist suddenly grabbed his full attention. He looked to find a black, slimy, wormy-type creature attached to his skin.

"What is…?" He tried to brush it off, but it wouldn't budge.

"Oh. Word worms. They're like leeches, but they only suck blood to leave a message." He laughed a low, throaty laugh. "It's like a fortune cookie gone horribly wrong."

If Sam hadn't been so preoccupied with getting the word worm off, he would've contemplated how, when, and where exactly this troll named Nehcterg would have ever visited a Chinese restaurant. But more pressing was the removal of this leech.

The troll stopped rowing, gave a little huff, and grabbed Sam's arm. Pinching the word worm on one end, he yanked it back like an old band-aid, removing it completely.

Sam winced as the pain traveled his entire body.

Dangling the word worm in front of his face, Nehcterg grinned. "Ah, that's a pretty good-sized one." He popped it into his mouth and ate it.

Sam closed his eyes and remained still, trying not to be ill.

The injury on his wrist measured three inches long and a quarter of an inch wide. Inside the puffy redness were letters embedded in his skin, but Sam could not read the message. "Is this Latin?"

"I suppose you want me to read it for you, too." More grumbling.

Sam glanced at Tallulah with his eyes raised. *A Chinese food-eating, Latin-reading troll with attitude. Great.*

"Says here 'YOU WILL FAIL'."

"Fail?" Sam thought about it for a moment. *"It's not prophetic…probably demonic."* He leaned over toward the dark water and yelled, "It won't work, leech demons." Sitting back up he realized the troll and Tallulah were both staring at him. He cleared his throat.

They sailed in peace—except for the bug-orchestra serenade—through the grove of ancient cypress trees, dodging each trunk and low hanging group of moss-covered vines.

Trying to make small talk, Tallulah asked about the name on the boat.

"Nehcterg. Yes, I named it after myself." He said it proudly, not caring who might rebuke his vanity.

"Your name's Nehcterg?"

He nodded.

"I'm S—"

"Yeah, I know. Sam and Tallulah. Been watchin' you. Couldn't take it anymore. Figured I better come and get you before you really got yourselves hurt."

"Thanks." Sam sat humbled by a troll.

"I know what you're looking for. I'll take you to them."

" 'Them'?"

"Yes 'Them'," Nehcterg said with an attitude bigger than the swamp. "Always the questions. Everyone always wants to know…" His complaints and ramblings continued for the remainder of the ride.

Sam tuned him out. Finally, a clue to what this whole mission was about.

Them.

Chapter Twenty-Three
White Diamond Heat

Hollywood

With the demonic Kong and the siren-witches defeated, the only thing left to conquer on the top floor of the Knickerbocker Hotel was the door in front of them.

Rebecca held her breath; Spencer turned the knob, while Ray and Armada observed from a few yards behind them.

Spencer had never opened a door so slowly in all his life. On one hand, he craved to know what was on the other side, but after all they'd gone through thus far, he wasn't sure he was up for it.

He continued turning until the door burst open, ripping the knob from his hand. A tempestuous gale sucked him and Rebecca over the threshold, knocking them to their knees.

Slammed by a raging windstorm, they found it difficult to even move. With eyes squeezed shut, Spencer slowly raised his shield at an angle against its raw force, and then he found the strength to guide Rebecca behind its protection, wrapping his arm tightly around her. He waited for the gust to ease, but it lingered longer than he expected, intensifying.

The sound of the howling wind pierced his ears, but he dared not move his position to cover them. With eyes sealed, Spencer wondered if they'd just found Hell. The air felt to be over 110 degrees, and humidity was non-existent. He couldn't even swallow. His skin felt brittle and tight, burning. The inside of his nose ached from the dryness. Minutes seemed like hours as they endured the windstorm.

When relief from the blast finally came, a strong wind still remained, but at least he could move and think. Braving the elements, he lowered his shield. Squinting against the lesser winds, he evaluated their situation.

The first place he looked was back toward the door. It was closed.

"What is this place?" Rebecca asked, even though she knew he didn't know.

Rising to his feet, he pulled her along with him. "We'll see." He grabbed the doorknob and turned, immediately releasing his grip. "Blazing hot," he said, inspecting his red palm. "And locked."

Rebecca looked at Spencer, donning a mask of braveness. "Guess we're on our own?" It was more of a statement than a question.

He nodded slowly as he considered what that meant.

They were dead center in a wasteland of hard-cracked dirt that could easily pass for concrete. Blown smooth, he could see nothing except the door for several miles in each direction. Only a ridge of odd-shaped, dark rock formations encircled them. Although the sunlight came from directly overhead, the unrelenting sky boasted blood reds, like a sunset in a nightmare. Unusual patterns in the ground crisscrossed the entire valley, resembling an odd system of train tracks—5-foot-deep trenches in the crusty dirt.

As options seemed scarce, he methodically scrutinized the rock formations for a plan. Rebecca stood next to him, also surveying the desiccated valley, her strawberry-blond hair whipping in the wind. She wrangled it into a quick braid.

"Water," he said.

"Where?"

"See where the rocks rise and then fall sharply? Looks like a waterfall."

Placing her hand over her brow to block the light, she searched through squinted eyes. "I see it."

"It's probably a five-mile hike."

Spencer took off his uniform coat and tied it around his waist. Rebecca did the same.

"You ready?"

She nodded and tried to swallow.

With a slow, deep breath he set a fast pace. Having no water was his greatest concern, especially since they'd only gone a few yards and he already felt like his scorched throat was the exhaust pipe of a semi-truck crossing the Sahara. The sooner they reached the waterfall, the sooner they could quench their thirst.

As they marched along the barren ground, the only change in their immediate surroundings was an occasional round indentation—crater-like holes that were as bare as the rest of the valley.

Rebecca took one-and-a-half steps to equal the distance of Spencer's stride.

He glanced down to find her face a bright red. He had lived at the beach and played in the sun his whole life. He was used to it, and his olive complexion allowed him more sun exposure than she could bear.

Somewhat delirious himself, he slowed to a stop and tried to think of a way to cool her down. As her eyelids fluttered and her eyes rolled back, he caught her before she hit the ground.

She perked up from the shock and embarrassment of almost fainting.

Spencer ushered her to the ledge of a crater to sit. "We can't stay long. Try to catch your breath."

Feeling helpless to shade her, considering their limited resources, he resorted to the only thing available. Untying his coat from his waist, he opened it up and grabbed the cotton fabric lining. A few quick yanks and the fabric peeled out, giving him almost half of a yard of material to work with. Folding it once, he faced her and placed it over her head, wrapping it into a perfect shield from the sun.

She looked impressed.

"Learned that in Saudi Arabia on a business trip. They have some serious sun there too."

"Much better," she whispered.

A trickle of sweat left his brow, but it dried completely before it reached his cheek.

"Let's go. At least when we're moving, we create our own breeze."

He felt like a piece of burnt toast. He was sure the next time they stopped he would find his boots had melted and atomically fused to his charred feet. Every step was pure agony. Ironically, his feet were so hot they felt ice-cold, painfully cold.

As they reached what he thought might be the halfway point, the winds began to intensify. He had wished the fearsome windstorm from before had been an unusual occurrence. So much for wishing.

He picked the deepest crater he could find for shelter, taking the same protective pose as before—his shield in front, an arm around Rebecca. The winds lashed murderously as the couple hugged the crater's sturdy wall.

Just as Spencer thought the storm might soon decrease, a new sound ripped through the valley. He refrained from peeking until it grew closer, matching the sound of a runaway locomotive. Shielding his face with his hand, he raised one eyelid and squinted so that his lashes were still partially covering his eye.

The giant spun dark, wide and fast as it gained momentum and grew nearer to their shelter. Spencer didn't know if they could outrun it, but he didn't want to experience its wrath.

"Run!"

The command was a guttural blast in a voice that he'd never heard escape his mouth before. He grabbed her hand and pulled her to a standing position while she turned to see their impending doom. Even in the whipping winds Rebecca's eyes widened as she caught a glimpse of the spiraling monster and she turned back around.

Without hesitation, they bolted out of the crater with semi-renewed energy and new motivation, sprinting as death chased them, thrashing at their heels. Despite their exhaustion, they maintained this maddening pace for a quarter of a mile.

Spencer looked back only to find the force of it tearing at the ground and obliterating the pieces into a fine dust that billowed like exhaust from a rocket. He now knew what the odd tracks were. The ground trembled and eroded right from under his feet like sand does when a wave retreats from the shore.

The force of the mere outer edge of it began to pick Rebecca up as if she weighed no more than a lock of her own hair. Through the thunderous winds, her scream slashed at every nerve in his body as she clung to the sleeve of his coat. Instantly, he grabbed her arm with both hands and spun around for more leverage, playing a deadly game of tug-of-war. Facing the giant was unnerving, but he kept his sights on Rebecca, digging both heels into the dirt and pulling back with all his strength as if he could match its power. If it got her, it would get them both; he wasn't letting go.

Her body lifted higher until she was parallel to the ground, the force of it pulling her like an enormous magnet. Desperation swelled to the point of combustion as he felt his hold slipping and the uniform's seam giving way. He tightened his grip, not afraid of breaking her arm at this point, but she still inched away, both her feet dangling at the edge of the vortex from Hell. Her scream wrenched his mind to the point of insanity.

With his feet now being dragged, Spencer shouted, "You can't have her!"

At that moment the force of the pulling decreased. It let her go.

Before she could hit the ground, he caught her and they fled as fast as her wobbly legs would go.

When the sound of it had faded behind them, they risked a glance backwards to observe what they'd escaped.

The long tubular spinning mass of dust-filled wind extended higher than they could see as it swept along the valley floor.

With both looking like they'd just survived the front lines in a battle, they watched it sway and bend as it glided toward the other side of the valley, leaving nothing but a scar in the crusty ground.

When it had vanished in the distance, Rebecca sobbed a tearless cry in Spencer's arms while he held her like she was back from the dead, eyes shut tight, squeezing as hard as he dared for fear of hurting her more. They said nothing. No words could follow such an occurrence. Only the 60 mile-per-hour winds spoke in angry gusts.

After a time, he felt it wise to keep moving, so he took her hand in his and gave her a look of bewilderment and pain. She mirrored his sentiments as they turned and resumed their quest.

They plodded along like the last-place runners of a marathon, their bodies limp, but still moving forward, laboring with each step.

Every fourth cycle the rhythms of their breathing patterns synchronized, but in between, their alternating breaths sounded like a steam engine leaving the station. The scuffling of their boots set the tempo, adding even more depth to the misery of the burdened beat.

Spencer put his head down and leaned into the oncoming steady gusts. Each foot landed like lead on the ground, as he tried to focus on just one step at a time, willing his feet to continue even though thoughts of giving up entered his mind. As long as he could hear her steps next to him, he'd keep going.

Braving the winds, he looked up to analyze their progress. He felt a rush of adrenalin as he realized they were only a few hundred yards away, but the excitement vanished when he saw no water—only sand and huge rock formations.

He stopped. "What?!"

She also stopped and froze at the sight. "A mirage." Her voice was pitiful and shaky, like she'd just read aloud a telegram making her a war-widow.

Like it could bring the water back, make it magically appear, they began to run toward the rocks, desperate to find even the smallest cupful.

As they reached the sandy dunes they struggled with each step as their tired feet sunk into the softest and finest sand they'd ever felt. The sand could have been rock for all they cared, though, because their spirits were sunk. To have come so far, to have survived the worst, and then to be rewarded with this was unthinkable.

Frustration overpowered Spencer. He thrust his sword into the gritty dune. Only half of it remained visible. Flinging his shield a few feet to the left, he fell forward onto his knees and then lowered himself onto the sand.

Rebecca soon followed, lying down next to him. "Mint-chip ice-cream. That's what I want. And then a movie. We could see that new Hitchcock..."

Without looking at her or responding to her delirium, he whispered, "I'm sorry."

"Wait... I think I have some money for our tickets."

Lying on her back in the soft sand, she dug into her uniform pocket. She pulled out the spectacles.

"Yes. Here it is."

Through her delusion, she slipped them on.

"Spencer, do you want mint-chip too?"

She held out invisible ice cream, dusting him with sand from her arm. He didn't answer.

She rolled away from Spencer and faced the other direction. "What about you, sir?"

Next to Spencer's sword stood a thin, ghostly body, made entirely of swirling white sand. Its long, gaunt face held dark hollows where eyes should have been. Her mind snapped awake.

"Spence."

He didn't move.

She sat up and her voice grew more intense. "Spencer, you won't believe this!"

Her small voice in his fading mind made enough of an impression for him to lift his head and squint at her.

"Over there."

He turned and saw nothing.

"You can't see it? Standing by your sword?"

It made no sounds and spoke no words. Turning its head and slowly raising its arm, it pointed toward the rocks. Moving at the speed of a cloud and just as gracefully it resumed its stare at Rebecca. And then, just as mysteriously as it came, it sifted like a light rain, vanishing into the spot where Spencer's sword pierced the sand.

"It told us to go to the rocks."

He laid his head down again. "Another mirage."

"I don't think so. We've got to try," she said, pulling at his arm. "It came from the place you planted your sword."

Hearing this made him hope. And it was this hope that woke him up. He stood, but he didn't brush the sand off himself.

With arms linked to hold each other up, they trudged over the powdery dunes until they reached the rocks that turned out to be much taller than he'd thought. In fact, they weren't rocks upon rocks at all. They were gigantic boulders, dwarfing them by comparison.

Thinking this terrain could at least offer them shade and protection from the elements, Spencer led Rebecca down a long, narrow opening between the boulders. The echo of their steps rippled up the stony walls until it floated up into the red sky, which, from where they stood, was barely exposed.

Inching along, they came to the opening of a massive cave that soared several stories high. They looked at each other in disbelief, relief, and pure joy. It wasn't the opening that drew them in, but the sound they heard inside.

Water.

They ran. With an explosion of energy, they ran inside the cave. They didn't stop until they jumped into the cool, dark river that flowed within its rock walls. The shocking chill was exhilarating as they splashed and laughed, drinking until they could drink no more.

Spencer put his head back and floated freely with the gentle current. Rebecca followed with a relaxed sigh, traveling beside him at a leisurely pace.

Giant stalactites stared back at them from the ceiling of the cave as they sailed. The formations were mesmerizing and not much like stalactites they'd seen before. These had a transparent consistency and shone like diamonds, even in the poor lighting. Reflections from their gleam danced on the water like starlight. In fact, embedded in the very walls of the cave, more diamonds shimmered.

As the speed of the current increased, the diamonds in the rock walls and floor grew more numerous, more illuminating. It was almost as light as the valley had been inside. Downstream it got so light the brightness overpowered, making it look like a dozen spotlights trained on them.

"We should get out," Rebecca suggested.

He agreed although part of him didn't want to leave the water. Yet the light fascinated him.

"Are these diamonds?" she asked mesmerized.

"Looks like it."

As they made their way downstream on the banks of the river, they squinted and tried to focus. Ahead and to the left they stood at the entrance of a tunnel that had walls completely covered with diamonds. Fire shot out from between the precious stones. The heat from the tunnel dried their clothes and hair. The brightness made it impossible to see very far inside.

"This is it. Old Joe wrote about it. The white diamond tunnel," she reported. "We're supposed to go through it."

"His notes didn't mention anything about fire though."

"No," she said, staring into the brightness. "Are we going in?"

"We've come this far."

Chapter Twenty-Four
Ice Labyrinth

San Diego

"You will need these," Armada said, holding out the cloaks.

Jack released the doorknob and took the shimmering fabric. He handed one to Katie, the other he tossed over his shoulder. When he turned back, the angels were gone.

On our own. Great. Letting a full breath escape at once, he returned his attention to the rusty blue door.

With the exhibit's rushing waterfall behind, and Katie and Jeremiah next to him, he turned the knob and pushed. The door resisted with the force of a bulldozer. Jeremiah and Katie joined the struggle, grunting and digging their feet in. With the efforts of all three of them, the door finally budged.

A vacuum released its pressure, hissing at them, as the door swung open like a slow-moving hearse.

The biting cold stung Jack's face like a hailstorm. "And I thought it was cold out *here*," he said, stepping into a foreign world. He threw on his cloak to block the Siberian chill. Katie and Jeremiah followed, sharing the other cloak, mouths ajar for what they saw.

"Which way should we go?" Katie asked.

"Which way *can* we go? It's like an optical illusion."

Forming an eerie fun house, a maze of pseudo-transparent walls of crystallized ice stood, daring them to move.

"It's like dry ice," Jack observed from the mist floating off the walls.

Putting her hand out to feel her way through the maze, Katie said, "How about this way?"

Jeremiah grabbed her hand before it touched the wall. "Look."

She followed the direction his eyes suggested. He pointed across the corridor to an unfamiliar, hairy animal that resembled a squirrel having a bad hair day. It appeared to be stuck to the ice, still alive, but much like a mouse caught in a sticky trap, pulling and twisting, trying to free itself. Pitiful, high-pitched squeals begged them for mercy.

"Don't touch the walls," Jeremiah said, staring at the squirming creature.

With close study of each wall, they moved slowly through the ice labyrinth, careful to stay in the middle of the corridors. Some walls looked like openings and some openings looked like walls. They could only tell the difference if they stood very close so their breath would influence the direction of the mist of the dry ice.

They passed two more stuck creatures. One had begun to decompose on the wall and nothing much was left of it besides the skeleton, but the other

271

squealed and flailed its limbs hopelessly. Katie looked away.

After they turned a corner, the vermin that had been squealing, hopped off the wall and began to follow them. It had camouflaged itself over a dead creature, and pretended to have been stuck, but now it skittered along the hard-packed dirt, keeping clear of the viscous walls and the Knights' line of sight.

They inched past another stuck rodent until Katie's love for furry things got the better of her. Slipping out from under the cloak she said, "Maybe we can help them." She reached out to try to free one.

"That's not a good ide—" Jack tried to warn.

"Ouch!" she exclaimed after the creature bit her hand in reply to her benevolence.

Before they could react to the injury, a hissing sound filled the corridor as steam blasted from a fissure in the cold dirt. The angry geyser shot up nearly twenty feet, touching the frozen ceiling and dissolving a hole in it.

Fierce quaking knocked the Knights to the ground as they watched from their knees as the walls pivoted and slid into new formations.

The walls traveled slowly, but persistently, keeping them on their guard. They rushed from hallway to hallway, avoiding contact with the ice.

From behind Jeremiah came the largest of pivoting walls. Jack could see that, unless he intervened, Jeremiah could be cut off. He lunged forward, pulling his son back toward his original position.

"Stay together," Jack ordered as another wall rotated behind them and closed a gap with a boom that echoed against the newly formed corridors.

When the geyser fizzled and the walls stopped moving, Katie found herself separated from the others.

In a panic she searched for a way around the frigid walls, but realized she was completely encased within the ice. She had no cloak to shield her from the sub-zero temperatures.

The bitter chill distracted her so much that, in her desperation, she accidentally touched the wall with her right hand, which, to her horror, instantly adhered. Gasping and pulling at her hand, she peered through the frosted ice at them, mortified that she'd forgotten to stay clear of the crystal maze. She could find no words. She couldn't even scream or cry.

Through her incapacitated hand, the heat was literally being sucked from her body. The intense pressure and cold crept through her bones like a cancer.

Looking around the network of ice and finding nothing of use to them, Jeremiah grabbed his dad through the two cloaks, and with one single blast of words he yelled in a voice ten times his size. "How do we get her out?"

Jack dragged his fingers through his hair and responded sharply. "I don't know."

Seeing her trapped like one of those hairy pests tormented Jeremiah. The panic settling in the pit of his stomach was stronger than any he'd felt of its kind.

Katie's skin was a frigid blue and her entire body shivered in the arctic-like air. Her beauty was stolen by the grimace on her face.

Jeremiah felt helpless as he watched her suffering. Consumed with frustration, he ripped off his cloak, letting it fall to the dirt. It was colder than any Montana winter he'd experienced, instantly prickling his skin with the raw chill. If she were cold, he would be cold right along with her. He stood a little taller, wanting to show her she was not alone.

Despite her own troubles, she saw his sacrifice and shook her head with fervor at him to replace the cloak. He didn't budge, except to begin to shiver in unison with her.

An unexpected voice distracted him from the cold. "You're just a pathetic child."

He wasn't sure if he'd thought it or heard it. His eyes inspected the entire length of the corridor. He saw no one except his father. In this dimension, he knew he should be able to see demons, but nothing manifested.

"Did you say something?"

Pacing back and forth, Jack was engrossed in finding a solution and shook his head in response.

"She wants someone her age; sophisticated."

The words echoed in his mind despite the logic fighting against them. He didn't want to believe them. The knights had taught him that, but deep down he did.

A new voice sounded in his ears.

"Can we help?"

In a flash, Jack and Jeremiah turned toward the female voice behind them.

Two women wearing hand-stitched animal fur, yielding crude spears, stood a few yards away. Their stance seemed non-threatening, but Jack still felt guarded. *Friends or foes?* he wondered.

"Who are you?" Despite the bulky coverings, Jack could see these women were extremely beautiful—or maybe it had been too long since he'd even noticed a woman.

As if they could read his mind, or maybe to appear more well-intentioned, they lowered their hoods exposing even more of their allurement.

The taller woman had short blonde hair and a fair-skinned, Netherlands-type of complexion. The animal skins she wore were a pristine white.

The other had jet-black curly hair pulled back in a coiled-leather tie. Her coverings were a cougar-brown, trimmed with black bear fur.

"I am Astra" the taller woman spoke. "And this is Nym. We can help you, but you must come quickly if you want to save her."

Jack was out of options. He looked at Jeremiah.

"I'm not leaving her," Jeremiah said as only a teenager could.

"He may stay with her if he prefers."

Jack nodded. "Put your cloak on. You can help her better if you're not frozen."

He looked through pained eyes at his son, not wanting to leave him.

"Okay, Dad."

After an exchange of sober expressions and no parting words, Jack turned to follow the women who were already strutting away. He jogged a few steps to catch up to their pace.

They made so many turns in the maze of ice, he knew he'd never find his way back alone. He was completely dependent on their goodwill. At least he hoped it was good.

After a half-mile trek, their pace slowed as they came to a large opening in the maze that seemed to drop off into nothing but darkness.

Nym sat down on the edge, her wooly-booted legs dangling over the side. Without explanation, she dropped out of sight.

Jack's heart skipped a beat as he lunged forward to see where she'd gone. At the edge he found what appeared to be black ice at his feet. *The black slide from Old Joe's notes.* Now he could see that it descended thirty yards before him, vanishing into the darkness below. Nym had already slid out of sight.

Although he was glad to find a landmark that seemed to validate the women as friends and not foes, he felt suddenly sick at the thought of having to actually use this slide.

Astra gracefully motioned for him to follow Nym. The sweet sound of her charming voice sent chills down Jack's spine.

"After you."

Chapter Twenty-Five
The Shack

Swamplands

Nehcterg continued to mutter as he navigated the boat through an ever-narrowing network of giant trees. Although there were several paths, his rowing didn't slow as they sailed along the murky maze. He was as familiar with the swamp as Sam was with Carthage.

As they glided along, Sam noticed the already dim light was getting dimmer. The fog had also grown thicker, suffocating the landscape. But the most disturbing thing was the absence of wildlife—or at least the absence of their sounds. Even Nehcterg had stopped talking under his breath. Only the sound of the oars hitting the water broke the smothered air.

A break in the trees revealed a rickety dock and boardwalk nearly overtaken by weeds and cattails. The troll maneuvered the boat toward it and tied it off.

"Well, I haven't got all day now. Move along," the hideous creature complained.

Sam hopped out reluctantly. Nehcterg may have been odd, but he was ironically the friendliest being they'd met. In a strange way, he trusted the cynical troll. As he held his hand out to help Tallulah disembark, she beat him to the question.

"Would it be too much trouble for you to tell us who 'they' are of whom you referred earlier?" Tallulah inquired with precise British politeness.

They both waited in awkwardness for an answer as Nehcterg untied the boat and began to row away without even a glance at them. The only words they heard him say were "How am I supposed to know? It's your mission…"

Sam watched until the boat disappeared in the trees. *Alone again.* Nehcterg was grouchy, but at least they weren't alone. He was sure the beating of his own heart was loud enough for Tallulah to hear through the silence.

Without collaborating with his counterpart, he led them along the tumbledown dock, choosing a careful path around the missing planks. Reaching the boardwalk, he found it was in much the same condition. With knee-high weeds poking between the boards, it was the only manmade object in sight, but from the state of it, a 'man' hadn't set foot on it for some time—or at least not one with handyman skills.

All too soon his feet came to the end of the boardwalk, and he found himself glancing back at Tallulah. "Want to try the path on the left?"

"That's a path?"

"More or less." He shrugged.

"Okay, but just keep a vine handy. I don't want another mud bath."

He threw her a half-grin and stepped onto the spongy terrain. Keeping one eye trained on the sky for killer wasps and one eye on the ground for overactive mud holes, he inched along the path. Abundantly lined with tall grass and moss-covered trees, the only sounds to be heard were the sounds of their boots as they sunk into the bog, and the plant life they scraped by, until a faint yet familiar sound invaded his ears.

"We must stop them."

Without hesitation he drew his sword.

"Trouble?" Tallulah asked.

"We're on the right path."

"On the right path to trouble?"

"Yep."

"Is it too late to choose the other path?"

His eyes scanned the area at a frantic pace, not wanting to be surprised, but could see nothing but plants and trees. However, the corrupt thoughts were everywhere and seemed to be on the move. They grated his mind like metal on metal. He wasn't sure where to look next until he caught sight of pinpointed, glowing-red eyes and heard the whisper of a hiss. A solid-ebony snake with no markings strangled the branches of two trees a few feet away.

With an explosion of power, he slashed through the serpent and the tree's limb all at once. It fell to the mud at Sam's feet, the thud sounding like a large bag of potatoes landing in a tub of oatmeal. As he recovered from the strike, he was astonished to see two snakes in front of him where the one had fallen.

He charged again, slicing through both of them easily with two fluid movements.

But to his horror, the two separated into four. Having not been trained in dealing with 'dividing snakes', he instantly decided to strike, but only once more. He connected with one of the four, of course forming a new fourth and fifth. Realizing the sword was only helping them to multiply, he lowered it and tried to block them with his shield. They surged toward him, avoiding this obstacle with ease. He panicked as he realized they appeared immune to his gifts.

They wrapped themselves around his ankles and then his wrists. Using good old-fashioned muscle, he slammed his snake-shackled right wrist against the nearest tree. No luck. The reptile appeared unfazed by the blow and squeezed even harder as the last one slithered its way up to his neck. Like a slimy vice, it crushed his throat until there was no more airflow. He dropped to his knees, pulling on the creature with all his strength. It made no difference. Sam was desperate for air, but the snake was not obliging.

Turning toward Tallulah, he found she was actively avoiding several serpents as well, trying to move them telekinetically, but having no success. Unable to speak due to the pressure on his throat, he grabbed her leg.

Doing a double take, she stated, "You're up a tree, aren't you?"

Her words began to mush together in a warbled, low-pitched mess. He watched several snakes attach themselves to Tallulah. Trying to shake them off, she flew straight up and out of Sam's line of sight. *Alone. Not good.* With the last bit of strength he could muster, he grabbed at the slimy noose and penetrated its textured skin with his raw fingernails. The swamp began to spin, and the world dissolved into bursts of black, blue and silver sparkling molecules, falling from an invisible ceiling. A face flashed before his eyes from the deepest part of his mind. *Hayley,* he thought. And then all went black.

A full minute passed before Tallulah returned to his side, herself now snake-free. Kneeling next to him, she pulled up her pant leg, exposing a leg holster. From it she drew a silver dagger. With a wild blaze in her eyes, she raised it over her head and then plunged it strategically into the serpent around Sam's neck. It hissed and looked at her in defeat and then went limp. She unraveled it and flung it into the trees like discarded, old piece of rope. The same followed with the other four snakes.

With the pressure off his limbs and neck, she checked for a pulse. She found it, but it was weak, and he wasn't breathing. Rolling him onto his back, she placed her mouth over his and blew two strong breaths, making his chest rise slightly. Silently she waited and watched.

"Sam! You've got a mission to complete here!" she commanded, but then she lowered her head and closed her eyes. *It wasn't supposed to be like this,* she thought with fists at her temples as she began to pray next to his lifeless body.

She lowered her hands, and turned her eyes toward heaven, waiting for guidance. She hoped

Armada would join her, but she remained the only warrior to aid Sam.

With new determination, she checked the pulse again. It was the same and he was still not breathing. She repeated the breaths. Nothing. All seemed lost, but then, after a few seconds, he finally gasped and coughed.

She closed her eyes and her body relaxed.

Sam took huge, labored breaths, cupping his throat with one hand. His throat burned like fire.

Tallulah kept watch as he recovered. She knew he didn't realize what she'd just done for him. She decided not to tell him.

"The snakes are gone, Sam. You're okay now."

She held out her flask. He tried a labored swallow.

As she watched for snakes, a small hill ahead and to the left piqued her interest. A faint and curious sound captured her full attention.

"Sam, do you hear it?"

For the moment all he could hear was his lungs being replenished. He didn't even hear the question. And he didn't care. The only thing he cared about at this moment was acquiring as much oxygen as possible

She said it louder. "Do you hear it, Sam?" Her face brightened with hopeful expectations.

That time he heard her and forced a few more swallows. He thought about sitting up, but then decided not to. Looking at her pleasant expression was his first clue to what she heard.

Feeling a little better, he lay very still, straining to hear it until a few notes rang through.

"Singing?" he asked, in a scratchy voice.

"A hymn."

The smile that grew larger on her face inspired Sam to sit up. But before he allowed himself to celebrate, he remembered the deceit that ran rampant in this place.

"It may not be what it seems," he warned.

It was barely loud enough to hear the words or to know who was singing. It reminded him of the way his mom and dad would play the radio late at night as they worked in the market downstairs, not wanting to wake him as he was supposed to have been sleeping in the apartment upstairs. It was never loud enough for him to name the title of the songs, but he knew the radio was on.

Swallowing some of the pain away, he stood, and then replaced his sword. Tallulah sheathed her dagger.

"Hey," he said, touching her arm.

She looked up at him.

"Thanks."

She nodded.

He wasn't sure how she'd saved hm, but her dagger told him she had,

"Up the hill?" he asked her, positioning his hand in the direction of the music.

She nodded again.

The music grew louder as they climbed the small hill.

She's right. It is a hymn. It sounded like several voices. Pretty good ones at that; with harmony, too.

As they crested the hill, a dilapidated shack came into view. The music was clearly coming from inside this pitiful excuse for shelter. Sam drew his sword.

They moved silently; but as quiet as they were, the inhabitants of the shack apparently seemed to know of their presence as the hymn was cut short.

All went quiet.

Sam and Tallulah stopped their approach within twenty feet from the deteriorated door. They waited. They waited for movement or noise, but neither came.

Without turning his eyes from the shack, he whispered, "Why is it always doors?"

The only course of action seemed to be to open it. Inside must be the 'them' of whom Nehcterg spoke. He hoped 'they' were friendly.

He nodded at Tallulah; she nodded back.

Even though it hurt his still-aching throat, he led with his shoulder and a war cry as he easily forced the rickety door to the ground. He stood in the doorway, ready for a fight, but what he saw put his aggression on a sudden hold.

In the corner, huddled together, several mud-covered people in haggard clothes stared back at him, wide-eyed, scared.

When he realized who they were, he dropped his sword. Complete astonishment controlled him now. Never in his wildest thoughts

284

had he conjured up the crowd that shivered in front of him—especially the man in the front. Slowly, the ragged group realized who he was as well and began to stand. But Sam could now only focus on the man in front. He was speechless, unable to move. He wanted to move, but it was like his feet were trapped in quick-setting cement. They wouldn't budge. He couldn't even breathe. *Is he real?*

Before anyone could speak, the man bolted over to Sam and tackled him in a gigantic embrace. "Sam!"

"Dad?"

It looked like him, felt like him, sounded like him. He wanted to believe it this time.

"It's me," Hank said, looking him square in the eyes.

"You're alive," he whispered, squeezing the air out of his father.

"Y'all thought I drowned, didn't you?"

"We searched, but…" Sam couldn't speak another word. His throat had closed up.

"Never mind that now. I'm okay." Hank exhaled, keeping a tight grip on his son.

From beneath the mud and filth came other happy, familiar faces. Faces from the past that Sam thought were long gone from his life, taken in tragedy, memorialized in the town square.

"Sam? Sam Wright?" The elderly lady hobbled over to him and craned her neck to look in his eyes. "Why, you grew up," said Isabella Chop with a chuckle.

Sam laughed, too. How many times had she told him to do just that when she'd caught him in the act of some sort of mischief?

Those with her were the other two "Model-A Widows", and the choir director, Brother Rogers, all believed to have been taken by the sea.

He glanced around at their humble abode. Talk about 'makeshift'. Survival looked like it had been difficult. He wasn't sure if he wanted to know how they'd done it, but he was glad to be taking them out of it— especially his father.

"Are you taking us home?" Gladys Littlejohn asked, grabbing his hand with her shaky, wrinkly one.

"Yes," he said, smiling down at her, "but we have one stop to make first."

Chapter Twenty-Six
Was Blind, But Now I See

Desert

"No way around?" Rebecca asked, staring at the flames that danced from the jeweled tunnel.

"Probably not," Spencer replied, also mesmerized by the fiery diamonds." I think we can avoid direct contact if we stay right in the middle."

"You 'think'?"

"Well, only one way to find out."

He stepped under the archway, surprised that he didn't have to duck.

"I'm right behind you." When she said right behind him, she meant it. They resembled contestants in a three-legged race: in sync, and close enough to have been tied together.

With each step they avoided the flames lashing out like daggers.

Naturally, Spencer's stride was much longer than hers, so the three-legged race strategy was not the best of plans.

Just stay in the middle, exactly the middle, she told herself as she felt the distance expand between Spencer and herself.

As if the flames weren't enough to deal with, the curved walls began to spin around the walkway like a kaleidoscope of death, instantly fooling them into believing they were tipping.

Their balance faltered. With feet planted awkwardly, in a sort of pigeon-toed stance, they bent slightly at the waist, their arms out to their sides like tightrope walkers. Remaining upright and away from those flames was their only concern. One misstep and they would land in the fire.

"It's hot in here, but not as hot as I would've expected with all these flames," she said.

Spencer glanced at Rebecca. "Wait."

Clearly motivated by a revelation, she watched as he unsheathed his sword. Without changing the position of his feet, he turned his torso to the right, allowing the flames of the spinning tunnel wall to engulf the end of the weapon. After a few seconds, he pulled it in close to him and inspected it. Cautiously, he touched the area that had been exposed to the flame; a quick pat at first, which multiplied into several quick pats as if testing the temperature of a baking pan. Being mindful of the sharp edges, he touched the blade for a longer time.

"It's cold."

Rebecca frowned and gave him a questioning look.

He replaced his sword into the sheath and this time extended a bare hand.

"Spence, don't!"

Her warning came too late. His hand already caressed the flames. She stared in disbelief as she

realized he must feel no pain. He didn't yank his
hand back in agony. Withdrawing his hand from the
so-called flames revealed not one blister or mark.

"Another mirage?"

She shrugged. "It looked so real."

He shrugged back.

With the fear of the fire squelched, they
turned their attention back to the spinning tunnel,
inching along. Upon reaching the end, a blinding
light overpowered them.

"Wish I had my sunglasses," Spencer said.

"Me too. I can barely open my eyes."

"Try your spectacles."

"Good idea." She slipped them on. "Much
better."

Spencer stepped out of the tunnel first and
found a place that appeared to have no boundaries,
no landscaping, and no buildings.

"It's just a bunch of… white."

The spectacles gave Rebecca the advantage
of seeing something additional: one white diamond
wall that measured fifteen feet high by fifteen feet
wide.

"Don't you see it?"

"What?"

"The wall? The diamond wall, right there?"
She lowered her spectacles, and then her view
matched his. Replacing them, she said, "You'll just
have to trust me. It's there."

Spencer drew his sword. They inched
toward the wall.

Rebecca's face sunk with a solemn expression as she drew in a large breath and stopped walking. "Oh my."

"What?"

"They're trapped."

"Who's trapped?"

"Looks like two men. Trapped in the wall. They're trying to get out. They're hitting the inner wall and shouting out to us."

"I can't hear them." He let out an exasperated breath. "I can't see them either. Hey, I can't even see the wall. How am I supposed to help if I'm working in the dark here?"

"Funny," she said at the irony of his statement. "But maybe you *can* help."

She held up her hand and touched the wall. "Right here. Strike the wall with your sword right here."

He looked at her for more of an explanation, but then realized this may be their only solution.

She motioned for them to stand back, and then she stood back and watched with squinted eyes as his sword hit the wall, sending the shattered pieces into oblivion.

Recovering from the strike, he stood up straight again. "Now I see them."

Two men crouched where the diamond wall had once served as their prison. They leaned on each other for support.

The younger, dark haired man wearing a captain's hat spoke first. "Who's there?"

"You can't see us?" Rebecca asked.

"It's just a big, white blur—no wait. I can see two figures now. Yes, it's getting clearer."

"How did you get in there?" she asked.

"I was hoping you could tell us that. All I know, is that it's probably been a couple years, too many years."

Through squinted eyes, Spencer took a closer look him. "Cappy?"

"Mr. Wetherholt?" The surprise in the question made the pitch of his voice rise.

"I don't believe it," Spencer said.

"How'd you find us?"

Spencer wasn't sure if the surprise in his voice was that they'd been found or that it was Spencer that found them. He was probably the last person Cappy would have expected to come to their rescue.

"It's a long story," Spencer said, not wanting to open that can of worms at the moment.

Cappy gave Spencer the kind of hug that men give when they greet each other and don't want to appear wimpy—lots of arms slapping backs, grunts and the like. "I'm sure glad to see ya."

Returning to his own personal space, Cappy glanced at Rebecca who waited patiently.

"Oh, this is my wife, Rebecca."

Cappy almost fell over from shock. "You're married?" He shook Rebecca's hand vigorously. "Nice to meet you. I can tell you've already had an interesting impact on his wardrobe. And a sword?" he joked.

"Like I said. Long story," Spencer said, chuckling. "Rebecca, this is Jonathan Kaplan,

291

Cappy for short. He used to be my chauffeur, my confidant, and my only real friend…until you. He led me to the Lord."

"Nice to meet you." She smiled.

"And this is my brother, Alex."

Cappy's brother shook both their hands with a profound look of gratitude, but with no words.

"How did you guys get here?" Spencer asked.

"The last thing we knew, we were out on Alex's boat for the weekend. In a blink we ended up trapped in here."

"You know when your boat went missing, I sent a team of my own out looking for you— even after the authorities gave up hope."

"Thanks, sir. Appreciate it."

Alex finally spoke. "So why did all this happen?"

"Again... lonnnnng story."

Chapter Twenty-Seven
Kiss the Cook

Ice Labyrinth

The descent on the black ice slide was surprisingly not terrifying, as Jack had thought it would be. After the thirty-yard plunge through the dark, it veered to the right and pushed them through a tunnel that gradually leveled off and spit him out into some wintry woods. He sat at the end of the tunnel absorbing the thrill of the moment. If circumstances had been different, he would have wanted to ride it again.

Nym replaced her hood as she waited by the end of the tunnel, looking unimpressed. *She has probably ridden it thousands of times,* he thought as he stood and waited quietly.

In one fluid motion, Astra appeared and stood as graciously as a gymnast performing her final dismount. She replaced her hood as well and took the lead, crunching the icy ground under her bulky leather boots through the thick collection of snow-covered pine trees.

As they pushed on, their gait increased to a jog. The further they traveled away from Jeremiah, the more he fought the urge to turn his thoughts to things beyond his control. His gut said this was the right course, but Jack hated leaving them behind.

From a low shrub to the right of their path a streak of teased-gray fur passed in front of Jack. He had to jump to avoid stepping on what he recognized as the type of rodent that had been stuck to the ice inside the labyrinth. Clearly these animals were seriously lacking in brains. It continued its course without regard for him and found refuge beneath another bush.

They began to climb an insanely steep hill. By the time they reached the summit, Jack was surprised he could still breathe at all. His legs felt like mashed potatoes, and he was about to black out.

But he was pleased to find the trees were thinning, giving way to a clearing that measured about an acre. In the middle stood a stone cottage that could have passed for the one in the Snow White story, sans the dwarves.. Oddly, he did hear a sweet, familiar melody coming from inside the cottage. A woman's voice hummed a tune that he couldn't name, but he knew well.

As he suspected, the two women led him straight to the door and stopped. Astra turned to Nym and flashed her a knowing look, and then looked at Jack. She opened the door and motioned for him to enter.

Taking a few deep breaths to slow his pounding chest, he tried to resume his regular heart rate.

The cottage was dimly lit. The only light came from a small window in the kitchen. Steam floated through the weak rays of sunlight as the humming continued. The familiar notes combined with a familiar aroma, and as he peeked around the corner into the tiniest of kitchens, he froze at the sight of a familiar woman standing at the stove. She was stirring the contents of a large pot. If this was some sort of demonic trick, he didn't even care. All that mattered was she was there.

She was alive.

But why was she here? Why was she taken here? Taken from him? Confusion overpowered his mind to the point of distraction. He could no longer think logically.

He must have gasped or maybe she just sensed his presence, because she turned abruptly and squinted at his back-lit figure. He stepped closer. Standing perfectly still, her mouth ajar, she dropped her spoon, but didn't seem to care.

They stood facing each other. Time stood frozen as the steam wavered between them.

"Jack?" Her voice was small and shaky.

He didn't respond with words. Instead, he bent down in a daze and picked up her spoon. Stepping closer, he handed it to her.

"Holly?" The smile on his face said it all.

"Jack?" Holly asked, her eyes brimming with tears.

She took the spoon without even knowing it, and then threw her arms around him. He lifted her off the ground and spun her around, his face buried in her hair. The spoon fell to the floor again, but neither of them noticed as they kissed each other through tears, laughter and disbelief.

295

"We must go." The harshness of Astra's voice in the doorway broke their trance. Nym stood beside her. "Nym, pack the tools and medicine. Holly, get the blankets."

Jack pulled back a bit from Holly, but he didn't let go of her. His countenance sobered as he looked at her through pained eyes. "Jeremiah's watching over a girl trapped in the ice labyrinth."

Holly's face went pale. "Jeremiah's here?"

"Uh, long story," Jack explained.

Astra continued. "I'll get the wood. Jack, would you please assist me?"

He forced himself back to reality enough to answer, but he refused to take his eyes off Holly. "Yes."

His thoughts shot back to Jeremiah and Katie. Prolonging the reunion with his wife was trumped by the urgency of the moment. Reluctantly, he let her go.

He watched Holly scurry away to gather the blankets and gloves, and then followed Astra to the woodshed.

As he loaded firewood onto a cart, he wished Jeremiah had been here. *He'll know soon. He'll have his mother back.*

Within minutes they had everything together and packed onto the cart. He figured Astra's plan had included a way to get the supplies down the enormous hill and then back up to the labyrinth. He was pleasantly surprised to know they wouldn't have to muscle the cart all the way to Katie.

The mode of transportation was fitting considering the snowy woods and high altitude.

With just enough room for the four of them and a cart of wood and supplies, a gondola hung amidst the pines as if they were on a ski trip. As it began its course, Jack estimated the maximum weight allotment, and held his breath as it creaked and moaned along the cable.

Holly sat next to him and they held hands like they did when they had dated. They didn't speak, but at this point there was too much to say for such a short trip. Besides, the anxiety level in the gondola was too high for conversation anyway. The feeling like too much time had passed to save Katie hovered over them like a thundercloud about to burst.

From inside the packed gondola, he observed the trail by which they'd come. The steep hillside they'd climbed looked even steeper from this prospective. Along the tops of the trees they sailed, dangling like a cinder-block ornament on a flimsy Christmas tree branch.

"I thought you drowned," Jack whispered.

"The last thing I remember was going under. I woke up in the cottage. I was alone and afraid until Astra and Nym arrived."

"We were sent to guard you until Jack came."

"Angels." Jack said.

They nodded.

"How did you find me, Jack?"

He gushed the story of Knighthood and their mission, Jeremiah, the zoo, Katie, Old Joe and everything.

It wasn't long before they were in view of the tunnel at the end of the slide. Dozens of the gray creatures skittered around on the platform on which they planned to disembark.

Astra sat a little straighter as she saw them as well. A look of concern on her face was mimicked by all as the cable groaned harder with the extra weight.

"Looks like they've chewed through the brakes again. And they're working on the cable. Jack, you and I will push the cart out first and then Nym and Holly will follow. It won't be stopping at the loop, so we've got to be fast."

The plan would've been successful, but the plan didn't factor in the quick progress of the chewing vermin.

At the first available space on the platform, Jack and Astra forced the cart out and turned to help pull the other two out, but the cable snapped, and the gondola crashed to the dirt landing. Nym jumped out upon impact. The cable started to drag the gondola back toward the sheer drop-off.

Holly was still inside.

Jack grabbed the pickaxe out of the cart and brought it down on the inside floor of the gondola and held on, buying them more time. Gritting his teeth and straining every muscle he had and some he didn't even know he had, he used every ounce of his strength. Astra held onto the doorframe and pulled as well.

Nym reached out for Holly's hand as the gondola tipped on the brink, but she couldn't connect.

Jack could feel his feet slipping and digging grooves into the cold dirt.

With an eerie "whoosh" the cable whipped free of the gondola and plummeted a hundred yards to the ground. The gondola teetered on the edge at the greatest angle before its free-fall would begin.

As the gondola left the edge, Astra jumped up on the side of the doorframe, reached down inside and yanked Holly out, throwing her toward the rest. But she came up short, grasping for anything to hold onto. Nym grabbed her wrists as the gondola slid off the edge. Astra defied gravity on her trek back to the landing—running in mid-air.

They cringed at the sound of the gondola hitting the ground and smashing into more pieces than they wanted to know about.

The angels continued pulling her to safer ground until she could manage on her own. While they all dusted themselves off, and their breathing began to slow, they watched as dozens of the evil rodents scattered back into their secret hiding spots.

"Well, now. Wasn't that fun?" Holly joked while her knees knocked.

Jack scooped her up in a hug. "I just got you back. No falling off mountains."

"Better keep moving," Astra said, pushing the cart toward the outer edge of the icy maze.

Corner after freezing corner, dread settled in Jack's stomach.

We've been gone too long, Jack thought.

Several rodents-from-Hell scurried past as they rounded the last corner.

Jeremiah knelt in the same spot by Katie's limp and imprisoned body. Her hand was still glued to the wall, her arm stretched above her, her body in a heap on the cold dirt.

Jeremiah was not looking at her trapped body though. His attention was drawn to what made the others stop cold in their tracks.

Above them shone a brilliant light that cascaded down to a floating, glowing being. The being was Katie, or rather her soul, which was rising up to meet the light right before their eyes.

Jack was shocked they would be privy to such a moment, but then realized they were in the spiritual dimension. He never expected to witness something like this though.

Jeremiah called out to her and she turned toward him. A look of pure joy on her face and a graceful, outreached hand sent a message of peace and acceptance. The entire group gasped when they heard her whisper, "Goodbye" to him. She turned and continued toward the light.

Speechless and stunned beyond anything he'd seen so far; Jack could not even move or think. It was beautiful, peaceful and joyful, but at the same time the heart wrenching agony of not being able to save her, slashed at his soul.

"No!" Jeremiah's scream pierced the moment. "It's not too late! Don't give up. She could come back to us. She's not gone yet. She's right there." He turned to Jack. "Dad, don't give up on her."

Jack swallowed and thought for no more than an instant. "I won't. He's right. Just because we can see her spirit moving-on doesn't mean it is *supposed* to happen now. If we couldn't see this we'd still be trying, right? Maybe we're meant to save her. Let's keep trying. Astra, what's the plan?"

She smiled as she stepped forward and delegated responsibilities to each person. The main focus was on building the hottest blaze they could. Within minutes the fire was taller than Jack, and the sound of it muffled all other sounds. With the ice softening up, they all attacked with shovels and pickaxes, coming closer to obliterating the wall with each blow.

They worked together. They worked quickly, keeping an eye on Katie's spirit, hoping their efforts weren't in vain. The light was diminishing, and Katie was gradually leaving their presence, almost fading into the light at a great distance.

A tremendous cracking sound was music to their ears.

Astra yelled, "Clear the area!" just before the partially melted wall crumbled down. They all worked simultaneously in thick gloves to clear the rubble.

"Her hand's free," Jeremiah laughed a nervous laugh as he held her hand in his gloved one. "Katie, you're free. You can come back. Don't leave us. You made it." He looked up to see only a trace outline of her glimmering soul, the light almost gone as well.

Astra motioned for the others the stand back. All obeyed except Jeremiah. He refused to let go of her hand. Astra worked around him. She rolled her in blankets and held her face with two hands. She spoke an unknown language.

A quiet reverent feeling passed over the rest of them as they felt like they had lost the fight, but then the faint light above them began to grow. With expectant, wide eyes, they stared at the light until it produced two figures that appeared to be descending. One was Katie, but it took a minute to recognize the other.

"Is that Nym?" Jack inquired.

"The Lord allowed Nym to retrieve Katie's soul. Jeremiah was right. It wasn't her time," Astra whispered.

And as Katie rejoined her body, Astra joined Nym and traveled into the light above.

Jeremiah felt energy surge into Katie's limp body. He broke out into relieved laugh, hugging her to him.

With a faint yet sassy tone, she complained, "It's about time you got me out of there. I'm freezing."

Jeremiah laughed even more through his tears at her response as he tucked his cloak around her shivering body.

He glanced toward the crowd to see a vision that knocked him backwards. His mother.

"She's real, Jeremiah. It's okay," Jack reassured him.

Jeremiah stared.

"It's me honey. I'm okay," Holly said, smiling ear-to-ear.

She rushed to her son on the floor and embraced both he and Katie. They both sobbed tears of pure joy.

"Mom!"

Chapter Twenty-Eight
Answers

Sam was past the point of exhaustion; too tired to be sleepy; too numb to feel anything, and wide awake as their Chargers landed at Rebecca's school. On the trip from Catalina his mind flip-flopped from Hayley to the return of his dad. Both had completely consumed his thoughts.

He knew dwelling on Hayley's abduction was exactly what the demons planned and wanted. He was sure she was being held in a similar manner to his father's captivity. Thinking of her in pain, alone, and frightened, tortured him. If the demons meant to get to him, they had succeeded. It crushed him to the core to not know how and where she was.

But even in the mist of this anxiety, Sam felt like he was the rope in a morbid twist of the game tug-o'-war because he was beyond happy his dad was alive. How could he feel such torment and happiness at the very same time?

Ray escorted them to the cafeteria building. The tables were set, candles lit, the music was low, and the aromas told Sam that angels had prepared this feast. Until the aroma enveloped him, he hadn't realized just how hungry he was. The moment they crossed the threshold of the room, their mud-caked, torn and otherwise smelly appearance transformed into shower-clean bodies wearing fresh new clothes—in the Knights' case: pristine, white uniforms.

At a substantial round table that sat about twenty, their meals waited under silver domes at each place setting. Sam's hunger pangs became acute as he stared into the shiny metal at his place, but he became distracted by his own warped reflection on the dome. His eyes were dark, bloodshot, and sunken, his skin pale, and his expression too care-worn for someone only seventeen.

Armada directed each team of Knights to report on their mission, making introductions as needed for the group. After this, he answered basic questions before they could be asked.

"By now you have realized you were abducted by demons, and everyone you know believes you drown. Do not worry too much about these things because you will step back into your lives as if nothing ever happened. *You* will know what transpired, but those left behind will not remember the tragedy or your absence. Your homes and lives will be completely restored. Ultimately, only time has been taken from you. God allowed you to be taken, to be used for his glory."

Isabella's petite hand rose into the air and Armada acknowledged her with a kind nod.

"But *why* were we taken?"

"You were specifically chosen by fallen angels to further their cause. They most likely studied you and your impact on those around them. They abducted some of you because you are key members of the towns they aim to destroy, but they were not allowed to kill you. You, for instance, Isabella, have the gift of discernment. Eleanor has the gift of hospitality, and Gladys the gift of teaching. By themselves these gifts may seem small, but when absent or ignored the entire infrastructure of a church could fail. The demons know this and prey on any weakness they can find. Your absence also decreased the number of prayers received for others in need. But the good news is that your return could be a silent voice behind a great revival."

He paused and observed the clean, but weary group.

"For now, your bodies need fuel and rest. Tonight, you will sleep at this facility and a special meal has been prepared for you. We thank the Lord for all his many blessings and ask this food be nourishment for your bodies. Enjoy it and rest well."

Most of the group practically inhaled their food. Sam lifted his dome, but, as hungry as he was, couldn't eat. Everyone was too busy enjoying the feast and the excited conversation to notice his unusual lack of appetite. From around his belt, he picked up the handle of Hayley's whip and admired the pattern of colors.

How can I eat when I don't even know where she is?

He replaced the dome, stood, and headed for Armada.

Ray intercepted him, grabbing both his shoulders. "Come outside with me."

Sam clearly objected, but still followed him out into the garden.

"How can everyone just sit there eating while she's gone? Doesn't anyone care about her? Why aren't we on our way to get her right now?"

"Sam, everyone is exhausted. Before they return home, they need briefing. Armada has orders, and he knows what he's doing. Part of his mission is overseeing the Knights. He hasn't forsaken her. And you won't do her any good without food and rest. You're not immortal."

"I hope she knows we're coming."

"She knows. She's a Knight. She can handle it."

Sam turned from Ray and walked the grounds of the school alone. Every second that ticked-by registered in his mind. Another second without her. Another second not knowing where or how she was. Another second she had to endure whatever the demons delighted in.

He didn't return to the crowd, but instead retired to his room in the dormitory.

***

Katie also just picked at her food, still emotionally shaken. She slipped out of the jovial dinner to the garden alone.

Jeremiah noticed. He gave her a few minutes of solitude before joining her on a bench under a willow tree. "Hey."

Although quiet, his voice startled her. She jumped a few inches off the bench, but then laughed at herself for doing it. "Sorry. I'm just still a little—"

"It's okay. I mean... are you okay?"

"Yes. I'll be fine."

"Did you want to be alone? Because if you want to be alone, I mean, I could leave if you want to be alone or something."

"No, I like the company." She grinned at his awkwardness.

With flushed cheeks he nodded, glad she didn't send him away.

Her grin faded. "I just can't believe how close I came to…"

An awkward silence sat between them. Jeremiah pushed the gravel with the toe of his boot, trying to think of something to say that wouldn't sound stupid or childish. Although he had chapters to tell her, he chose the silent route.

"Your dad told me you wouldn't leave me alone; you wouldn't give up on me."

He glanced at her and then returned his focus to the gravel.

"Thanks."

He held his breath and closed his eyes as she leaned in and kissed his cheek. Then he turned to look at her, finding her eyes brimming with tears, glistening in the moonlight.

Jack approached, crunching noisily through the pebbled path.

"There you are. Your mother sent me looking for you," Jack said. "See, she's back for less than a day and she's already keeping tabs on you."

Jeremiah half-grinned.

Jack thought about his son and all he'd been through— not an average day for a thirteen-year-old. He had fought for Katie's life when everyone else had just accepted she was gone. He had become something more than a thirteen-year-old. Right then and there he decided to give the kid a break.

"*Jeremy*, I think we should head back to the group."

Jeremiah straightened up on the bench. "What?" He couldn't believe what he'd heard as he scrutinized his dad's face.

Jack grinned.

His son stood and almost came eye-to-eye with him. Grinning back, he said "No, Dad. It's Jeremiah." And then he walked back toward the cafeteria as if he had never begged to be called Jeremy.

Jack was caught off-guard, but he enjoyed the moment. For once there was no fighting, whining, epic debates, or shouting matches.

Katie stood up and shrugged. "You two can never agree, can you?" This time it was her turn to grin.

Returning to the cafeteria, they found the meal now finished and the dishes cleared.

Ray then stood and asked, "Hank, Pete, Isabella, Gladys, and Eleanor, would you please

309

come with me? We'll be discussing your return home."

They followed him out a side door while the rest waited in anticipation of Armada's directions, but there were none. Instead, a familiar scene appeared—one the Knights hadn't seen for quite some time. For Holly, Jeremiah, Cappy and Alex it was overwhelming, unbelievable.

The cafeteria faded and gave way to the gigantic Golden Staircase. Its pure gold steps flashed like sunlit mirrors. The stairs ascended and then blurred into the bright light from above.

"What's going on, Dad?" Jeremiah asked.

Before he could say anything, Armada spoke. "You have also been chosen to join the Knighthood of the Angel Realm. Holly, Jeremiah, Alex, and Cappy, follow me." And with that, in classic Armada style, he turned and began to rise without looking back.

The dumbfounded-four turned and looked at the Knights.

Jack waved at his wife and son. "Come back soon."

Jeremiah was the least surprised of all and felt like a king. He'd traipsed after the Knights so much he already felt like one—even had his own ring and battle wound to prove it. Glancing over at Katie he was glad to find her looking at him. He would come back more of an equal to her. He turned and started climbing.

Cappy shot Spencer a 'what do we do now' look.

"Don't worry. Enjoy the ride," Spencer shouted at his friend.

It was only a few brief moments until the staircase had disappeared. Tallulah, Spencer, Rebecca, and Jack stood alone in the cafeteria exchanging knowing smiles.

Chapter Twenty-Nine
Return to Carthage

In the nearly vacant dormitories, Sam thought sleep was impossible. With his mind wrapped around Hayley's absence, and with the mountainous decibels of snoring coming from his roommate, Jack, sleep finally found him not long after his body touched the sheets.

It seemed like only minutes snoozed by before Ray stood at their door.

"Time to move. We've got visitors. Get to the Chargers."

Half-asleep, Jack bolted out of bed and rushed to the hall, assuming Sam was close on his heels, but Sam had other ideas.

In the dim light from the hall, his eyes fixed on an object of opportunity. In his haste, Jack had forgotten to take his satchel containing the cloaks. Without wasting a moment, Sam grabbed it and threw a cloak over himself, hiding the satchel beneath it as well.

And then they were upon him. Beams of light slashed through the dark room like blades as they searched all around him, oblivious to his presence. Two officers performed a cursory search and left just as abruptly as they'd come. Sam let out a breath, but remained frozen, waiting and listening.

Heavier footsteps echoed in the hall. Their more casual tempo mocked Sam's nerves as he tried to breathe shallow. As the steps approached his doorway they slowed and stopped. St. James flicked on the overhead lights with a sly finesse. Sam felt naked even though fully dressed and under a cloak. He was sure St. James could see him like he had at the Casino, especially as he moved closer and squinted his eyes almost looking directly in Sam's eyes. The tiniest of squeaks escaped from the floorboards beneath Sam's left foot. St. James glanced down, shifting his own weight until he created the same noise. He even lifted his nose inhaling, searching.

Sam found out just how stealth the cloak made him when he felt the officer's arm whoosh through his chest. St. James didn't react. But electrified, breathtaking air swept through Sam's body. Sam fought to keep his composure; fought to hold his breath; fought to remain hidden.

The dwarf-sized, dread-lock demon entered and stuttered through his report. "The dorms are clean. We've been through each room. They must have left already, in pursuit of the girl."

"Good. Good."

"Do you think they know she's in—?"

"Keep silent. The walls may be listening."

Sam celebrated his spy tactics. St James may have stopped the demon mid-sentence, but he didn't stop its thoughts. And he didn't keep Sam's gift from working.

"Ignis Fervens… in Carthage…" the demon thought.

Hearing the demon's thoughts made Sam's stomach churn with disgust. He wanted to rush out from his perfect hiding place and dispose of the creature, but instead he remained stealth and waited until the footsteps diminished before moving to the Chargers.

Ray was waiting for him by the spirit horses. "Thought you might've enrolled in the school," Ray kidded, shaking his head at Sam.

"She's being held in a place called Ignis Fervens,"

"Is that in Carthage?" Ray asked.

"Yes, but I've never heard of any place named that," Sam said.

"It is probably a location only seen in the spiritual realm," Armada said.

Sam exhaled, wishing they were already there. Looking over his shoulder as the Chargers took off, he noticed several well-placed officers standing guard, unaware of the Knights.

The sun was just rising and therefore giving Sam a postcard view of the landscape. He drank it in like a fine wine. But as intoxicating as it was, the need for sleep ranked higher than the view. Sam didn't mean to doze off, but the steady rocking of the beast was much too comforting. He leaned forward on Lightning and passed out from sheer exhaustion.

He awoke with a jolt. He knew they must be close to home because he felt re-energized. He felt like he could take-on anything.

They landed in the middle of the town square.

"So this is Carthage?" Rebecca inquired. "It's quaint. I like it."

Sam smiled at her compliment.

A low-laying fog blanketed the ground throughout the square.

More fog. Great, Sam thought.

Standing in one spot and pivoting a full 360 degrees, Sam's senses were heightened, processing any and all information leading to Hayley.

He swore he could hear her voice—just a few syllables—but it was definitely her. They sounded strange, maybe distressed. As he moved in her direction, he drew his sword and analyzed the situation.

Her voice came from Charlie's diner about 50 yards away. With Spencer to one side of him and Tallulah to the other, he set a brisk yet cautious pace. When the large picture window came into view, the three Knights stopped with the fog swirling around their feet.

It was Hayley's voice. Sam was mortified.

She wore a pink sweater. Her hair was clean and smooth unlike the last time he'd seen her at the bell tower, in fact she practically glowed as she sat at the table by the window, sipping a chocolate malt through a bendy straw in one of those tall glasses. The dark sleeve of a leather jacket leaned on the table. It was Nick's turn to take a sip of the malt.

Sam couldn't move. They were laughing and sitting close. He couldn't believe he'd been so worried about her while all this time she'd been with Nick.

Nick placed his arm around her waist and pulled her in close to him. Sam's jaw dropped and his face turned ice-cold as he watched as their lips came within an inch.

Suddenly, Nick pulled back from Hayley abruptly as if by a force other than his own. And then black ooze seeped up his torso from below. It gushed up over his head and began to pull his body straight down. Hayley reached out for him, yelling his name, but she appeared strapped to her chair. His arms and legs flailed as he grasped for anything. From the blackness bulged demonic figures that grabbed at him like flames licking at wood, and then hauled him down into the abyss.

Sam didn't move.

After all the training and fighting and surviving he'd done, Sam just watched Nick perish into the blackness, regardless of Hayley's screams and Nick's cries for help.

He let his sword fall from his hand and down into the fog. And then he realized what he was doing (or wasn't doing) was a mistake. Flooded with guilt, he reached too late into the fog and tried to reclaim the sword. As he moved his hand, the fog grew around him, detaching him from everyone and everything else. There was still no sword as he realized he had never heard it hit the ground. The next thing he knew, he was floating in the clouds, unable to discern which way was up.

"Sam?!"

When his eyes focused on the face in front of him, it took a few seconds to shake the dream. Part of him was still upset, but most of him was grateful it had not really happened.

"Wow. You must've been really tired if you fell asleep on a flying horse!"

Chapter Thirty
Ignis Fervens

Empty streets and columns of smoke rising from dozens of homes and businesses on spiritual fire greeted the Knights upon their arrival in Carthage.

Not one person walked on the sidewalks of the square. The streets were devoid of vehicles, although the traffic signals still changed their hue automatically: green, yellow, red, green, yellow, red. Shop doors were closed with shades pulled. It was Saturday afternoon, and the square that was usually the hub of activity was a smoldering ghost town.

An eerie dread swelled up from Sam's gut, settling as a lump in his throat. He swallowed, but the lump remained. The theater, the bank, and Charlie's Diner were all smoldering. Sam was relieved that Spott's appeared untouched.

"Where is everyone?" Tallulah asked.

"I don't know where everyone is, but I just found Ignis Fervens on one of Joe's maps. It's in the gymnasium of Carthage High School," Rebecca said.

They rode to the school. From their vantage point in the sky, they could see the football field and the bleachers were full of fans, and the parking lot was jammed with vehicles. An announcer's voice squawked from the speakers.

The Knights dismounted near the gym.

"That's the State Championship game." Sam told the group. He said it with regret hidden well and with much relief in finding an answer to why the square was empty.

The school was not free of flames as well. Even the bleachers were on fire and the crowd appeared hostile. Armed officers settled disputes and had some troublemakers in cuffs. Parents screamed at their misbehaving children.

Mayhem, Sam thought.

Sam felt the twinge of regret as he heard the announcer yell out the names of his former teammates and the plays they were making, but that was not his focus now.

The gymnasium stood in front of them— the same building that always smelled like sweaty socks and Coach Benson's chewing tobacco, but now, hundred-foot flames shot out from it.

Sam and Tallulah stood out in front, facing the building. Spencer, Rebecca, Jack and Katie were close behind. Ray and Armada appeared beside the Knights.

"Let's do it," Sam said.

Tallulah raised a hand to open all four sets of glass doors at once. Walking with a similar, purposeful stride, they entered the foyer. Nothing out of place there. Without slowing their pace,

319

Tallulah opened the next set of doors that led to the main part of the gymnasium. But they stopped unexpectedly when they felt the heat.

Through the open doors a blast of heat and wind escaped the gym, knocking Sam to the ground. As he lay on the floor, he stared up at the unusually amber-colored tiles. Time slowed and sounds swirled together as if he might lose consciousness. One strong inhale brought oxygen back to his empty lungs. His face instantly felt flushed as if sunburned—pulled tight with radiant heat escaping from his skin. The stench of sulfur made him gag and cough.

Feeling as if he'd adhered to the floor, he pulled himself to a sitting position. It was no surprise for him to find the other Knights on the floor with him, but he was shocked beyond belief when he found Ray and Armada there as well.

Sam attempted to wrap his mind around what it meant for angels—at least of Armada's rank—to be knocked to the ground.

Watching quietly, Sam observed as each Knight realized Ray and Armada had fallen. No one said a word. They didn't have to. Their expressions said it all—wide eyes and dropped jaws. But they managed to hide their shock quickly. It took a few moments before any of them stood.

Sam knew who angels were. He knew they weren't omnipotent. He knew there were different ranks, different levels of power, but even so, he had felt more confident with angels in the group.

*If Armada's not powerful enough, then what are **we** doing here?*

A red glow escaping from the gym was not a friendly beacon.

But they would enter this unfriendly place whether they wanted to or not. Sam drew his sword to strike at the demon pulling at his feet, but he found nothing there. His eyes widened as he realized he was moving toward the gym doors, sliding uncontrollably as if on a conveyor belt. Reaching out, he grabbed at a trophy case, trying to slow the pace. This gravitational pull had wrapped around each of them, dragging their squirming bodies across the threshold until the foyer doors slammed behind them.

Now trapped inside, and still being pulled, Sam plunged his sword into what should have been the gym flooring to slow himself down, but instead the floor turned out to be volcanic rock. Spark shot out where his sword scraped the dark rocks.

He forced his eyes to look up, away from his skidding feet to analyze his surroundings. No sweaty socks or chewing tobacco, but he could still see the gym. It was the less dominant of the dimensions, as if he were seeing it through smoked glass.

His feet were sliding toward an angry river of lava. Two enormous, black pillars rose out of the lava, which was swift and glowing, with giant bubble hot spots, bursting and splattering.

Across the magma, Sam's watery eyes scanned the rocky, looming hill until he saw at the crest a glossy, ebony throne. It was empty. Sam wasn't sure if this was a good thing or a bad thing.

Whatever sits on this throne, outranks Armada.

As he continued to slide against his will toward the molten rock, the sweat poured down his face, but gave him no relief from the pressing heat. He breathed shallow breaths as the dryness stung the back of his throat.

His sword seemed to make little difference, except for the offensive grinding noise it made, so he withdrew it from the rocks and searched for another way to slow his progress.

"How do we stop it, Ray?" he called out as he dug his boots into the coarse rock.

Before Ray could answer, their feet abruptly stopped sliding.

And then they heard them coming.

At first it was only a steady, far-off rhythm, but then it grew into a thunderous marching of hostile troops behind them. As if from another dimension, they appeared in a flash, their ranks closing-in behind the Knights.

"Skulks," Ray informed.

Sam turned to face them and drew his sword. They halted and stood at attention— perfectly aligned rows of ebony-skeleton, demonic soldiers with tumultuous lava innards brewing within their bony, black ribs. Their black bones shimmered like obsidian. Through the sweaty sting of his squinted eyes, he detected slight grins on their black skulls.

They didn't move. They didn't breathe. Each of them stared blankly ahead. Some of them wielded bow and arrow, and others held swords and black shields—not shields of a glossy black like their bones, but more like an emptiness, a black hole.

A casual voice interrupted the face-off.

"I thought you might arrive soon."

The throne was now occupied.

Danakrius, in his usual tailored, black suit, black shirt and black tie, sat comfortably. The widow's peak of his jet-black hair came to a perfect point on his strong brow. From this peak it was slicked straight back. Handsome enough for celebrity status, he looked ready to receive an academy award for lead actor.

Armada whispered, "Danakrius."

"Yes, Armada. I'm glad you remember," the prince mocked.

Armada didn't respond; didn't react.

"It really is a shame you have all gone through so much trouble only to fail now."

With a wave of his finger the Skulks marched forward ten steps, causing the Knights to edge toward the lava.

No way out. Sam was unsure whether he'd thought it or a demon had.

He couldn't consider the choices for long because the Skulks reached back into their quivers and readied their bows. Slipping their arrows between their ribs, the tips ignited from the lava in their torsos.

They took aim.

As if regular demon arrows weren't bad enough. Fire demon arrows, Sam thought.

The Knights took cover beneath their shields and behind large rocks by the edge of the lava-river.

The first wave of arrows rained down on them.

A piercing heat and pain surged through Sam's entire body, but then localized in his left shoulder. He looked down to see if his arm was still attached, finding a solid slice on his shoulder. His uniform sleeve was on fire. Without much forethought, he smacked at the burning, smoky fabric—making the pain worse. Inspecting his arm, it looked to him like it was cut clear down to the bone, but at least he could still move it.

Gritting his teeth, Sam peered over the ridge at the enemy line. Armada was closest to the Skulks. Several arrows pierced his shield, but he was unharmed. Before they could reload their bows, he easily destroyed rows of Skulks at a time.

But, from Danakrius's bow, from across the boiling red river, flew a single flaming arrow, over the Knights and toward the angel's back.

"Armada!"

Sam screamed it, but he was too late. The angel didn't even have time to turn. The arrow pierced his upper back between the shoulder blades and traveled straight through the front of his chest. The tip was still on fire, poking through his garments. He fell to his knees.

Armada wailed an unearthly cry. Sam had never heard an expression of pain like this before.

Jack, Spencer, and Sam rushed to Armada and ushered him behind a boulder. They gawked at the wounded angel with the flaming arrow sticking out of his torso.

Desperate to find help, Sam searched for Ray. He found him on the front line engaged in sword combat.

Ray flattened a dozen Skulks as Sam watched, but then found one that appeared immune to his offense. It countered every strike without much effort and then positioned its shield in front of Ray.

The angel's sword was sucked from his hand and into the black hole of the Skulk's shield. Ray's entire body followed.

Sam couldn't believe what he'd just seen.

Ray was gone. He was just gone. And Armada lay writhing in pain beside Sam.

Angels have failed. The Knights will fail. Again, Sam didn't know if he'd thought it or not.

Armada rolled onto his side, took a deep breath and pulled the arrow out. There was no blood and no sign of physical injury, but he was clearly in pain as he breathed erratically, gasping for relief.

Sam watched his chest rise and fall, labored and sporadic. "How can we help? Can we do anything?"

"It will pass in time. The wound is … only spiritual."

From across the lava, an eerie voice interrupted them. "I could have sent more arrows, but I chose just one for effect. I thought it was simple—more meaningful." Prince Danakrius mocked. "And there is something *else* that may be meaningful to you, Sam."

Hearing Danakrius call him specifically by name made him cringe. But he cringed even more when he heard a familiar voice float down from the top of one of the pillars rising fifty feet out of the flowing magma.

"Sam? I'm here!" Her voice was shrill and desperate as she looked down from the platform. Ragged and shackled, she cried down to him. "I'm up here!"

She's alive. "Hayley!" He yelled it so loud his throat hurt. His breathing accelerated and he scanned the area for a solution.

"Hey! Help!" sounded another familiar voice. It was Nick, in his football uniform, clearly distraught on the other pillar.

She will die.

Before he had a moment to consider the source of the voice in his head, the ground began to shake. A low, quick rumbling grew into a jolting, rock-splitting quake.

Sam watched in horror as the pillars tipped and swayed with each tremor. Hayley and Nick were tossed around like ragdolls on tethers, hanging off the pillars.

More of the ledge crumbled from beneath Sam's feet and another round of flaming arrows forced them to take cover as the earth rocked.

One of the arrows pierced through the edge of Sam's cape, the fire spreading through the material. Feeling the intense heat through his uniform, he cut the cape off with his sword and threw it into the river below. With the earth still shaking, he nearly fell in with it, but Jack grabbed his arm, pulling him to safety. They watched as the material combusted in midair and disintegrated before it even touched the surface of the oozing river of molten rock.

The earthquake rumbled-on, leaving a network of deep crevices.

Danakrius laughed. "You will not survive this day."

Chapter Thirty-One
Standard Issue Armor

As more Skulks prepared for another round of assaults, the Knights dodged the new-forming cracks in the rock.

From behind the ranks of skeletons and resembling the cavalry, Jeremiah, Cappy, Alex, and Holly—newly trained Knights, improved Sam's outlook.

Now surrounded, the skeleton-demons scrambled to implement new strategy.

Jeremiah stepped forward and played an unusual looking horn, resembling a cross between a trumpet and a Shofar of ancient times. The sound waves shot out like lasers, crushing three rows of Skulks immediately.

He looked down at his instrument. "Works pretty good."

Holly was all grace amidst the chaos as she rode her own Charger and took sharp aim at skeletons one-by-one with her sword.

A huge smile covered Jack's face as he watched his wife and son and their newly acquired skills.

"Jack! Isn't she beautiful? Her name is Skye!" Holly said as she flew past the group.

Sam was confused when he saw two Skulks stabbing their own kind in the back. *Was this rebellion among the ranks? Orders gone wrong?* It took most of the army by surprise until the rebels were the only ones left standing.

All the Knights waited for the rogue creatures' next move. The skeletons began to change shape into their true identities—Cappy and Alex.

"Dude," Alex said as he high-fived his brother.

"Dude," Cappy echoed.

"Cool gift," Spencer whispered to Rebecca.

With the current threat of flaming arrows gone, the Knights applauded their new counterparts.

A growl from the dark throne behind them rattled across the river, showing Danakrius's strong disapproval.

With a snap of his fingers a fresh batch of Skulks were summoned and the ground shaking intensified. Jeremiah was taken down by falling rock. Flaming arrows speared Katie and Tallulah. Sam was horrified as he witnessed the rest of the Knights fall into the widening crevices one-by-one: Holly, Rebecca, Cappy, Spencer, Alex, and Jack.

Sam was the only remaining Knight.

He sat next to Armada, defeated. "Armada, what do I do?"

"You've forgotten your armor."

"What do you mean? I'm wearing it."

329

"You are wearing it, but you don't trust it. Your battle is not with flesh and blood, but with rulers, powers, and authorities. You are protected against their worst."

Rising to his feet, Armada staggered over to a nearby rock. "They have been deceiving you."

Sam also rose, intending to lead the angel back to safety behind the ridge of rocks.

Armada raised his sword above his head and then thrust it into the rock, exposing and impaling the Skulk—the one that Sam had been hearing. It had hidden under a cloak, disguised as a rock, stealth to all the Knights.

The demon sunk into the abyss with a toddler-tantrum, high-pitched protest.

Armada was abruptly sucked through the air. Against his will, the angel flew over the river, his angelic body crumpled forward, clearly lacking strength.

Hayley, watching from the pillar, cried out, "Armada!"

Danakrius smiled as the angel fell at his feet, dust speckling his freshly pressed suit pants. Stepping back, he bent down and dusted them off. Standing upright, he turned toward Sam across the lava.

Sam gaped at the scene.

He felt his right arm involuntarily jerk forward, pointing directly at Danakrius, who had his hand out as if to catch something. The force pulling on his arm ripped Sam's ring from his finger.

Before he could blink, Sam found himself kneeling in the middle of the gymnasium floor. No sign of Danakrius, lava, Skulks or anything from the spiritual dimension.

A familiar, eerie laugh echoed in his mind as he realized he could still hear Danakrius's thoughts.

Sam rose to his feet, completely at a loss for what he could do now. He hated the sound of the beast. He wanted to switch-off his voice. Instead, he stood completely still, listening for anything, any way back in, any hint of hope.

With his heart pounding, he waited. The pause was unbearable.

Sam could only imagine the two angels coming face-to-face.

"I will have a party later in your honor, Armada. You will fail now."

Bitter frustration washed through Sam's veins like arsenic.

Helplessness poured over Sam until, injured and kneeling before him, Jeremiah appeared. Wincing, he lifted his head toward Sam, and reached up with one hand.

"I thought you might need this." At this he sucked air through his teeth, in an attempt to deal with the pain.

Jeremiah's ring lay in his palm.

The last time he'd seen Jeremiah, he was under a rock pile, unmoving.

"God willing, I'll be back for you."

Jeremiah laid his head on the glossy floor.

With the borrowed ring on his finger Sam reentered the spiritual realm.

Sam's shield instantly collected fiery arrows. He knocked them off against a boulder and then saw Danakrius lording over Armada, his sword aimed effortlessly at the fallen angel. Sam needed to cross the river. He had no plan after that, but crossing was a first step.

Scanning the area, he found the answer to his problem waiting faithfully by the crevice into which Holly had fallen. Skye waited for her faithful mistress, shifting her weight and scratching her hooves on the crusty rocks.

In one huge leap, Sam attempted to mount the vaporous beast but found himself instead on the ground as it denied him the ride.

Jumping to his feet, he then grabbed her bit and pulled her head down to Sam's eye level.

"Skye, let me ride you."

With a whinny the flying horse obeyed. Skye turned and scooped him up and they soared over the lava. Upon its descent, two skulks were there to greet them. Sam was ready for them—obliterating one and seriously wounding the other.

Perched on Skye, he was instantly mortified as he watched Prince Danakrius's sword plunge into Armada's side.

Sam sat on the Pegasus, stunned. "No," he whispered and then reminded himself, "He will recover. But now we face them alone."

Before Sam's eyes, Armada faded into shades of grays and blacks.

Instantly a pillar of white flames shone down on the angel. Without warning, it pulled him straight up toward heaven.

"It was unwise to come back," the demon bragged.

Danakrius acquired Sam's sword and sent him flying backwards fifty feet.

He then walked nonchalantly to Sam. Standing taller than him, a smug smile grew on his face.

The first wave of assault hit Sam with such force, Sam's ears rang. A pressure weighted him down into the rock. It grew heavier and heavier and more and more uncomfortable. He could barely breathe. Short, shallow breaths were all that kept him from passing out.

"You won't be getting this one, Danakrius."

Sam knew the voice well, but he thought he must be hallucinating.

The distraction allowed some relief from the pressure—enough to lift his head and see it was his father speaking to Danakrius.

The demon let go and slowly turned toward Hank.

Sam was dumbfounded. He sat up. Not only his father, but his mother as well donned the Knight's uniform. And they were flying.

Flying!?

He was completely flabbergasted.

Between them, and arm-in-arm, Nick sailed along, his feet dangling. They escorted him to the other side of the lava river.

Sam saw Nick sprint for the gymnasium doors.

Danakrius appeared amused by this. "My soldiers will deal with him later."

His parents returned. Sam couldn't process what he was seeing. It was too overwhelming. Both of his parents wielded swords, and when they landed in front of Danakrius, they wasted no time initiating their offensive attack.

Danakrius seemed bothered having to draw his sword. With a 'here we go again' stance, he humored them with a lukewarm defense.

Sam reclaimed his own sword from the rocks and joined his parents in the fight.

"Get Hayley," his dad grunted between strikes without looking at him.

Without delay, Sam bolted onto Skye again. He rode the flying horse to the top of her pillar. There was just enough room for Skye to land on the obsidian prison. As her hooves touched down, he dismounted.

He couldn't resist grabbing Hayley up into his arms for a moment. Then he took her by the shoulders, directing her away from the chain's origin.

She stood anxious and hopeful.

With a wind up made for the World Series, he struck her metal tether with his sword. Sparks burst from the sudden friction of the metals colliding. She was free.

"You might need these," he said, handing her whip and gloves to her.

The Charger whisked them off the pillar only for them to see Danakrius send his parents careening over the lava and against a boulder on the other side.

Skye reared back as Danakrius appeared directly in front of her. Before Sam and Hayley could even react, he snatched Hayley and sent Sam and Skye hurtling several yards away onto the rocks.

Both landed hard. Sam rolled like a stuntman, and then scrambled back to his feet. Skye bounced a couple of times before coming to rest. She tried to lift her head, but then put it back down.

Sam assessed the situation:

His parents were out cold— or worse.

Hayley dangled by invisible tethers over the magma.

No angels.

No Knights.

Alone.

Danakrius's voice crept into Sam's mind like a cold razor blade. *"She will die now."*

Desperate for a plan Sam frantically glanced left and right.

Hayley spied a Skulk's bow targeted for Sam's back. From her precarious position, she cracked her whip at the creature and the tip of the whip brushed against its black shoulder blade just enough to bring it to its knees in a slow approach to the abyss. It fell forward with its arrow still pulled back. And there it remained, jerking a rapid series of spasms on the volcanic rock.

An idea hit Sam like a meteor. "My armor. Father God, I trust You."

Sam looked at Skye. She struggled to her feet, shook her mane, and stomped a hoof in protest for the fall.

In a game-winning sprint and leap, Sam sprung onto Skye's back, and maneuvered straight for the injured, and still trembling, Skulk, stopping long enough to grab its bow and an unused arrow. Jamming the arrow between its ribs, he lit it, burning his hand as he fumbled with the bow.

I've got one shot. That's all I need.

Danakrius turned his head back toward Sam just as the arrow left the bow. He saw it coming, but it was too late to avoid.

As it pierced the dark prince's body, black smoke shot out from the entry point. His body became hollow and withered as if filled with nothing. Vacant, dark eyes blinked once as he screeched through a blackened, ghostly-shaped mouth.

Sam turned his focus from the demon's demise, to see Hayley plummeting toward the molten rock. Her scream sliced through his ears like a guillotine.

He and Skye flew into a blur toward the lava. Sam's legs felt like they were about to disintegrate from the heat, but it didn't slow the flying horse.

Just before Hayley plunged into the fiery ooze, Sam saw sparks as her whip lashed itself around a rock formation. Clinging for her life, she swooped toward the shore—her cape dragging across the river, instantly bursting into flames.

Skye flew directly behind her swing. As Hayley landed, she rolled which snuffed most of the fire. Skye landed next to her and Sam wasted no time dismounting and putting out the rest of flames. They embraced, and Sam let out whispers of gratitude for her safety.

Their attention was then drawn to the final stages of Danakrius's demise.

The churning abyss opened in front of the dark throne. Danakrius sank down slowly, with fierce protest. The newly summoned Skulk army followed their leader into the blackness like a tangled pile of bones.

Bruised and scorched, but not broken, Sam and Hayley, still locked in their embrace, watched the beasts disappear and the ground close up.

A few moments passed before either of them could move, but gradually they stood.

"You alright?" Sam asked.

"Much improved, just recently. You?" Hayley returned.

"Couldn't be better." He gave her an exhausted yet proud smile.

Skye interrupted their exchange with two stomps. Sam turned and rubbed her mane.

"Well done," he told the Charger.

She bobbed her head.

Looking across the glowing, red river he saw that his parents were now conscious and helping the rest of the Knights to their feet. The demonic affects were fading.

Sam picked up his sword and stood on the ebony throne. With the passion of a warrior, he drew his sword and raised it straight up. He hollered-out a ruckus, inspiring the rest of the Knights to send out a celebratory shout in response. The sound of victory bounced from rock to rock.

After replacing his sword in its sheath, he put his hand out for Hayley to join him on the throne, but she hesitated.

Something caught her eye. She bent down and picked up an object. Smiling, she opened her hand, revealing Sam's ring. He took it from her palm and then slipped it into his pocket. Safe-keeping for Jeremiah later.

Sam took Hayley's hand in his and then pulled her up onto the throne with him. Holding her face in both his hands, he let his eyes soak up every inch of her beautiful, dusty, tear-streaked face. He looked at her with enough gratefulness to fill the oceans.

And then he kissed her.

All around them, while their eyes were closed, the hellish landscape faded, giving way to the ordinary gymnasium. The Knights gathered around the throne, still cheering.

Spencer yelled, "It's about time he planted one on her!"

Chapter Thirty-Two
Wild Sunflowers

Once outside, they sat in the cool grass under a large pine tree and reflected on what they'd been through; what they'd achieved. Carthage had won the fight on the football field and in the gym. The crowds were dispersing, and the day had turned into twilight.

"Do you think all the demons have fled?" Katie asked.

Hank shook his head. "Every town has a few scouts at least. It's up to the community to keep them at bay."

Sam stared in awe at his parents. They were Knights! They had some serious explaining to do.

Hank continued. "It'll take time for the town to recover spiritually from an attack of this magnitude."

"Where's Tallulah?" Hayley asked.

"She said something about going home," Deb said.

Sam's attention was drawn to his old hunk of junk in the parking lot. "What? Let's go find her," he said, grabbing Hayley by the hand and heading to where he'd left his motorcycle. Taking their rings off, they joined the real world again, although it didn't feel real at the moment.

Truth be known, he just wanted to get away with Hayley— just the two of them. Away from everything. With her behind him on the dragonfly, everything seemed right again.

Sam was too wrapped up in the exhilarating ride, too pumped from the victory, too excited about Hayley to notice anything unusual right away when they arrived at Tallulah's house.

However, Hayley tuned-in to it the moment the house was in sight.

"A for sale sign?" He was still oblivious. "Is she moving?"

"Sam, the house is vacant."

They stared at the empty house.

"By the looks of that sign, it's been there for a while. Look at the vines that have grown up the post," Hayley said.

It was slowly dawning on them.

"She was…" he started.

"…an angel," she finished.

In disbelief, they looked all around the property looking for more clues to prove it, which took them to the gazebo in the back yard.

"Maybe we could see something in the spiritual realm?" he suggested.

Replacing their rings, they were surprised to find all the Knights, except Sam's parents, were landing their Chargers on the front lawn.

Hayley announced, "Guess what! Tallulah's an—"

"Your parents told us. Angels among us," Spencer said.

"She had to go home for recovery. Your mom said she took several arrows," Rebecca said.

"Will we ever see her again?" Hayley asked.

"I have a feeling we will. Your parents said she was around when they became Knights." Katie said.

"When was that?" asked Sam.

"When they were your age." Jack reported.

Sam's eyebrows rose. They really had some explaining to do. "Where are my parents?"

"They said they'd see you at home," Katie said.

Sam liked hearing that. Both his parents. At home.

"Well, we just came by to say goodbye," said Spencer.

"I'll drop you all off and lead your Chargers back to my place… until next time," Jack said.

Sam estimated the hugging and hand shaking went on for a half-hour. Twilight had succumbed to night before the Chargers and the Knights flew out of sight.

Sam and Hayley hopped on the dragonfly and sped past a row of giant, wild sunflowers trimming the property's edge.

When they arrived at the Goodman Ranch, he drove around back to the kitchen door.

"So, what about Nick?" he asked, hoping he'd be able to survive the answer.

"What about Nick?"

"You know. The last time I was here I saw you kissing him."

"You *saw* that?"

He nodded. "Uh-huh."

"Well, if you knew anything, you'd know it wasn't me kissing Nick, it was *him* kissing me."

"What's the difference?"

"The difference is that I hit him with a pot to make him stop."

"You hit him with a pot?"

"Right in the face."

"The bruise."

"Yeah, I *almost* felt bad about that. And he felt bad about the whole thing. He even gave me flowers to say he was sorry."

"I brought you those flowers, Hayley. They were from me."

"So, you…"

As her voice trailed off, he pulled her close and kissed her goodnight. It was the kind of kiss that is accompanied by an imaginary string orchestra.

***

He should have been tired by now, but the wind in his face on the way home kept his mind replaying everything. Just thinking about Hayley could keep him awake for the next week, let alone his gifts, the angels, Archai, the Chargers... Add to that, defeating the reigning demonic prince of the North American region and he could have a serious case of insomnia.

As he turned the corner to the square, he could see the lights were still on in the market and he could see his parents through the window. They looked so ordinary. They looked so amazing.

A movement in the shadows by the market's front door caught his attention. He stopped the motorcycle and looked intensely toward the movement. When he saw who it was, he hopped off the bike and dropped to his knees. Jumping all around him, they licked his face and rolled onto their backs for a scratch.

"Lancelot! Guinevere!"

The End.

COMING SOON...

to **AMAZON.com...**

KNIGHTS OF THE ANGEL REALM

A SPIDER'S WRATH

(KOTAR BOOK #2, The Prequel)

&

**KNIGHTS OF THE ANGEL REALM
A BIBLE STUDY GUIDE**

Ways you can support authors:

- Purchase and read their books.
- Leave reviews on Amazon.com, Goodreads, etc.
- Recommend their books to friends and family.
- Post with links to their books on social media.
- Give their books as gifts.
- Visit the author's website/blog or follow them on social media, and leave constructive, friendly comments.
- Buy merchandise related to their books, if available.
- Attend author speaking engagements or book signings.
- Request books from your local library and book/gift stores.
- Sign up to be on their e-mail list.
- Form a book club.

Please visit me!

Website/Blog: GretchenRhue.com

On Facebook: Gretchen Rhue, Author